A LADY MOST WAYWARD

DARCY MCGUIRE

Boldwood

First published in Great Britain in 2025 by Boldwood Books Ltd.

Copyright © Darcy McGuire, 2025

Cover Design by Head Design Ltd.

Cover Images: Head Design Ltd, iStock and Shutterstock

A CIP catalogue record for this book is available from the British Library.

Paperback ISBN 978-1-83603-572-5

Large Print ISBN 978-1-83603-571-8

Hardback ISBN 978-1-83603-570-1

Trade Paperback ISBN 978-1-80656-024-0

Ebook ISBN 978-1-83603-573-2

Kindle ISBN 978-1-83603-574-9

Audio CD ISBN 978-1-83603-565-7

MP3 CD ISBN 978-1-83603-566-4

Digital audio download ISBN 978-1-83603-567-1

This book is printed on certified sustainable paper. Boldwood Books is dedicated to putting sustainability at the heart of our business. For more information please visit https://www.boldwoodbooks.com/about-us/sustainability/

Boldwood Books Ltd, 23 Bowerdean Street, London, SW6 3TN

www.boldwoodbooks.com

To Brennon for being the bestest big brother ever, and to Erin for being such a fierce advocate for our most vulnerable. And to Derek, my forever.

CONTENT WARNING

This book contains references to suicide. Reader discretion is advised.

1

Olivia Smithwick shrank deeper into the shadows. For the first time in her thirty-six years, she fervently wished to disappear. Which wasn't like her at all. Generally, Olivia craved the spotlight. But not tonight. In the Mayfair mansion, no longer her home but still full of haunted memories and broken dreams, she would love nothing more than to become one of the dust motes spinning into infinity.

Holding her breath, she prayed the god-awful butler didn't peer too deeply into what had once been Olivia's bedroom.

The bloody idiot should be looking for a new job, not snooping around in this mausoleum the night before the new owner takes residence. Fool!

If he were a fool, then Olivia was stark raving mad. To come back here, when so much was at stake. While intimately acquainted with madness, she had no intention of revisiting the asylum that held her captive in Germany for ten long years: a fate decided for Olivia by her now-dead husband.

I'd rather join Percy in the fiery pit of hell than go back there.

Percival Smithwick had not been a kind husband or a good man. Olivia knew she couldn't find joy in the arms of any man, but Percy took sick pleasure in making her life as unpleasant as he could. Right up until the moment he met his fate at the hands of Ivy Cavendale, one of the Queen's Deadly Damsels. They were a small but fierce force of women led by the powerful Duchess of Dorsett.

Lady Philippa Winterbourne.

Unbidden, the memory of cobalt eyes framed by dark lashes, a crimson mouth that would tempt even the angels to sin, and so much glorious black hair, Olivia's fingers twitched to test its texture, filled her mind.

She scowled, ruthlessly reminding herself Lady Winterbourne was the enemy and someone Olivia despised. The indomitable duchess helped to catch Olivia's husband while completing a secret mission for Queen Victoria.

Because she is so special, the bloody ruler of all England trusts her with hunting down the most dangerous lords in her realm.

A fact Olivia found both impressive and irritating.

Percival had been one such lord. Based on the evidence Philippa and her Deadly Damsels discovered, they could prove Percival was the dreaded Wolf, second-in-command to the Crow who led London's most secret and insidious brotherhood. The Devil's Sons. And devils they were, working to enslave young girls and boys in a flesh trading ring stretching far into Europe.

After Olivia's friend Ivy helped capture Percy, Philippa used her influence with the Queen to ensure he was kept in Newgate prison. None of the Damsels had faith the system would hold Lord Smithwick accountable for his crimes, but neither did they expect the brotherhood to take matters into their own hands. Yet that is exactly what the Devil's Sons did. An unnamed criminal, no doubt a minion of the brotherhood, was tasked with ensuring Percy's secrets stayed hidden forever. He murdered Percy in his cot before he could stand trial.

But I escaped.

Even in her perilous circumstance – breathlessly waiting to see if the cursed butler was going to discover her hiding in her old bedchamber or go pack his bags and bugger off – Olivia smiled at the memory of her fist slamming into Philippa Winterbourne's far-too-perfect face. The crunch of Olivia's knuckles against Philippa's cheekbone was more satisfaction than she'd felt in... forever, actually. Not that she was angry with Philippa for helping to catch her husband. Far from it. Olivia loathed Percival and the brotherhood. She hated what he made her do on behalf of their treacherous mission to victimise London's most vulnerable so they could line their own pockets. Olivia was thrilled her bastard of a husband had finally been stopped. She also knew she deserved to share in Percival's fate. But that didn't prevent a shiver of triumph at getting one over on the far-too-proud, always-right, better-than-the-whole-bloody-beau-monde Duchess of Dorsett.

The butler sighed heavily, turned, and walked out of the room, gently shutting the door behind him.

Olivia nearly melted into a puddle of relief on the parquet floor, which was premature at best as she still had a dangerous task to complete. She couldn't relax yet. Not until she'd found the hoard of money and jewels she had hidden in preparation for her eventual escape from Percy. She hadn't planned on circumstances being quite so dire, but Philippa had complicated matters exponentially by putting Olivia's name at the top of the Queen's most-wanted list. Still, Olivia's end goal was unchanged. Freedom. Although now, instead of retiring to her dowager house in the country, she would need to leave England entirely. She could hardly show her face amongst the beau monde, knowing the duchess was hunting her down like some feral prey.

Infuriating, horrible, awful woman! I finally escape my hideous marriage, and now I face the threat of imprisonment.

Which, at the root of things, felt the same to Olivia. Both ensured she had no control. No autonomy. No chance of living a life that might bring any hint of happiness or contentment.

So, I shall take fate into my own hands. As soon as I get my blasted money.

She could book passage on a ship bound for America and hold onto hope for a future there where she might finally decide what path to walk. Alone, but free.

'It will be a fresh start. For me and for Hyacinth. She will thank me one day,' she whispered into the dark room, needing to hear the words so she could believe them.

Pressing her lips together in a firm line, she refused to cry at the thought of her daughter. Not once during the sixteen years since she brought her sweet girl into the world had Olivia ever imagined Hyacinth would hate her with such burning rage. Then again, she never believed Percival would rip them apart when Hyacinth was only six years old, condemning Olivia to ten years of hell in an asylum while he poisoned her daughter with lies about Olivia choosing to whore around Europe instead of raising Hyacinth.

When Percy finally summoned Olivia home, whatever fantasies she created of being welcomed into her daughter's arms were shattered as the girl stood like a stone, hands clasped together so tightly her knuckles were white, eyes hard, head full of her father's falsehoods. In the few months they'd had together since her return, she'd made precious little headway with her daughter.

'Fucking bastard. I hope your last moments were as horrifying as the ten years I suffered.' It wasn't lost on her that she was cursing a dead man in an empty room, but she didn't care.

Likely, his last breath was taken with a large amount of fear and dread, and she couldn't dredge up an ounce of pity for him. Being murdered in a Newgate prison cell was hardly a peaceful end. But it was no more than he deserved. Given his role in decimating countless innocents, it was rather fitting he met a violent end. But the damage he wrought during his life didn't end when his heart stopped beating. Indeed, Olivia was still reeling from the repercussions of his sins, as were countless innocent victims of his crimes.

Anger always focused Olivia, and so she chose that over grief. She couldn't lament her stolen past with Hyacinth or her uncertain future when so much still needed to be done. If she wanted any chance of a life beyond the next few days, she needed to retrieve her hidden treasure from beneath the loose board under the huge bed, collect her daughter, and leave the continent before Lady Philippa Winterbourne and her band of Deadly Damsels found Olivia and delivered their vigilante justice.

All her hope rested in the velvet bag containing a small fortune, safe in its hiding spot, waiting to be collected.

The magnificent mahogany bed had been stripped of its sheets and blankets and stood like a grand lady completely naked in the centre of her chamber. An unbidden image of Lady Philippa Winterbourne, standing just as grand and just as naked in Olivia's bedroom, painted a blush across her cheeks.

'Hardly. She is the last person I would ever be interested in bedding. I hate her.'

A true statement, but hate and attraction weren't mutually exclusive.

'Just bloody inconvenient. And impossible. She would rather string me up by my neck than look at me,' Olivia muttered as she crept quietly across the floor, avoiding the creaking board to the left of the bed. 'And I would much prefer hitting her again. Repeatedly.'

Grateful for the split riding skirts that offered her freedom of movement, she crouched and felt under the bed for the divot she had created in the wood when first prying it free. She lifted the board and slid it back. Her fingers wrapped around the velvet bag stuffed full of jewels, gold coins, and any other valuables Olivia was able to secret away while Percy was busy completing tasks for the Devil's Sons. Thankfully, the man lost track of little things like lost necklaces or missing coin purses when he was focused on his work. After all, who had time to count the silver when one was so busy procuring innocent children and delivering them to evil men with insatiable appetites?

'And I helped him.' Olivia felt the bile rise in her throat. How could she blame Hyacinth for hating her when Olivia loathed the woman she had become? No matter that she did it all to protect her daughter. She had become as sick as the monster she despised. 'But I can change all that. Once we are free of this place, I will make amends. For Hyacinth and the others. I will find a way.'

Pulling the bag free, Olivia's heart stuttered as her stomach rolled in a queasy wave.

It was far too light.

'No. No, no, no!'

Scrabbling with the drawstring, she ripped the bag open and plunged her hand inside.

Empty.

Her finger caught on the sharp corner of a calling card. It was the only thing left in the purse. The only thing Olivia hadn't put there. Suspicion dawned as nausea turned into something else. Something harder. Colder. Far more deadly.

She pulled the card free and hurried over to the window, drawing aside thick curtains. A silvery moon hung in a black sky, but it spilled enough light over the dark purple card for Olivia to make out the gold script.

Lady Philippa Winterbourne, Duchess of Dorsett

The Queen's Deadliest Damsel had left her calling card. The one person Olivia needed to avoid at all costs now held her only key to escape.

'All right, Lady Winterbourne. You want me to pay you a visit?' Olivia stood tall, pulling back her shoulders and letting rage fill her with courage. 'I shall pay you a visit you won't soon forget.'

* * *

Nothing felt quite as decadent as silk on the skin. Philippa sat at her dressing table as Delacroix brushed her thick hair and expertly twined it into a braid. She ran her fingers over the slippery fabric. Her banyan was deep purple with a black damask pattern. It was not lost on her that even her bedclothes were in hues of mourning. The beau monde long believed her choice to wear only the darkest colours was in honour of her late husband. They were wrong. He was not the person for whom Philippa still grieved.

The streaks of silver at her temples were a striking contrast to the ebony tresses. Not prone to false modesty, she also knew her pleasing face and figure could be used to her advantage in a world that valued beauty over wit or character. Philippa had once detested her features and the unwanted attention they brought, but she quickly learned how to use her appearance as she did most everything else. It was a weapon she honed to cut, maim, and dismantle.

'Thank you, Delacroix, that is all for tonight.'

Her lady's maid had been with Philippa over nineteen years. Since the day she was thrust into the position of duchess, Delacroix had been her constant companion. She watched Philippa struggle to maintain the guise of a happy marriage to her much older husband. She helped pick up the pieces he left behind after his nightly marital visits during the first months of their union. It was Delacroix who supported Philippa as she learned how to fight back against Lord Winterbourne, both physically and, more importantly, with her mind. Her heavily accented words of encouragement reminded Philippa she was no man's puppet, and a bond had developed between them that the years only strengthened.

The French woman held strong opinions on every subject and never hesitated to voice them, but tonight, she was oddly quiet.

'Are you well?' Philippa raised a perfectly sculpted eyebrow.

Delacroix wrinkled her nose. Her light-brown hair was pulled into a neat twist, and her flawless skin made it impossible to accurately guess her age. But Philippa knew she was cresting her fourth decade because they shared the same birth year.

'*Oui*, I am perfectly fine. It is for you I worry.'

Philippa turned to face her maid. 'Nonsense. Why would you worry about me?'

Shrugging, Delacroix's lips curled down at the corners. 'Ever since that woman punched you in the face with 'er fist, you 'ave been different.'

The last thing Philippa needed to be reminded of was her disastrous encounter with Lady Olivia Smithwick. Summer's heat had quickly faded into a crisp autumn, but Philippa's feelings of embarrassment – a rare emotion for her – and outrage – a much more familiar one – had not faded with summer's warmth.

Olivia Smithwick's flawless face flitted through Philippa's mind as it did countless times a day. It was infuriating to be plagued by the only woman Philippa would happily forget. But she couldn't shake Olivia from her thoughts.

Only because I intend to hunt her down. For my Queen.

While Philippa was always sharply focused on the cases she investigated for Queen Victoria, never before had a suspect haunted her thoughts the way Olivia did. Mayhap it was because she was also the only person to catch Philippa unaware and deliver a cheap shot to her jaw.

Philippa absently rubbed her fingers over the spot where Olivia's knuckles had smashed into her cheek. The mark she left was no longer there, but that didn't stop Philippa from feeling the echo of Olivia's blow.

She had left an invitation for the despicable woman. One she secretly hoped Olivia refused. Because for the first time in Philippa's life, she wasn't sure how to win this particular battle. And that worried her.

'I'm fine. I'll be even better once we capture Olivia Smithwick and force her to name the leader of the Devil's Sons. I grow weary of the chase. I'm ready for the kill.'

'So brutal. Do you never tire of always being the blade?' Delacroix pursed her lips and cocked her head to the side. Her dark gaze was far too assessing.

'The world doesn't need another soft woman. Not when innocents must be protected from men like the Devil's Sons.'

'But you are not chasing a man this time.' The maid didn't try to hide her sly smile. ''ave you finally found someone worth your interest?'

Philippa's sexual inclinations were never a topic of conversation, but after so many years together, certain secrets were impossible to keep hidden from her lady's maid. Delacroix had once made it clear that, were Philippa interested, she would be amenable to extending their relationship into something much more intimate. But while Philippa respected Delacroix's sharp mind and even sharper wit, her heart belonged to another. She could never betray her lost love by engaging in a relationship with another woman. Even if that woman was someone she respected and admired as much as Delacroix. In point of fact, Philippa hadn't been tempted by others, though there had been more than just her maid's offer of companionship over the years. Lusty widows with enough confidence to risk flouting the laws of society, sending messages of illicit invitation, or lady-wives trapped in marriages with no chance of fulfilment making furtive overtures for a more intimate friendship with the Duchess of Dorsett. But no matter how beautiful or tempting these women might have been, her heart was still completely enthralled with her first love, a girl who had been in the grave for over twenty years.

Liza.

The only woman Philippa's heart ever claimed. The reason she insisted on wearing colours of unending sorrow. Because Liza was lost to her forever, and with her, Philippa's only chance of finding happiness in the arms of another. Liza, two years Philippa's junior, was only eighteen when she chose death over endless torture from the doctors running the asylum where her father imprisoned her. And all for the crime of loving Philippa.

Liza was gone, taking with her the light that had once glowed in Philippa's soul.

Two decades had passed, but sometimes, grief made it feel like mere moments since Philippa's whole world shattered.

She pushed back her shoulders, clenched her teeth, and reminded herself she was born a fighter. For warriors such as she, love was only ever a dream. Liza's death taught her to melt loss and pain into the crucible of vengeance. Her late husband only deepened those lessons until she beat her emotions into a blade stronger and sharper than the finest steel. She learned how to wield that weapon with the skill and courage eclipsing any of her male counterparts. Liza's death allowed Philippa to understand the value of holding powerful men accountable for their sins. She knew their brethren never would.

And she found an unlikely ally in Queen Victoria. The young monarch knew too well the danger of allowing a man complete control. Having grown up under the watchful eye of her mother's attendant, Sir John Conroy, and being subjected to the cruel system of rules her mother and Sir John devised and named the Kensington System, Victoria had little patience for men wishing to exert their power over her. A few veiled conversations when Philippa was first presented to the Queen at her coronation brought to light a shared kinship between Philippa and the newly crowned monarch. That tentative friendship only grew deeper over the years, culminating in a proposition by the Queen to the duchess. It was an offer Philippa couldn't refuse. A chance to put her rage to good use while providing purpose to her life. She would do for other innocents what she could not for her sweet Liza. Protect them by any means necessary against power-hungry lords with far too much control. Philippa became the Queen's first Deadly Damsel.

Now, their small army numbered four more women and their partners, and Philippa was grateful. Tasked by the Queen to take down the vile group of peers orchestrating a flesh trade of maids and orphans from London to Europe was only becoming more dangerous. Each lord they uncovered was more powerful than the last and more deadly.

Olivia knew the identity of the final link in this rusted chain. The head of the triad that ruled the Devil's Sons. The Crow. Philippa meant to get that name from Lady Smithwick at any cost.

She refocused her attention on Delacroix. 'The only thing that interests me about *that* woman is the information she can provide.'

'*That* woman. There is a saying in France, you know. You cannot truly 'ate someone if you 'ave not first loved them. When you speak of this woman, I see the fire of 'atred in your eyes, but is that so dissimilar from the 'eat of passion?'

Philippa glared at her maid in the mirror. 'There is a saying in England as well, Delacroix. A maid with too many opinions will find she is a maid no longer.'

Delacroix's gallic shrug expressed more than words ever could. ''ave it your way. I shall keep my thoughts to myself. But it wouldn't kill you to talk about your feelings every once in a while.'

'And it wouldn't kill you to *stop* talking about them. Starting now. Goodnight, Delacroix.' Philippa blinked, schooling her features to remain carefully blank. Delacroix was right about love and hate being two different faces of the same coin. But Philippa held neither love nor hate for Olivia.

More like lust and loathing, which is a different currency altogether.

That was a penny she kept rubbing between her fingers each time their paths crossed. Infuriating as it was to admit, Philippa was attracted to Olivia. While she had felt the whispers of desire before with other women, never had it lingered in her blood, sinking into her bones, infiltrating her thoughts at the most inopportune times. Knowing they were enemies did nothing to dull the sharp edges of her awareness when the fair-haired beauty invaded Philippa's space. Highly inconvenient, but her borderline obsession with the woman she needed to hunt wasn't something she was willing to admit to herself, let alone her already too intuitive lady's maid.

'Goodnight, Your Grace. I 'ope you are able to sleep without a certain blonde vixen 'aunting your dreams.' The smug maid smirked as she sashayed out of Philippa's bedroom, softly closing the door behind her.

'Really. Between Delacroix and Stokes, I get no respect. They seem to forget it is I who pay their wages.' Philippa stood, brushing her hands down her robe in brisk flicks. Restlessness stole through her like the warning howl of wind before a storm. Glancing at her bed, she knew sleep was impossible tonight.

Far too many thoughts crowded her mind, and an edgy need for movement tightened her muscles. There was only one solution. With the servants all sent to bed and her butler, Stokes, long since retired to his own chambers, the ballroom would be completely empty.

'I love fighting in the dark,' Philippa murmured as her feet led her through the echoing halls. This wouldn't be the first night Philippa trained until the sky began to lighten with dawn's arrival. It wouldn't be the last night she tirelessly wielded sword, dagger, and cudgel, practising the steps of life's most dangerous dance. Her insomnia was a carry-over from youth, but after years of battling with her body's refusal to succumb to sleep, Philippa knew the best solution was to accept her restless spirit and soothe it with movement. After hours of physical exertion, she would be so weary, she might find a few moments of sleep.

Tonight, she would train with the katana and wakizashi swords. She had been studying the Niten Ichi-ryū method of sword fighting for close to a decade. It required complete focus, and all other thoughts, even those of a cursedly beautiful marchioness, had no room to cloud her mind if she were going to give her blades the attention they demanded.

Fluidity, adaptation, rhythm, control.

She repeated the mantra silently as her body flowed like water over stones, the blades an extension of her arms, effortlessly cutting through imagined foes. Her fascination with other cultures' battle techniques had allowed

Philippa to learn fighting patterns many English noblemen were not expecting. The teachings of Miyamoto Musashi – originator of the Niten Ichi-ryū method – emphasised taking the offensive and controlling a fight from the onset. Strategies no man expected from a lady, especially a duchess. It gave Philippa another advantage in her war against opponents who were often bigger and sometimes stronger, though rarely more skilled.

Philippa moved across the ballroom floor, her steps light and sure, sweat dripping as she discarded her banyan. She fought in only loose silk pants and a flowing sleeveless top that allowed her limbs complete freedom.

Hours passed, or perhaps only moments. Her muscles began to burn. She focused on controlling her breath as the blades sang their war song. Peace descended, all her racing thoughts became silent as her body glided through practised movements. She relished the calm seeping into her soul.

The sound of a throat clearing broke her focus, and she froze. Slowly straightening from her fighting stance, she kept her swords at the ready and spun to face her adversary.

2

Lady Olivia Smithwick was lit by a silvery moon. The pistol in her hand flashed in the pale light. She stood in the centre of the ballroom, glowing like a Valkyrie come to carry Philippa's spirit to Valhalla. Some unnamed emotion stalled Philippa's heart mid-beat. For a breathless fraction of time, they stared at one another, warriors each assessing the other for weakness.

'You received my invitation.' Philippa forced her lip to curl into a confident smile. She refused to acknowledge the prickling rush of heat washing over her skin.

'I did.' Olivia's clear voice rang through Philippa's nervous system like a lightning bolt, as infuriating as it was thrilling. The woman's hold over Philippa was unaccountable. And unacceptable.

Focus on the mission. This is my chance to capture the wayward woman and discover her secrets. That is all I care about.

'I'll admit, I didn't think you would come.' Philippa slid her bare foot to the right, stepping slowly closer as Olivia countered Philippa's approach with a matching evasive step, her pistol following Philippa with nary a tremor of nerves.

'How could I resist an invitation from the infamous Duchess of Dorsett? A woman whose high and mighty ideals are only eclipsed by her own hypocrisy.'

Rarely did a person dare insult Philippa. And never in her own ballroom, pointing a pistol at her chest. Her heart kicked hard against her ribcage as pleasure bloomed low in her belly. An enemy willing to openly engage in battle. How delightful. Not that she found *her* delightful. Just the opportunity to fight her.

Now that's sorted, what was she accusing me of? Ah, yes.

'Hypocrisy? What a fascinating relationship you have with reality, Lady Smithwick. If we are discussing duplicity, perhaps we should turn our focus to your recent behaviour. You claimed to be Ivy Cavendale's friend, then delivered her into the hands of your husband. He would have killed Ivy had she not been ready to fight.' Philippa would never forgive Olivia for putting her friend and protégée in such danger.

Lord Percival's plan to infiltrate London's poorest orphanages, kidnap children to fill orders of twisted men, and sell those innocent souls into a short life of unspeakable horror was foiled by Lady Ivy Cavendale and the help of her now-husband, Commissioner Edward Worthington. But not before Ivy was grievously betrayed by Olivia. For that alone, the woman deserved to be punished.

Lady Olivia swallowed as her chin wobbled.

False tears from a false woman. I will not be swayed by this deceitful beauty.

'The last person I wanted to hurt was Ivy. I had no choice. Not that you would understand anything about desperation, would you? Sitting here in your ivory tower. The world bows down to the Duchess of Dorsett. Confidante to the Queen. Richer than Croesus and colder than the Cailleach. You have no idea what it is like to know your heart lies in the hands of a monster. There is nothing I won't do to reclaim it. Even betray my friend.'

'You admit to being heartless?'

'I admit nothing to you.'

'Who still holds your heart, Lady Smithwick? Your husband is dead. Are you not now free?'

'What woman is ever free in this world? Even you are beholden to society's chains, Lady Winterbourne. Hiding your true nature behind the guise of a glamourous duchess for fear of the beau monde rejecting you if they saw who you really are. But I see you. A violent creature terrified of her power being challenged.'

'I've yet to meet a man with enough courage to try.'

'Thank God I'm not a man. And I'm not afraid of you.'

'Then you are a fool.'

Olivia's full lips hardened in a tight line. She lifted her brows, defiance clear in every sinew of her body. 'No more foolish than you for trying to intimidate me, Your Grace.'

It was dangerous to fight angry. Emotion clouded judgement and made it easier to misstep. But Olivia's words sparked a fire in Philippa. 'I am no one's fool,' she hissed as she leapt forward, taking Olivia by surprise.

Philippa moved like a whirling dervish of speed and skill. Olivia barely adjusted her aim before the flat of Philippa's katana blade smacked Olivia's wrist, breaking her grip on the pistol. Philippa could have easily adjusted her strike to cut off Olivia's hand, but the woman had beautifully shaped fingers. Again, not that Philippa cared about the woman's hands. It's just that it would be a shame to ruin her favourite nightclothes with Olivia's blood.

The pistol crashed to the floor. Philippa expected Olivia to scramble away or chase after her weapon. Instead, the contradictory woman leapt forward, catapulting herself at Philippa and gripping her around the waist, wrestling her to the floor. It was a stupid move that could have easily ended in Olivia's death given Philippa's superior weaponry. But instead of using her blades to incapacitate the woman, Philippa fell back against her assault. She hit the floor hard. Olivia's body landed on top of her, crushing Philippa onto the parquet.

Her hesitation cost Philippa. She couldn't use her blades in such close quarters and needed to drop them if she wished to defend herself. And she needed to defend herself because Olivia wrapped those beautiful fingers – *fingers I should have severed when I had the chance* – around Philippa's neck. Olivia's other hand shackled Philippa's right wrist and pinned it over her head.

Concentrate. Stay calm. There is always a weakness. Find it.

But Philippa found it hard to concentrate when Olivia's fingers, instead of tightening around her throat, tickled the fine hair just behind Philippa's ear. The woman's scent, an intoxicating blend of honeysuckle and vanilla, seeped past Philippa's guard like a drugging poison. Philippa bucked up with her hips, but Olivia flexed her hand hard enough for fear's sharp thrill to spiral from Philippa's belly to the tips of her fingers and bare toes. She was achingly aware of Olivia's body pressed against her own. The woman wore a hideous grey gown that scratched against Philippa's exposed skin. The dress was better suited to a maid than the glamorous Marchioness Brightmore who so quickly captured the attention of the beau monde earlier this summer upon her return from a decade abroad. Olivia's sensuous figure was hidden by a high neck and long sleeves, but Philippa felt every supple curve and lean line as Olivia tightened her thighs around Philippa's waist, pinning her lower half to the floor.

'Return the contents of my purse, Your Grace, and I shall leave you in peace. Refuse, and I shall leave you in pieces.'

* * *

Olivia was still trying to pull her thoughts together after watching Philippa train.

She had been hiding in the corner of the ballroom, waiting for the servants to go to bed before seeking out Philippa's bedroom. Then, like a gift from the heavens, a light had flickered down the hallway. The door creaked open, and the duchess had appeared in the cavernous room, her face illuminated by a single candle.

A gasp had caught in Olivia's throat before she swallowed it down, cursing herself for three times a fool. The duchess' beauty was renowned in the beau monde. The dramatic contrast of midnight hair and silver streaks, pale skin, and bold, crimson lips – a colour Olivia knew the duchess enhanced with cosmetics despite Queen Victoria's decree that a plain face was most appealing. Perfectly sculpted cheekbones, eyes the colour of a stormy sea.

Lovely. I'm waxing poetic about a woman determined to see me hang.

But only a blind fool could deny Philippa's sharp beauty. And Olivia was neither.

Instead of attacking immediately, she had indulged her fascination for the deadly woman, telling herself she only watched Philippa gliding across the ballroom floor, the steel of her blades flashing in the moonlight, to better learn her foe's skills.

I must understand her strengths if I am to take advantage of her weaknesses.

And what Olivia learned had disturbed her in the extreme. Because the duchess appeared to have no weaknesses. Philippa moved so quickly, she was like a bird of prey effortlessly twisting, sliding, and leaping in a pattern impossible to predict. Her black silk pants and loose top fluttered as her long braid whipped behind her. The wickedly dangerous blades were unfamiliar to Olivia, and certainly nothing like the massive broadsword of the highlanders, or the much thinner rapier preferred by most lords of the beau monde. One blade was just longer than Philippa's arm, the other about half that size. She had wielded them as extensions of her body, arcing and slicing in movements closer to dance than the brutish thrust and parry Olivia had seen when lords duelled. It was mesmerising.

Olivia had only intended to watch for a few moments, but she became lost in Philippa's violent beauty. She might as well have been a child gorging on the sweet ices served at Gunters with no parent near to temper her voracious appetite. But, as with all temptations, there was grave danger in such gluttonous indulgence. Because the longer she had watched Philippa, the more convinced Olivia became that she could not defeat this woman. Not if she played by the rules. So she had determined to break them, starting with bringing a pistol to this sword fight. Albeit a pistol she didn't know how to use, but Philippa need not know that.

Forcing her body to move before she melted into the cracks of Philippa's polished parquet floor, Olivia had pushed down the confusing blend of emotions gripping her chest in a tight squeeze and making it hard to breathe.

I must remember why I'm here. She is my enemy. And I must vanquish her if I have any hope of a life beyond this madness.

She had attacked without hesitation, which brought her to this moment, straddling a very angry duchess, her hand wrapped around the woman's throat.

'Return what you stole,' she demanded.

She deserved a chance to escape and restart her life. After fighting so long to escape the prison created for her by cruel men, she had earned the right to control her choices. The only person standing in her way was trapped between Olivia's thighs.

'You really expect me to hand you the one thing keeping you from escape?' Philippa's pupils were blown wide, betraying her seemingly calm demeanour.

Olivia should have tightened her hand around the woman's delicate throat. Jasmine and frankincense wrapped around her, muddling her thoughts. Instead of pressing her advantage, Olivia's fingers gently caressed over the soft skin behind Philippa's left ear. The hitch in Philippa's breathing confirmed one suspicion Olivia had about the duchess. There was more simmering between them than just vengeance and justice.

'Not willingly. But yes. I think we can both agree my money isn't worth your life. You already think the worst of me, so it shouldn't stretch your imagination to believe I will kill you if you refuse.'

Philippa strained forward, lifting her head from the floor, pressing her throat harder into Olivia's hand. She bared her teeth in a feral smile. 'Do it then. I dare you. Because you will get nothing from me.'

Ridiculous, stubborn, impossible woman!

She was calling Olivia's bluff. It was the worst possible outcome. Olivia was desperate, but she wasn't a killer. She needed the money, but she couldn't end someone's life for it. Even if that person enraged her. And now Philippa knew Olivia's weakness.

With a frustrated scream, she shoved Philippa back to the floor, taking petty satisfaction from the thunk of Philippa's head hitting the wood panels. Getting to her feet, Olivia scanned the room and found her pistol as Philippa stood and reclaimed her blades.

Olivia backed slowly to the open window.

'You know I can't let you leave, Lady Smithwick.' Philippa slid one foot forward, holding the blades in front of her in a fighting stance.

Olivia re-aimed her pistol at Philippa's chest, for all the good it would do. She had taken it from where she knew Percy kept his guns, but she had no idea if it was loaded, how to load it if it wasn't, and what to do to make the thing go bang. Given that Philippa kept calling her bluff, her only option would be to throw the heavy thing at the duchess if she attacked with her wickedly sharp blades.

'And I can't let you catch me. There is far more at stake here than you'll ever know. You've no idea the power of the Devil's Sons. Running is the only choice I have left.' The words tasted bitter. Cowards ran, and that is what she was.

'Who is their leader?' Philippa took a sidestep that brought her closer.

The pistol shook as Olivia's throat closed, making it impossible to speak even if she wanted to reveal the Crow. Which she would never do. It would mean more than just her own death. He would destroy her daughter. Slowly. Painfully. While he forced Olivia to watch.

'I can't tell you that.' Olivia stepped back, closer to the open window. The curtain fluttered against her calf.

'Why?'

Olivia choked out a laugh, though nothing about this was funny. Her one chance of escaping England was gone. Because of this woman. Someone fighting for justice and truth. Someone Olivia both admired and hated in equal measure.

And someone I desire most fervently.

She blinked, forcing the inconvenient truth into the same dark pit where her honour and kindness struggled to survive.

'Because the cost is too dear.'

The door closest to Philippa opened. An older man in a long nightgown and sleeping hat burst into the room, a candle in one hand and fire poker in the other.

Several things happened at once.

Startled by the man's sudden appearance, Olivia swung the gun toward him, pulled the trigger, and learned it was loaded.

Plaster exploded in a cloud of white as a bullet lodged in the wall – thankfully well above the gentleman's head.

The portly man in the nightgown dropped to the floor in what must have been a dead faint.

Philippa spun toward him and screamed, 'Stokes!'

Olivia turned and leapt out of the window, landing hard on the grassy lawn below. She didn't turn to see if Philippa followed her. She ran.

* * *

Philippa sipped her whiskey-laced tea and tried to listen to the conversation swirling around her. It was early afternoon, but the day had already been long. After determining her butler had only succumbed to shock and not a bullet, she spent the remainder of the early morning getting Stokes back to his bed, ringing for a doctor to check on her curmudgeonly patient, and organising the repair of her ballroom wall. Olivia had left quite a mark. With those tasks complete, she sent invitations to the Queen's Deadly Damsels. It was time to make a war plan.

'I can't believe she almost shot poor Stokes. Although, you've been threatening to do that for years, Philippa. Perhaps she meant to do you a favour.' Millie Drake sat on the settee opposite Philippa. Her wild, red curls were swept into a high knot with tendrils left to frame her freckled cheeks.

'Millie! That isn't funny. The poor man could have been seriously injured.'

Ivy Worthington, pale and lean in a sapphire dress that complemented her crystal eyes, slapped Millie's arm. She and Millie had been friends since childhood and often interacted like sisters, though they could not look more opposite. Millie's figure was lush where Ivy's was lithe. Millie's bright-copper curls and rosy complexion reminded one of a warm summer afternoon while Ivy's blonde hair and pearl complexion inspired thoughts of a winter moon rising over snowy fields.

'She makes a point, though.' Hannah Killian stood next to the fireplace. She had one hand in her pocket and the other held a glass of whiskey. 'Philippa has been threatening to use Stokes as target practice since long before I moved into her house.' Hannah was the illegitimate child of Lord Winterbourne. Upon her mother's murder, Hannah had nowhere to turn except for Philippa. The duchess extended an invitation for the fourteen-year-old girl to live with her and trained Hannah as her first protégée. It was a highly unusual arrangement most women would never allow, but Philippa was not most women. She was grateful to Hannah's mother for diverting her husband's attention away from Philippa. As far as she was concerned, she owed her husband's mistress a great debt, so when Hannah arrived on her doorstep covered in blood and needing sanctuary, Philippa didn't hesitate to offer what protection she could.

Hannah became Philippa's first Deadly Damsel, and while the duchess had never particularly longed for children, Hannah made her appreciate the benefits of progeny. She wasn't Philippa's daughter by blood, but the duchess loved Hannah with a fierceness every mother felt for their child. It was something she rarely admitted, even to herself.

Of course, her affection for Hannah didn't stop the young woman from nettling Philippa.

'Perhaps Olivia was trying to offer you a bribe. Stokes' life in return for the jewels you stole.'

'Her idea of bribes is just as horrific as her idea of friendship.' Philippa looked meaningfully at Ivy. A crimson blush stained the young woman's throat and cheeks in splotches.

'I know you never trusted her, but Olivia was kind to me.' Ivy picked up a sugared tart and nibbled the edge.

'She lied to you, kidnapped two orphans, and would have watched her husband shoot you like a dog in the street. If that is kindness, I would much prefer cruelty.' Philippa's voice shook with barely controlled rage. Despite her best efforts to remain aloof, the women she trained had all captured a piece of her heart. The very idea of one of them being harmed filled Philippa with fear she could not tolerate. She did what she always did when faced with a vulnerable emotion and transformed it into anger.

Ivy returned the tart to her small plate and carefully licked sugar from her finger. 'We are missing something. I don't think Olivia would willingly align herself with these men. You didn't see her expression that night. She was torn. Haunted by her choice. The Devil's Sons must have some kind of leverage over her.'

'Have you spoken with her brother? Mayhap he has some information we could use to find her.' Penny frowned into her lap, fiddling aimlessly with a button on her skirt. Philippa respected the maid-turned-marchioness. She had proven herself to be smart, resourceful, and loyal. Once Millicent's lady's maid, Penny took a position in Lord William Renquist's house in an undercover attempt to capture an evil lord. But it was Liam who captured Penny's heart when she realised he was secretly working with the Queen to dismantle the Devil's Sons. Their love story sparked quite the scandal as a maid took on the mantle of marchioness, but no one was more deserving of such good fortune as Penny.

'The Lord High Chancellor came to me the week after Percival Smithwick was arrested.' Philippa remembered the meeting well. The usually reserved man, second only to the Queen in power and influence within the realm, was nearly beside himself with worry for his niece. 'His biggest concern was finding Olivia's daughter. While he expressed deep grief over his sister's choices, he has given her up as lost and is only focused on Hyacinth's safety. If we find Olivia, she will face the hangman's noose, and if we don't, she will live the rest of her life as a fugitive. But Hyacinth could have a proper life. The young girl is only sixteen. This summer was meant to be her debut into society. He fears Olivia has taken the girl against her will and is holding her somewhere.'

Ivy shook her head. 'Olivia would never do anything to harm her daughter. She spoke often of trying to repair their relationship.'

'Did she speak often of her loyalty to you? Because she certainly lied about that.' Philippa failed to keep the poison from her tone.

'Not everything she said was a falsehood. She may have been deceiving me about our friendship, but she wasn't lying about her daughter. I'm sure of it.' Ivy spoke with quiet conviction.

Philippa raised a brow, pressing her lips together to keep insults about Olivia from spilling forth.

'Does he know of our work? Being so close to the Queen, I'm sure she has revealed certain facts to him.' Hannah crossed the short space between the hearth and a velvet wingback chair, smoothing her skirts before she sat.

'Based on his request for me to seek out his niece and return her to him, a good guess would be yes. According to the Chancellor, his sister's extended absence during Hyacinth's formative years left quite a rift between mother and daughter. He took the girl under his wing, and he's sick with fear for her safety.'

Millie tucked a crimson curl behind her ear. 'I can't picture the Chancellor showing any kind of extreme emotion. I only met him once at Ivy's charity ball, but he was so composed. Even when you informed him of his brother-in-law's crimes and his sister's escape. As I recall, he clenched his jaw and his left eye twitched. Hardly someone who would be overcome with feelings.'

Philippa lifted a shoulder in a shrug. 'He was more expressive with me. I think he's had time to process the dangers facing his niece. The last thing he wants is for this to be made public. The scandal of it would ruin Hyacinth's chances of finding a normal life.'

'It was clever of him to spread rumours that Olivia and her daughter escaped to the countryside during the scandal of her husband's imprisonment and murder,' Hannah mused. 'If the beau monde were to catch wind of Olivia's involvement with her husband's dealings, or discover she is missing, it isn't just Hyacinth who could be ruined by gossip. The Lord High Chancellor's entire career could be in jeopardy.'

'It's bad enough his brother-in-law was one of the leaders of the Devil's Sons. Has the Queen said anything to you?' Ivy looked to Philippa, her clear eyes wide with curiosity.

'She told me the Lord High Chancellor Hardgrave went directly to her after the charity ball and told her everything. He is committed to helping us root out the last leader in this group, but Hyacinth's safety takes priority for him. He promised the Queen any loyalty he had to his sister died the night she helped Percival kidnap the orphans and turned Ivy over to her husband.' As a rule, Philippa trusted very few men, but the Lord High Chancellor, while reserved and stiff in his demeanour, had shown true fear when speaking of his niece. She was certain he would do anything to get her back, and that kind of desperation wasn't easy to fake.

'So what is the next step?' Penny asked.

'We need to track down Olivia's whereabouts, determine if she has her daughter with her, rescue the girl, and capture Olivia.' Philippa was determined to achieve this mission quickly and put the entire affair behind her.

'Simple as that.' Millie's eyes flashed with mischief. 'We should have this buttoned up in no time.'

'I'll talk to Edward. I'm sure he would let Reading help us. The man is a marvel. He can comb through piles of paperwork and find one tiny piece of evidence that cracks the case.' Ivy stood. 'I'll go to Scotland Yard directly and see if Edward is available.'

'I suppose there are some benefits to being married to the Commissioner of Scotland Yard.' Hannah winked at Ivy as the pale woman's blush re-emerged.

'Or at least being married to the man who hired Reading as his secretary,' Millie added, standing to join Ivy. 'I must be going as well. Drake is meeting me at the milliner for a new bonnet.'

'I imagine he'll look quite dashing. Mayhap something with blue ribbons to bring out his eyes?' Penny's smile was infectious. The very idea of Major General Drake in a frilly bonnet with his scarred face and the physique of a bare-knuckle brawler had even Philippa fighting a smile. Penny rose, brushing crumbs off the settee. 'I should take my leave as well. Liam promised to take me riding in the park before we lose the light. He insists I'm getting better, but then his opinions about me are often skewed.'

A pang of longing resonated in Philippa's chest. She was accustomed to living alone and appreciated her solitude, but seeing the women she mentored all partnered with men perfectly suited to each of their strengths and weaknesses filled her with a strange longing. Not for a man.

Saints preserve me from such a fate.

But for a partner. Someone to sit with in front of the fire as evening darkened the sky, sipping whiskey and tea, discussing the day's events. But her chances for domestic tranquillity had never been good. A sapphist faced serious challenges to hide any romance behind the guise of passionate female friendship, but Philippa had the added complication of guilt and sorrow to navigate.

Liza's face drifted into her mind, fresh with youth, fuzzy with time, and achingly familiar. Hollow loneliness grew sharp edges of grief.

Some people are meant to walk their path alone. There's no point lamenting that which cannot be changed. I committed myself to Liza, and nothing will sway me. Not her death, and certainly not some blonde siren who belongs in a prison cell, not floating around in my head like a phantom temptress. And why am I thinking about Olivia... again?

Philippa forced her attention back to Hannah. 'Are you off as well?'

Hannah tilted her head, her gaze assessing. 'I can stay for one more cup of tea. Shall I pour?'

Hannah busied herself with refreshing Philippa's tea while the other ladies made their goodbyes and bustled out in a colourful swish of lace, silk, and cotton.

Hannah knew Philippa best of all the women and was the least afraid. The petite woman didn't want another cup of tea. She wanted to speak with Philippa alone. 'Say what you want to say, Hannah.'

Handing Philippa a fresh dish of whiskey-laced tea, she turned to pour her own cup, conveniently avoiding eye contact with Philippa. 'I've been thinking about something you told me once.'

Philippa raised an eyebrow. It was a look she had perfected in her early years with Lord Winterbourne. Generally, she found it an effective tool in convincing others to think very carefully about their words before saying something stupid. 'I'm surprised you remember anything I say; you certainly never seem to follow my advice.'

Hannah tsked. 'Your advice is not always as sage as you believe it to be. But this particular time, I think you were spot on.'

Philippa huffed out a breath. 'I am always spot on,' she muttered.

'You told me, "All creatures deserve love." You also said no woman should be ashamed of her desires.'

Philippa felt heat rising from her chest to her neck. She hadn't blushed since she was a girl. She wasn't about to start now. Forcing another sip of whiskey down her suddenly dry throat, Philippa focused on that burn instead of the heat emanating from her core. 'Women spend far too much time being ashamed of their feelings, while men have no trouble demanding their wants be met at any cost. I am not ashamed of my desires, but neither do I intend to discuss them with anyone.'

'I remember feeling similarly that night. But it didn't stop you from poking your nose into my business when I was too scared to admit my attraction to Killian.'

'You think I'm scared?' Philippa snorted. 'Of my desire? Please. Do I strike you as a woman who feels fear for anything?' It was an evasive question designed to reveal little. While Philippa trusted Hannah implicitly, being vulnerable with anyone was out of the question. It invited far too many emotions, and emotions were like a feral cat. Just as prone to scratch and claw as snuggle and purr.

'I think you fear letting people close.'

First Delacroix, now Hannah. Damn these women and their blasted opinions.

It mattered little that their opinions happened to be correct.

'I am simply cautious with my friends. Few people are worthy of my time. You and the other ladies are exceptions to that rule.'

'But is friendship enough? Or do you wish for more? For a special companion?'

'Like a cat? It would ruin the furniture. And dogs are far too needy.'

Hannah exhaled slowly through her nose. 'Not a pet, Philippa. A partner. I know you won't admit it, but something about Olivia has unsteadied you. It would be easy to paint her as an evil woman, unworthy of love or affection. But what if you are wrong?'

'What does her guilt or innocence have to do with anything?' Philippa was used to being a step ahead of most people. She did not like this feeling of confusion. It was bad enough that Philippa kept thinking of Olivia. Why was Hannah bringing her into this discussion?

'If she is innocent, then you would have no reason to dislike her.' Hannah glanced up from her tea. 'And if you had no reason to dislike her, you might find a few reasons to like her.'

Jittery nerves thrilled through Philippa. She stood, pacing in staccato steps. 'This is a nonsensical argument. I don't want a companion. Having desires is very different from wanting to act upon them. And, lest we forget, Olivia Smithwick is guilty of attempting to aid her husband in terrible crimes. I suspect she also kidnapped her daughter and is holding the poor girl against her will. The only feelings I have for the woman are outrage. The only desire I have is to catch her and force her to face justice.'

Hannah watched Philippa pace. 'What if you are wrong and she is not guilty?'

'You were there that night. You heard Ivy tell us how Olivia could have stood against her husband, but she did not. Instead, she willingly sacrificed Ivy to his homicidal machinations. I am not wrong about this.' Philippa spoke unflinchingly. Because she needed her words to be true.

Standing, Hannah walked to Philippa and put a reassuring hand on her arm, squeezing softly. 'We are all wrong sometimes, Philippa.' She leaned forward and pulled Philippa into a hug.

Philippa wanted to wrap her arms around Hannah and accept the gesture of support. She wanted to lean into Hannah's strength, if only for a moment. But leaning on someone else only invited a devastating crash when they left. So, she remained stiff and unyielding in Hannah's embrace.

Hannah pulled back, her eyes meeting Philippa's gaze with a frankness few dared show the duchess. 'You were right when you told me we all deserve love. And I am right when I tell you that "all" means "all". You aren't exempt from this.'

Philippa pressed her lips together, hating the thickness closing her throat. 'I have had my chance at love. I don't want another.'

'Sometimes, what we want is not what we need, Philippa.'

'And sometimes, it is the exact same thing.'

Hannah blinked twice in quick succession. It was the only indicator that Philippa had been too harsh in her rebuke, but it was enough. Philippa forced her tone to soften. Hannah wasn't trying to attack her, after all. She was trying to help. Even if Philippa didn't need any help. 'It is getting late. You should return home to Killian before he starts to worry and organises a military offensive to rescue you.'

Hannah tucked her hand into her pocket and stepped away from Philippa. 'I do hope we catch Olivia. Mayhap justice will look a little different than we expect once we hear her side of things. Ivy is right. Something is amiss.'

'The only thing amiss is her belief she can escape me. I will prove beyond any doubt she is guilty.'

Philippa noted the look Hannah gave her before she walked out the door. A look calling Philippa ten times the fool.

3

It was an undeniable truth that azalea bushes carried with them a great many pokey branches and at least twenty of those branches were stabbing Olivia in the arms, legs, and side.

As soon as she had escaped Philippa's, she knew she must return. There was no hope of booking passage to the Americas without her money, and Philippa was hiding it somewhere in her mansion. Probably in her bedchamber.

Olivia had determined to come back to Philippa's and keep watch on the front door. The duchess had to leave eventually, and then Olivia would sneak in, ransack the woman's room, and find her goddamned money. If it wasn't in Philippa's room, she could swipe some of the duchess' endless jewels to make up the difference. Chances were great that the pampered prima donna wouldn't even notice.

But not long after she wiggled into the leaves of the rather robust hedge between the front yard and the street beyond and discovered the azalea's afore-mentioned sharp branches, carriages started to arrive. Lady Hannah Killian was first. Then the maid-to-marchioness Penny Renquist. Lady Millie Drake and Lady Ivy Cavendale – *not Cavendale, Worthington, now she married the Commissioner of Scotland Yard* – were last, and their carriages came almost at the same moment. As Olivia watched the women greet each other in the drive and exchange hugs, guilt, self-loathing, and jealousy created a cocktail of heaviness in her chest. Ivy had been a true friend to Olivia. She was a rare creature in the beau monde. Honest. Courageous. Kind. All of the things Olivia was not. When Ivy offered loyalty and trust, Olivia betrayed the young woman in the most devastating way possible.

Perhaps I don't deserve to escape. I should turn myself in and face the consequences.

But to do so would put her daughter in grave danger. If Hyacinth's whereabouts were discovered, the Crow would come after the girl. He'd promised Olivia if she did not follow orders, her daughter's life would be sacrificed. Olivia certainly wasn't following his orders any longer.

She had only betrayed Ivy and helped Percival to kidnap the poor orphans because the Crow was using Hyacinth as leverage to ensure Olivia's obedience. But that fateful night had created a window of opportunity for Olivia to take her daughter and run. So she created a new plan. A dangerous endeavour that would end in their freedom or absolute failure. And the biggest risk to her success was the bloody Duchess of fecking Dorsett.

Olivia was struck with a mad thought as she watched Ivy's coachman manoeuvre the smart little carriage around the far corner of Philippa's mansion to park near the mews. If she could convince Ivy to forgive her, mayhap the woman might be her ally. Help her reclaim her money and evade Philippa's pursuit, for surely the duchess was calling together her Deadly Damsels to plan Olivia's capture.

Ivy always saw the good in others, even when it was barely recognisable. Mayhap she would see that same shimmer of worthiness in Olivia. At the very least, she might loan Olivia some money so she could leave this very day, collect her daughter, and set sail. It was a dream too good to be true, but fate was giving her another window. She had to climb through it.

Carefully extracting herself from the angry azalea bush, she brushed off errant leaves and snuck from topiary to fountain to rose bush until she cleared the front windows of Philippa's Belgrave mansion. She skirted the side of the impressively large home and found herself in the cobblestone yard.

A maid emerged from the kitchen and dumped a bucket of murky water into a grate. She glanced at Olivia but barely acknowledged her. Looking down at her grey dress and ragged coat, Olivia imagined she looked like any other servant on a task assigned by her employer. Walking with confidence over the cobblestones, Olivia passed a group of men standing in a small circle smoking pipes and discussing horseflesh. They had to be the various drivers of the carriages that had just deposited Philippa's friends on her front step.

Olivia breezed past them, turned the corner of the stables, and found four coaches parked next to each other. The horses stomped and huffed out puffs of warm breath. Olivia stiffened and bit back her cry of alarm. She had always found horses to be beautiful creatures best observed from a distance. She gave them a wide berth as she made her way to Ivy's carriage.

Twisting the silver handle of the barouche, Olivia slipped inside. Drawing the curtains, she pressed herself into the far corner and waited.

A million disastrous scenarios played out in Olivia's mind before the carriage dipped and the springs squealed in protest as Ivy's driver pulled himself to the top box. The driver clucked at the horse and the carriage lurched into a slow roll over the cobblestones of the mews, then the gravel of Philippa's drive. He was pulling to the front of the house to retrieve his mistress.

'This is a terrible plan. What was I thinking?' Olivia hissed. Desperation must have stolen her wits. Ivy was going to open the door, see Olivia crouched in the corner of her carriage, scream bloody murder, and that would be that. 'No. She'll give me a chance. I know she will.'

Before she could counter her own ridiculous argument, the door swung open. Ivy was holding the driver's hand as he assisted her in alighting. Her face was turned away from Olivia, her lips tilted in a sweet smile.

'Thank you, Jacob,' Ivy murmured before turning to find her seat.

A seat that was partially occupied by Olivia.

Olivia couldn't stop the tears from filling her eyes as she pressed a finger to her lips, silently begging Ivy to remain quiet. If she were wrong about Ivy, she would lose everything.

Ivy's mouth fell open, and her pale-blue eyes widened in shock.

'Is everything all right, my lady?' the coachman asked from behind her. Ivy was blocking his view of the carriage's interior.

'Please.' Olivia mouthed, her gaze never leaving Ivy's face, willing the woman to forgive her.

'Just a spider on my seat.' Ivy made a display of slapping the velvet squab. 'I frightened it off. Please take me to Scotland Yard; I need to speak with the Commissioner.'

Oh dear.

Scotland Yard was the very last place Olivia wanted to be. As Ivy shut the door, panic filled Olivia. She opened her mouth to speak. Plead. Beg Ivy to listen to her, but now it was Ivy pressing her finger against her lips and shaking her head.

'Not yet,' she whispered.

Ivy sat next to Olivia on the small seat and waited for the carriage to roll forward. The sound of the street became louder, and Ivy turned to face Olivia.

'What the Devil is going on, Olivia?' Ivy's face hardened into angry lines.

'Oh, Ivy.' The tight rein Olivia had kept on her emotions snapped. Tears streaked down her cheeks as she tried to catch her breath. 'I'm so sorry.'

'Why? Why did you do it? Did our friendship mean nothing to you?'

The time for hiding her past was over. As quickly as she could, Olivia attempted to explain her predicament, starting with the asylum where she had been imprisoned for ten years. 'Percival only brought me back from Europe because he needed someone to provide an entrance into the orphanages. Who better than his charity-minded wife? And Hyacinth's debut into society was just another weapon he wielded against me. He swore to force Hyacinth into marriage with one of his oldest and most perverse friends if I didn't agree. His own daughter was nothing more than a bargaining tool for Percy. He knew I would do anything to protect her. I *will* do anything still to ensure her safety. But I should never have betrayed you like that. I should have found another way. You must know, if I'd seen a different path, I would have taken it.'

Ivy leaned back against the squabs, her face shifting from anger to disbelief, until finally settling into a carefully blank expression. Which worried Olivia exceedingly.

'Why can't you come forward? Expose the Crow? End this horrific ring of flesh trafficking?'

'He is more powerful than you'll ever know, Ivy. And who would believe me? I have no evidence of his involvement. Revealing his identity would only condemn me to death and my daughter to a fate even worse. Leaving here is our only option.'

Ivy shook her head. 'Philippa is determined to catch you, Olivia. She has people watching the docks and main roads exiting London. I'm going to Scotland Yard right now to have Edward and Reading begin investigating all the potential places you might hide. You have no money, no allies. How will you possibly escape?'

'I was hoping you might help me. If you could loan me even a little coin, I promise I will repay you once Hyacinth and I are settled abroad.'

Olivia's stomach dropped as Ivy slowly shook her head.

'I can't. I won't betray Philippa and the other Damsels.'

The fight seeped out of Olivia like blood from a mortal wound. 'Then I am lost.' Her stomach cramped, and she bent forward. She couldn't remember the last time she'd eaten. A bone-deep fatigue washed through her as hope ebbed.

But her daughter still needed her. She couldn't just give up. Not until there was no other choice. Forcing herself to straighten, she gripped Ivy's hand in hers. 'Please know I am sorry for my actions. You were always a true friend to me. I only wish I could have been the same for you. If you will extend one more kindness I do not deserve, let me out at the next stop. I know you are duty-bound to tell the others I was here, but at least give me until you reach Scotland Yard to sound the alarm. All I ask is for a chance.'

Ivy squeezed Olivia's hand. 'What if there is another way?'

Olivia's brow drew down in confusion. 'What do you mean?'

'I have an idea.'

4

Philippa's life was not immune to intrigue. As a secret agent of the Queen, one expected a certain number of clandestine meetings in the middle of the night. But she didn't anticipate receiving a note from Ivy instructing Philippa to meet her at a coaching inn on the outskirts of London. According to Ivy's note, Reading had made an important discovery, and if they hoped to catch Olivia before she slipped away entirely, they must make haste.

Upon arrival at the bustling inn, Philippa instructed her driver to feed and water the horses but stay ready to leave at a moment's notice. She climbed the steps of the inn, ignored the stares of several travellers, no doubt awed to see the infamous Duchess of Dorsett gracing such a plebian establishment, and inquired as to the location of Lady Ivy Worthington. The innkeeper blushed to the roots of his thinning blond hair.

'She booked the private dining room, Your Grace. Just through 'ere.' The man bowed repeatedly as he led Philippa past the common room, down a narrow hall, and opened a scarred oak door to reveal a dimly lit sitting room. The room was crowded with a small dining table and four rickety chairs, a faded settee with the stuffing coming out of busted seams, a crackling fire in the far corner boasting a dusty hearth, and a side table covered in various plates and bowls of steaming food. None of this was particularly noteworthy, but what did stop Philippa in her tracks were the two occupants of the room.

Ivy stood near the fire, her finger tapping incessantly against the teacup in her hands. A clear sign she was anxious.

She bloody well should be anxious.

Because standing behind the table, a glass of sherry in her beautiful fingers, wild ringlets catching the warm light of the fire, her full bottom lip caught between blunt teeth, was Olivia Smithwick.

A wave of something hot, forbidden, and unwanted washed through Philippa.

Damnation.

'I suppose it's too much to assume you are delivering her to me.' Philippa directed her words to Ivy, but she didn't look away from Olivia. She didn't trust the woman not to run or try and attack. Philippa removed the fan from her pocket and thwacked it against the palm of her hand. Most assumed it was merely decorative; few knew it was also deadly. The frame was steel, and lace hid a razor-sharp edge that could easily cut through any number of things. Cloth, rope, flesh. Whatever might be impeding Philippa's progress.

'You have every right to be angry, but I'm asking you to listen.' Ivy's voice was calm even as crimson splotches appeared on her neck.

'I have every right to be angry? What about you? It was *your* life she risked when she abandoned you to her husband. You could have died.' Philippa realised her voice was becoming shrill. She also acknowledged her emotions were spiking. Taking a deep breath, she forced herself to calm down. 'How could you let her trick you once more, Ivy?'

'I told you she would never listen. She's far too stubborn to hear reason. Especially if it contradicts what she thinks is true.' Olivia glared daggers at Philippa. As if she had the right to be incensed about anything. The bloody woman should be kissing the ground Ivy walked on and singing her praises for not immediately handing Olivia over to the Bobbies.

Rage spiked once more, and Philippa took three sweeping steps past the table to face Olivia. The woman's eyes widened. She stumbled back. Philippa felt a thrill of power. 'What I *know* is true.'

'You aren't right about everything all the time, Duchess,' Olivia fairly hissed, regaining her composure and stepping forward until she was almost nose to nose with Philippa. The sweet aroma of honeysuckle washed over Philippa, tempered by warm vanilla. It was an oddly comforting scent, and she hated that it emanated from Olivia. 'I was false with Ivy. I admit that. I put her at risk, and I hate myself for it. But I had no choice.'

Caustic mirth bubbled up within Philippa. 'Please. There is always a choice.' She leaned closer, expecting Olivia to back away. But she held her ground, green eyes blazing, her chest rising and falling with rapid breaths.

'Perhaps for lofty duchesses with more money than wit. But not so for me. If I did not betray Ivy, I would lose my daughter forever. I did what I had to do. I can accept that. But I won't accept your judgement of me, Lady Winterbourne. You know nothing about me or the torture I've had to endure.'

Despite her best efforts, a crack splintered in Philippa's confidence.

What pain have you suffered?

No. She didn't care. It didn't matter. The why of Olivia's choice was not nearly as important as the actual decision.

'I don't care what you've experienced, Lady Smithwick. I care about protecting the innocent.'

'Exactly. Just as Olivia is trying to do for her daughter.' Ivy jumped in, placing her cup on the table as she drew closer to Philippa. She squeezed Philippa's arm. 'I think, given time, you might both realise you are more similar than different. Which leads me to my proposal.'

Philippa ripped her gaze from Olivia to blink at Ivy. 'What possible proposal could you have for me and this woman that doesn't end in her death?'

'You taught me not to back down from bullies, so I won't let your words dissuade me, but I will remind you that jumping to conclusions is never a wise strategy, Philippa.'

Ivy's censure stung, even more so because she had a point. Philippa battled with annoyance and pride. It was glorious to see Ivy stepping into her own power, but she would prefer the woman didn't use her newfound confidence to contradict Philippa.

Trouble, thy name is woman.

'Fine.' Philippa stepped away from Olivia and exhaled. 'Tell me your idea, Ivy. I can't promise to agree, but I will at least listen.'

Olivia rolled her eyes. 'Oh my. What a gift you've bestowed upon us. You'll *listen*. How shall we ever show our gratitude, Your Grace?'

'You could start by losing the sarcasm, Lady Smithwick. Much like that dreadful frock, it hardly flatters you.'

Which was an absolute lie. Even in the plain clothes of a working woman, Olivia was stunning. Her figure rivalled that of Venus. Cheeks flushed a rosy pink that only highlighted the pale glory of her wild curls. Her full lips distracted Philippa every time she bit the bottom one, and her emerald-green eyes flashed with defiance, begging Philippa to meet her on the battlefield and pit her will against Olivia's.

Olivia narrowed her eyes and rested a hand on her hip. 'Have you any suggestions on what might improve my appearance, Lady Winterbourne?'

Bloody hell. She caught me out on that one.

Rage and a disconcerting excitement she only felt when warring made it difficult to devise a witty reply. Thankfully, Ivy saved her from having to try.

'We are getting off track. Philippa, we need to uncover the identity of the remaining leader for the Devil's Sons. Olivia, you need to be guaranteed safe passage away from England for you and your daughter. These goals are not mutually exclusive. I think we can help each other.'

'Letting this woman get away with her crimes is the antithesis of our goals, Ivy. If you are so remorseful for your previous choices, Lady Smithwick, then make up for that now by revealing the Crow.'

'Not until I know my daughter is safe. Help me get her away from England, promise me she will remain hidden and protected, and then I will tell you everything. You can take me into custody, march me in front of the House of Lords and subject me to their judgement, or execute me yourself if you wish. My life means nothing to me once Hyacinth is safe. This is my bargain, Duchess.'

Philippa's spine stiffened. Never before had someone used her title as an insult, but the disdain in Olivia's tone was sharper than the edge of Philippa's fan.

'You would willingly turn yourself in?'

The infuriating woman's throat constricted, drawing Philippa's eye to the hollow of her neck. How soft was her skin, just there, in the dip between her clavicles?

I don't care about her skin.

But guilt washed through her at the rogue desire to know if Olivia tasted salty or sweet.

'Yes. Once my daughter is safe, it doesn't matter what happens to me.'

Something tight squeezed around Philippa's ribs. Much as she despised Olivia, it seemed wrong for the woman to so easily sacrifice herself.

'How do I know you'll hold true to your bargain?'

Olivia raised a pale brow in a close imitation of Philippa's signature look. *Not bad. Quite intimidating.*

'I suppose you'll have to trust me. Just as I must trust you won't betray my daughter's safety for your own pursuit of glory.'

Philippa narrowed her gaze. 'I pursue justice, Lady Smithwick. Glory tends to find me all on its own.'

Olivia muttered something sounding suspiciously similar to 'Arrogant prig.'

'Do we have a deal?' Ivy asked, a smile tipping up the corners of her wide mouth.

Philippa rarely agreed to deals she hadn't carefully brokered. She certainly didn't join with enemies, even if they were focused on a shared goal. But mayhap Olivia was right. Sometimes, there was no choice. Even for a duchess.

Olivia knew the identity of the Crow. She also agreed to willingly turn herself over to Philippa once her daughter's safety was guaranteed. Wasn't that worth joining forces for a time? And the fact she didn't trust the woman only made it more imperative to join with Olivia and watch her every move.

Keep your friends at a distance and your enemies close.

'I promise to protect your daughter from any danger, and once her safety is assured, you will reveal the identity of the Crow and accept whatever punishment the Queen deems appropriate. Do we have an accord?' Philippa held out her hand and her breath, hoping Olivia didn't see the glaring hole in Philippa's proposal.

Olivia's gaze flitted from Philippa's hand to her eyes. Pressing her lips together, she exhaled through her nose and shook her head. 'You swear to me you will do everything in your power to ensure no harm befalls Hyacinth?'

At least that was something Philippa could answer with complete honesty. 'I do.' Only safety for Olivia's daughter would come in being reunited with her uncle, not sailing off across a treacherous ocean to live in a country of outlaws and wild creatures. Not that Olivia need be privy to that particular detail.

Reaching out her delicate hand, Olivia took Philippa's, surprising the duchess with her firm grip. An electric punch of current burst from Philippa's palm, zinging up her arm. Olivia gasped, and they both pulled free of the handshake.

'What the Devil?' Olivia hissed.

Philippa shook out her hand, clenching her fingers into a fist to dispel the jitter of energy. 'We must have built up static electricity. Damn carpet.' She looked at her feet and ignored that the floorboards were bare, making her explanation patently ridiculous.

'Lovely. Well, you need to change, Philippa. You have a lot of ground to cover if you're going to make the Cornish Coast in time.' Ivy clapped her hands together.

'Cornish Coast? What the bloody hell is in Cornwall?'

'Charlestown Port, actually. Hyacinth is there, and so is a ship bound for the Americas.'

'But you certainly can't embark on your journey as the Duchess of Dorsett. You'll draw far too much attention,' Ivy explained as though she were talking to one of her orphans.

Olivia's face bloomed into a smile that should have worried Philippa if she wasn't too busy trying to clear the buzzing from her head. The woman really was far too attractive.

'I don't understand.'

Ivy bent to retrieve a carpet bag. 'You shall be taking a leisurely trip to the coast for a holiday with your closest friend and companion.'

Alarm bells clanged somewhere amidst the haze Olivia's smile created in Philippa's thoughts. 'Pardon?' She tried to keep her voice calm. When one was the Duchess of Dorsett, one did not succumb to something as common as nerves.

'In this bag are the travelling clothes for one Miss Honoria Smith. A bluestocking spinster who spent most of her life as a governess and is splashing out for a much-deserved trip to the sea with her chuckaboo.' Ivy shook the bag.

Olivia lifted her hand and wiggled her fingers. 'That's me. Mrs Lavinia Brown. A widower whose pension allows me the freedom of travel with my dearest friend.'

Philippa blinked three times, slowly, waiting for the scene in front of her to disappear. She must be experiencing a waking nightmare. It was the only reasonable answer.

'I am to be a spinster. On a trip. With my... friend?' She nearly choked on the word, for Olivia was the last person she would consider as a friend. 'To Cornwall of all places? That's at least a fortnight by coach. Why don't we take the rails?'

Ivy waved away Philippa's question. 'Honoria and Lavinia couldn't possibly afford tickets on the train, and they enjoy more rustic modes of travel. Just think of the time you'll have to become better acquainted. When you finally reach the coast, you'll have no doubt of Olivia's guilt or innocence. I'm certain.'

Ivy's statement did nothing to reassure Philippa. It did raise her suspicions that there was more at play here than a simple decision about trains versus carriages. Was it possible the Damsels were working against Philippa and trying to force her to get to know Olivia? Surely, they wouldn't be so devious.

I did train each of them to be exactly that. Blast and damn.

'I shall check on the coach and leave you to change, Honoria.' Olivia had the audacity to wink at Philippa, her cheeks rounding as she smiled once more. Before leaving, she pulled Ivy into a tight embrace that did not cause a flare of something hot and uncomfortable in Philippa's chest. 'Thank you for your faith, Ivy. Whatever occurs, I will always treasure our friendship.' Olivia pressed a kiss to each of Ivy's cheeks in a display of affection Philippa could never allow for herself. Such open acknowledgement of intimacy only made one vulnerable to hurt and disappointment. She had been hurt before. Most grievously. She wouldn't allow fate another chance to wound her.

Olivia swept from the room in her dismal grey gown, somehow taking some of the light with her. Which was nonsensical.

'Let me help you change, Philippa.' Ivy came forward, turning Philippa to begin unbuttoning the row of tiny pearls holding her dress together. She resisted pulling free of Ivy's grasp. It would be impossible for her to change alone, but Philippa wasn't used to anyone but Delacroix helping her with her toilet.

A new thought emerged.

'Dear God. How are we to get along without a lady's maid between us?' The very idea of helping Olivia remove her dress to don a nightgown, or tangling her fingers in the woman's wild curls to create a reasonably neat coiffure, created a fluttering in her belly akin to a charm of hummingbirds beating their wings in a frenzy. And the buzzing was back in her head.

'You'll be fine. The travelling clothes I packed for you are all far simpler than your gowns, and your hair will look just as well in a chignon as it does with all these braids and curls.'

'What about Stokes? The other ladies? What excuse will you give everyone for my absence?' Philippa realised she was speaking too quickly, but her words raced as swiftly as her thoughts.

'I shall tell them the truth. You are following a lead on Olivia. Stokes will be pleased as punch to rule the roost for a few weeks, and the rest of us will keep searching for evidence against the Devil's Sons.'

'Do you think she'll stay true to her bargain?' Philippa let her jewelled gown fall from her shoulders, revelling in the moment of weightlessness before taking the much simpler and dowdy day dress of printed cotton. The travelling costume was a lavender hue far lighter than anything Philippa would choose. A wave of nausea rolled through her as she stepped into the narrow skirt and shoved her arms through the sleeves. It felt like a betrayal of Liza to don such light colours. She was meant to be in perpetual mourning. Yet here she was, about to embark on a journey with another woman, wearing the clothes of a merry spinster. It felt terribly wrong. And terribly exhilarating.

'I think, despite her earlier behaviour, she is an honourable woman.'

Philippa's snort was cut short as Ivy tugged the back of the dress together to button the simple wooden clasps.

'Will you do me one favour, Philippa?' Ivy asked as she finished the last button and stepped back.

Philippa turned to face the young woman who had once been as timid as a church mouse and now had the courage to stand against the Duchess of Dorsett. Not an easy task for a seasoned warrior, let alone a once-wilting wall-flower. 'Perhaps. What is it?'

'Give yourself the opportunity to be wrong.'

Philippa raised her brow. 'Since when is being wrong an opportunity?'

Ivy smiled. 'Since being wrong lets us grow. Forces us to change. Invites a little unexpected wonder into our lives.'

Philippa stepped away from Ivy. 'Is that what you're hoping this trip will accomplish? Unexpected wonder?'

Ivy shrugged, her eyes widening in false innocence. 'I'm just trying to help you accomplish your goal.'

Philippa raised a brow. 'What goal might that be?' Before Ivy could answer, she shook her head. 'Never mind. The last thing I need in my life is unexpected wonder. It sounds dreadful.'

Ivy's laugh did nothing to calm Philippa's nerves.

The lean woman led the way to the door. 'Not nearly as dreadful as the tedium of always being right.'

Philippa wanted to dismiss Ivy. She was close to fifteen years Philippa's junior. What could she know about life that Philippa hadn't already experienced three times over?

She might know a thing or two about wonder.

Philippa silenced the voice. She had no time for such ponderings. Wonder left her life the night Liza died, and she wasn't about to invite it back in. Instead, she squared her shoulders and prepared for a long journey in a small carriage with her sworn enemy.

5

The carriage jerked to the left. Olivia put out her hand to avoid smashing her shoulder into the squabs. Her back ached, her left foot had gone numb, and she had to empty her bladder.

'Must you constantly be shifting in your seat? You are worse than a child.' Philippa sat across from her, their knees almost touching in the small coach. They couldn't take Philippa's more luxurious conveyance as it was emblazoned with her crest and would leave no doubt in anyone's mind who was travelling the road to Cornwall. Ivy had taken Philippa's carriage, and they had hired a coach with a surly driver who stated upon meeting them he didn't think women should travel alone without a male companion. In his estimation, it wasn't safe.

'Oh, but we have you to protect us.' Olivia led with flattery.

'We are far safer alone than with any man.' Philippa followed with abrasive honesty.

That had been hours ago, and since the carriage rolled out of the inn's drive, Olivia was determined to keep her mouth shut and her eyes on the window as dawn crept over the sky, painting the clouds pink and yellow. Better to stay lost in her thoughts than attempt any conversation with the arrogant woman across from her.

The task would have been much easier if Philippa's jasmine and frankincense scent weren't surrounding her like a blanket. Or if her knee didn't keep bumping against the duchess'. Or if her gaze didn't keep wandering to Philippa's brazenly painted mouth.

She was torn between anger at Philippa, who clearly thought Olivia measured somewhere between a sea slug and a parasitic worm, and fear the duchess might come to her senses, and demand the driver take them directly to Scotland Yard. Olivia couldn't speak to the beautiful, horrible, infuriating duchess with any semblance of control, so she stayed silent. But Philippa seemed intent on poking her into some kind of reaction with her constant verbal barbs.

'If I had known I would be travelling with someone incapable of sitting still for more than two minutes together, I might have rethought my choice.'

Fine. If you wish to provoke me, I shall meet you tit for tat.

'Tell me, Lady Winterbourne, when did you first realise you were a sapphist?'

There. That should keep her quiet.

But instead of sputtering, or offering blatantly false denials, or doing as Olivia hoped and remaining quiet, she merely stretched her crimson lips in a smile that didn't reach her cobalt eyes. 'Ah. There is the mean-spirited woman Ivy refuses to see.'

Olivia opened her mouth to spit back a retort, but Philippa kept talking.

'I was twelve.'

Shock kept Olivia's mouth open until she remembered to snap it shut. The duchess was actually admitting something intensely personal about herself. To Olivia.

Because she plans on killing me when this is through. She needn't worry about me spilling her secrets when I'm six feet under the earth and rotting.

'Are you surprised at my honesty? I'm sure it's a novel experience for someone who lives in deceit. I think the moment I really knew was when sunlight caught my best friend's hair. A breathless need to run my fingers through those strands nearly felled me. I've never met a woman in my life with hair more beautiful than hers.' Her gaze flicked to Olivia's ringlets and then quickly back to her face. 'What about you, Lady Smithwick? Or will you dissemble?'

Olivia lifted her chin. The duchess was trickier than Olivia expected. If she avoided her question, she would prove herself a liar. Something Olivia was desperately trying to change. But if she admitted the truth, Philippa would know something just as intimate about herself as she now knew about Philippa, and she would lose the upper hand in this verbal sparring match.

In the end, she decided on honesty. 'Eighteen. I was newly wed, and the marriage bed held no charm for me. Although I didn't act on my impulses until later. I suppose I hoped the attraction for Percy would grow with time. It did not.'

'With a husband such as yours, I'm not surprised.' Philippa's dry assessment of Percival was hardly flattering but completely accurate.

'He wasn't overtly cruel. At first. But when he discovered me with my lady's maid five years into our marriage, he was... displeased.' Olivia broke eye contact with Philippa as a distant memory resurfaced.

'Filthy, invert, whore!' Percival grabbed Olivia by her hair, wrenching her from where she crouched protectively over her lady's maid, Daisy. Thank God Hyacinth's nursery was two floors above them. At least she need not fear her daughter would hear Percy's raging anger.

Daisy's eyes were huge with fear. She screamed as Percival hit Olivia with an open hand.

Olivia tasted blood, but she felt no fear. She felt nothing at all. Everything went numb.

Her fingers unerringly brushed over her cheek. His first smack hadn't been his last that fateful afternoon. One punch had been so hard, the white of her eye had turned red for days. Pulling herself out of the past, she forced a brittle smile. 'I suppose I'm a liar and a cheat. Disrespecting my marriage vows, with a woman, no less. You must be so pleased to find out my past matches your overall impression of me.'

Philippa held her gaze. Olivia wished she could read the duchess' thoughts. But likely, she didn't want to know the inner workings of Lady Winterbourne's mind. Still, her words surprised Olivia. 'Disrespecting an institution that disrespects women is hardly a sin in my eyes.'

Olivia shrugged. 'So, I suppose I'm just guilty of lying to my husband.'

Philippa's lip curled. 'Hiding your true nature from your husband may be the only thing we have in common.'

It wasn't a compliment, but neither was it a cutting remark. Olivia looked at her lap and smiled. 'She was such a lovely girl. Daisy. When she kissed me the first time, I finally understood what all the fuss was about. Like champagne fizzing in my belly and through my veins. Percival sacked her and sent her away, but at least he didn't whip her. I didn't even get to say goodbye. I think he thought he could beat the Devil out of me. That's what he would say, at any rate, when he was issuing his punishments.'

'Based on the rumours about you, it would seem your husband's efforts were successful. Though he wasn't able to inspire your fidelity.'

Olivia looked out the window as rain began to splatter against the glass. She hated the rumours Percival sparked about her. But she used his vitriol against him when he finally brought her back from the asylum. 'Ah, yes. His wayward wife, throwing herself at any lord with an ounce of wit or charm. Surely someone with your skills in investigation can see through such a blatant lie. He raged for months after discovering me simply kissing my maid. Can you imagine his wrath if I engaged in such infidelity with men?' She turned to stare at Philippa. 'But then, maybe your ability to discover the truth isn't quite as developed as you thought.'

Philippa shifted her foot. It was a subtle move that put her leather boot between Olivia's sturdy travelling shoes. Tension stretched between them like a violin string. Olivia moved her foot just enough to brush against Philippa's boot. Like a bow dragging across the string, a resonant vibration sang over Olivia's skin.

'He lied about your many conquests?'

'He did. Daisy was my only indiscretion. Percival destroyed her and kept me locked away for a decade as punishment.' Olivia shifted her foot back and stiffened her spine, breaking the invisible tie connecting her to Philippa.

'Men are singularly spectacular in their capacity for cruelty.' Philippa's low voice barely carried over the sound of rain on the roof and the crunch of gravel beneath the carriage wheels.

'Another thing we have in common. Our view of men. Miraculous.' Olivia glanced at Philippa and was struck by the flash of pain in her eyes. 'Was your husband equally brutal?'

Philippa pressed her lips together as if holding back the words by sheer force of will.

Olivia shook her head. 'Never mind. It is none of my business. I think we are approaching our next stop.' Relief at being able to escape the small space crammed with unspoken words was only eclipsed by knowing a privy waited several moments away.

The driver gave them surly instructions to be back at the carriage in no less than ten minutes. That's how long it would take to trade horses. They needed to be on their way to make the next inn before nightfall as it would be a long day of travel. 'It's not safe on these roads at night. I won't risk me life for two silly ladies in a rush to start their 'oliday.'

As Olivia walked around the inn to find the necessary – a dilapidated shack near the far corner of the property, surrounded by forest – she passed three men standing in a tight circle, smoking cheroots. Two wore the clothes of gentlemen. Their boots were shined to a dull sheen. Well-fitted trousers showed off their muscular legs while each of their jackets was tailored to emphasise wide shoulders and narrow waists. One wore a tall hat; the other's head was bare. The third must have been a steward, for his clothing showed more evidence of wear, his hair too long to be fashionable, his boots scuffed and worn. One of the gentlemen tipped his hat at Olivia, a mischievous glint lighting his dark eyes. She returned his smile with one of her own, though nothing about the man appealed to her. It was mechanical to respond to men's interest with feigned appreciation. It caused less of a fuss than dismissing them out of hand.

When she emerged from the necessary a few minutes later, the gentlemen had wandered to the edge of the property and directly in her path, blocking her way to the front of the inn.

'Hullo, love. Where are you travelling on this fine day?' the man with the hat asked.

A bold question and one he would never dare ask if he knew her status as a marchioness.

Olivia ducked her head, looking at him through her thick, golden lashes, presenting the perfect picture of a shy maid as fear, ancient and elemental to any animal of prey, thrilled through her. 'My party is waiting for me, sir. I've no time to dally.' She attempted to sidestep the gentleman, but he anticipated her bid for escape. Olivia nearly crashed into his chest as he matched her move-ment. He put a hand on her hip, ostensibly to steady Olivia, but his fingers tightened against her in a gesture far too familiar.

'Unhand me, sir.' Olivia stepped back and slammed into the other lord. The steward had circled around to cover her left side. She was hemmed in between three men with the forest behind her.

Stupid! I should have been more aware.

'What we've in mind won't take much time, love.' The lord behind her had a high, nasal voice, as though someone were pinching his nose. His giggle turned Olivia's blood cold.

How long had she been gone? A few minutes at most. Surely Philippa would come in search of her if she wasn't back to the coach in time. But how long might it take for these men to hurt her? Minutes at most.

The man behind her gripped Olivia's arms, holding her still as he pressed his pelvis to her bottom. The ridge grinding against her left no question as to his intentions. They could easily drag her into the woods and do whatever they pleased.

Olivia opened her mouth to scream, but before any sound escaped, the man in front of her issued his own cry. His hand flew to his temple before he collapsed in a heap. Blood seeped from between his fingers, but he didn't move.

'Bloody hell!' the steward to her left squawked.

Philippa stood behind the fallen man. She took up Olivia's entire range of vision. Spinning in a swirl of lavender cotton, she flicked her fan open and swept it through the air. For a mad moment, Olivia thought Philippa was attempting to attack the steward with nothing more than a buffeted breeze. But when the edge of the fan sliced across the man's neck, blood bloomed in a thin line. It wasn't deep enough to be fatal, but the steward's eyes bugged from his head as he pressed both hands against his throat and fell on his arse.

Philippa held a pistol in her left hand. Faster than a hawk descending upon its prey, she stepped forward, her arm extended, the gun a flash of silver in Olivia's periphery. The man holding Olivia grew impossibly still. Swivelling her head to the side, Olivia could see the indentation of Philippa's pistol against the man's forehead. The sound of the gun being cocked stalled her heart. If Philippa pulled the trigger, both she and the man holding her would be caught in its blast.

Dear God. I am going to die next to this privy.

'Let her go, or I shall blow your head clean off.' Philippa's voice was calm and clear. Strangely, it quieted the rush of blood pounding in Olivia's ears.

The man instantly released Olivia, pushing her away. 'Here now, madame. There's been a misunderstanding. We were just helping the young lady return safely to her carriage.'

Olivia stumbled back, her breath ragged as she pulled air into her lungs.

'Truly? Is that so? Were they just helping you?' Philippa flicked her gaze to

Olivia long enough for her to see the rage burning there before the duchess refocused on her prey.

'Hardly.' Olivia was amazed at how calm she felt. It must be shock.

'I thought not,' Philippa replied.

The duchess flipped the pistol and caught it in mid-air. She held it by the muzzle like a cudgel and cracked the ebony handle hard against the man's temple. The sickening sound of metal hitting flesh created a strange reaction in Olivia. Satisfaction.

The man crumpled to the ground in a heap at Philippa's feet. She looked down at him as though he were no more than a pile of excrement in her path. Exhaling, she tucked the pistol into her pocket and turned to survey Olivia.

'I can't even let you go to the privy alone without disaster striking.' Turning from the various bodies strewn about the yard, Philippa heaved a sigh. 'You are trouble, make no mistake about it.'

'You aren't seriously going to try and blame this on me,' Olivia spluttered. Outrage quickly overshadowed her shock and fear. 'What were you thinking, putting the gun to his head like that? If you'd pulled the trigger, we both would be lying on the ground in a pool of blood. What then?' It was so much easier to be angry with Philippa than terrified of what might have happened.

'Then I could have our delightful driver turn his mule cart of a carriage around and take me back to Belgrave Square. But alas. I saved you instead. I'm already regretting it.'

Pompous prig!

Olivia strode forward on legs strengthened by rage. She didn't stop until she was almost nose to nose with the indomitable duchess. 'You are a horrible woman.' *Not my best insult.* 'I don't like you.' *True, but hardly scathing.* 'And that dress looks dreadful on you.' *Better.*

Philippa leaned closer. Olivia couldn't stop her eyes from focusing on the beautiful woman's mouth. It should be a sin to stain lips so dark, highlighting the delicate cupid's bow, emphasising her plump bottom lip, making Olivia want to nibble on her like a berry. The nerve of this woman.

'Then by all means' – Philippa lifted her hand and brushed it over Olivia's cheek, along her jaw, down the centre of her throat to rest just below the hollow of her neck – 'stop looking at me.' She shoved Olivia hard enough for her to nearly land on her arse. Only swift feet and a determination not to let the despicable woman win enabled Olivia to remain standing. Philippa strode past her and down the path toward the carriage without a backwards glance. 'Best hurry along before another disaster finds you.'

'I *hate* her.' Olivia cursed, taking a moment to catch her breath and wait for the tingling echo of Philippa's fingers on her skin to dissipate.

* * *

A painful truth was becoming impossible to ignore. Philippa had grown soft. As they pulled into their final stop for the night – a large coaching inn that started as a stone cottage but had been haphazardly added onto with various spurts of material and architectural inspiration to accommodate its many guests – Philippa dreaded what they would find within.

A lumpy mattress full of bed mites. No whiskey. Watered-down wine. Boiled mutton. Stale bread. Delightful.

She hated to admit it, but she missed Stokes. The man might live to vex her, but at least he knew how she liked her meals. He would have already ridden ahead, ensured her room was clean, brought a case of her favourite Scottish whiskey, and apprised the innkeeper of her importance, ensuring some modicum of service.

Dear God. I sound like a pompous prig. I've brought men to tears with the raise of my eyebrow. I've levelled criminal networks with nothing but my wits and a pistol. I've trained four young women to become the Queen's Deadly Damsels. I can manage a few nights of rough travel.

Which forced Philippa to confront another uncomfortable fact as they climbed down from the carriage and made their way to the steps of the inn. Olivia was woefully underprepared to protect herself. Something that should bring Philippa some sense of satisfaction. After all, the less skilled Olivia was in fighting, the greater advantage Philippa had when it was time to battle her nemesis.

Not that her lack of training helped me when she punched me.

Just remembering that night in August when they apprehended Olivia's husband was enough to have Philippa thwacking her fan against her skirts in agitation. She should have seen the woman. Olivia was wearing an iridescent dress, of all things. It had clung to her figure like a second skin, catching the light and making Olivia glow like an angel.

A fallen angel.

Not that Philippa was one to judge a woman for taking what she pleased. Unless what she took was Philippa's pride.

Despite her inherent brightness, Olivia had found shadows deep enough to keep her hidden that night, and when she did leap at Philippa, the duchess froze. Which she never did, and for good reason. She hadn't even lifted her arm to protect her face when Olivia smashed her fist into Philippa's cheek.

Mortifying.

But it was more than that. After seeing Olivia's painful lack of fighting prowess with the men by the privy, Philippa had to admit a terrifying truth. She *let* Olivia catch her unawares in August. And she did it again in her own ballroom. When she could have struck, she held back for reasons she didn't wish to examine.

Because I like her.

Impossible. She was the enemy. Philippa hated her. She couldn't possibly like someone while also hating them.

Love and hate. What did Delacroix say? Two faces of the same coin...

Shaking her head, she reared back from the idea. She certainly didn't love Olivia, nor did she want to entertain the possibility of such treasonous thoughts. She loved Liza. And Liza was dead. Love was in her past, not her future, and certainly not her present. She wouldn't think about why she hesitated in attacking Olivia. Instead, she would focus on the men who hadn't held back.

They could have so easily overpowered the slight woman. And not because they were stronger or better armed, or more powerful. Simply because Olivia had never been taught the skills of fighting. It was infuriating that women were subjected to the whims of men for one reason alone. The male species believed themselves to be physically superior. Regardless of whether the woman in question was Philippa's friend or foe, the situation was unacceptable. She would need to think of a solution.

'Excuse me, good sir, do you have any available rooms for me and my travelling companion?' Olivia had sashayed her way to the bar, leaving in her wake a trail of staring men. Philippa could hardly blame them. Even in her wrinkled grey dress, bereft of the glamour and jewels she normally wore, she was breathtaking. Her pale hair formed a wild mass of ringlets that refused to stay contained in a simple twist. Philippa was slightly transfixed by Olivia's hair. When she spoke of Liza having the most beautiful hair she'd ever seen, her tongue tasted the lie even as her heart felt the oily guilt of betrayal. Yet it was undeniable that Philippa had spent far too many minutes in the carriage wondering what Olivia's hair would feel like between her fingers. The woman's eyes reminded Philippa of a jungle cat and sparkled with untold mischief as she blinked innocently at the innkeeper. Her full lips parted in a shy smile.

Such a consummate flirt! And a sapphist.

It was a wonder. But also a seeming truth, for why would Olivia lie about such a damning reality? It threw a new light on the woman's carefully curated coquetry in front of men. Her seductive behaviour was all a façade designed to provide her with some sense of power. Now Philippa knew Olivia's secret, it was easy to discover her tell. Olivia twirled a finger in one of her ringlets, tugging gently on the strand whenever she spoke to men in that breathy, wholly distracting way.

She's never once twirled her hair while talking to me.

Philippa wasn't sure how she felt about that, much like everything else in relation to Olivia. The woman had her at complete odds.

The innkeeper gave Olivia an appraising glance. 'We're full to busting. We've only got one room left and it's not near nice enough for a lady like your-self.' He winked.

Olivia tittered.

Philippa curled her lip in disgust.

She elbowed her way to the bar, her hip brushing against Olivia's as she slapped her palm on the scarred wood. 'Is it clean?'

The innkeeper's brows rose, and he took a half step back. 'Clean enough.'

Tapping her finger on the bar, she contemplated how quickly she could rip the man's moustache from his now-twitching lip.

Not worth the mess.

'We'll take it.' She reached into her pocket and withdrew three guineas. 'And somewhere for our driver to sleep.' It was more than enough money to cover the cost of a room for each of them, including the horses. The innkeep-er's eyes bulged at such a display of wealth. 'Do you have any private dining rooms, or only the common one?'

The man swallowed loudly as he stared at the coins. 'W-we've got one private room, but it's being used.'

'Well, of course it is. I'm sure this fine establishment hosts many grand

guests. Two lowly spinsters such as us shouldn't expect such fine treatment.'
Olivia glared at Philippa before turning back to the innkeeper.

Damnation. I suppose I'm not acting like a middle-class spinster.

'We would be more than happy to take our meal in our room. Can you
send someone up with it?' Olivia smiled sweetly at the man as she stepped
hard on Philippa's toe. Thankfully, Philippa's boots were made of leather and
offered some protection.

'Of course, madame. I'll have my wife show you up.'

The man may have been married, but that didn't stop the slimy toad from
staring at Olivia's chest as he palmed Philippa's coins. She re-evaluated the
merits of removing his moustache and a portion of his upper lip with her
dagger.

'You're too kind.' Olivia's purred reply was enough to make Philippa gag.
The man tipped an imaginary hat as he disappeared to find his wife.

Turning, Philippa rammed her elbow into Olivia's ribs, unable to hide her
smile as air exploded from Olivia in a whoosh.

A young woman hurried from a dark opening that no doubt led to the
kitchen. Sweat dripped from her brow as she wiped her hands on a stained
apron.

'You the two ladies me 'usband spoke wif?'

Philippa nodded.

'This way, then. We've got mutton stew or fish pie fer supper. I don't 'ave
many 'ands to spare, so if you're wanting to be waited on, it won't be quick.'

A strong woman leaning toward stout, the innkeeper's wife led them
through the common room, past a crowd of travellers ranging from working
men in homespun shirts and worn breeches to titled lords in great coats and
hessian boots until they reached the staircase. It leaned like a drunken man
against the far wall. Philippa counted three women in the crowd, all of them
huddled close to their male companions. Smoke from the fire, various pipes,
and cheroots created a haze that hovered by the wood-planked ceiling. It
blended with the melange of seasoned meat, sweaty men, and freshly baked
bread. The scent followed them as they ascended the stairs. Philippa's nose
twitched, but it wasn't an unpleasant smell. Just rather earthy.

'We'll have the mutton stew. And bread, if you have any.' Philippa had
spied a crusty loaf on one of the tables. If the stew was inedible, at least they
could fill their bellies with bread.

Olivia was behind Philippa, but the duchess didn't need to see the marchioness' expression to know she angered the woman with her over-reaching order.

Good. The sooner you realise I am in charge, the easier this trip will become.

'Please don't worry about how long it takes to bring our food. We're in no hurry.' Olivia graced the innkeeper's wife with a smile, crinkling the corners of her eyes as they stopped next to a door at the end of a dim corridor. The woman turned and stared at her for a moment. This wasn't the false expression of comeliness Olivia used on the woman's husband. This was genuine and beautiful.

Damnation. She is dangerous.

Philippa knew her own features were highly regarded in the beau monde despite how far she strayed from the conventional standards of feminine beauty. She was dark edges, sharp lines, and deep colours. High cheekbones, strong limbs, bold features, and even bolder actions. Her beauty was a weapon she had honed, fierce and formidable. But Olivia embodied the ideal English rose. Hair so fair it shone white in the candlelight. Creamy skin. Pink lips. Large eyes prone to blinking innocently while flashing with naughty mischief. She wielded her weapons with far more finesse, and Philippa was beginning to believe she was just as lethal with her assets as the deadly duchess was with her blades.

'Ahh.' The innkeeper's wife put her hands on her hips and assessed Olivia. 'I see what 'e was fussin' over. I thought it were those shiny coins, but turns out summink else was striking 'is fancy.' She broke into a coarse laugh that ended on a cough. 'Thick in the 'ead that man if 'e finks 'e has a chance wif the likes of you.' She handed a set of keys to Olivia.

Olivia's petal cheeks darkened to rose. 'I'm not sure I understand what you mean.'

Philippa snorted at such patent falsehood. 'She understands exactly what you mean.' She stepped in front of Olivia, shielding her from the woman. 'That man was lucky to find himself a wife as well suited to him as you are. He would be a fool to look elsewhere.' Philippa's statement could be read as a compliment or insult, and she wasn't sure herself how she meant it, but she stretched her mouth into the semblance of a smile. 'If you have any whiskey, we'll take a bottle of that as well.'

Raising her brows and puffing out her cheeks, the woman rocked back on her heels. 'Aren't you as fine as you please? I like that. 'e wouldn't dare make eyes at the likes of you for fear of losing 'is bollocks, sad shrivelled peas that they are.'

Philippa's lips twitched, but she refused to smile. 'I stand corrected. That man is hardly deserving of a woman like you.'

She nodded. 'Too right. But 'e's better than me last 'usband and prolly not as grand as me next one.' She laughed again. 'We ain't got no whiskey, or brandy neither. Gin, wine, or ale. Take yer pick. I'll 'ave one of the girls bring it up when they get a chance.'

'Wine.' Olivia poked her head from behind Philippa. 'Wine would be lovely.'

The innkeeper's wife turned and swept back down the hall.

'What if I preferred gin? Or ale?' Philippa stepped back so Olivia could fit the key in the lock and open the door.

'What if I preferred fish pie instead of stew?'

'Do you?'

'I suppose you'll never know.' Olivia looked over her shoulder at Philippa and winked.

What is she about? We are enemies. One doesn't wink at an enemy. Unless it's right before one thrusts a blade through their heart. She's trying to play me the way she's played everyone in this inn. But I'm not an easy mark. And I never lose.

Philippa tilted her chin, clenched her teeth, and strode into the room. 'Damnation.'

There was only one bed.

6

'Well, at least it's large.' Olivia stared at the bed instead of turning to look at Philippa. 'Unless you'd rather sleep on the floor.' Because she certainly wasn't giving up her side of the mattress.

Philippa's exhalation of air was more expressive than any man's string of curses. 'This is unacceptable.'

Olivia moved around the bed and examined the rest of the room. It was large enough to allow for a dressing table with a bowl and pitcher of water on the western wall. Soap sat on a dish next to a cracked mirror. In the corner between the dressing table and bed was a folding screen decorated with painted flowers, allowing some privacy when they changed into their nightclothes. There were two small windows on either side of the table with a candle on each sill. A small fireplace crackled cheerfully on the wall opposite the bed. Next to the door was a desk complete with a padded stool. Compared to the tiny cell Olivia lived in for ten years at the asylum, this was palatial.

'This is quite charming.' She turned to face the duchess, daring the bold woman to contradict her. 'Not all of us need a suite of rooms replete with servants, silk sheets, and plush furnishings.'

Philippa's laugh was sharp. 'Please. You are just as accustomed to the finer things in life as I am. Don't pretend to be thrilled with our accommodation.'

Pampered princess.

'You have no idea what I am accustomed to, Duchess.'

'I know you were born the daughter of a viscount and spent your child-hood in a smartly appointed townhouse in Mayfair. I know that you came into society with much fanfare, a diamond of the first water, top of every wealthy lord's marriage list. But Percival Smithwick, though not as highly titled as some of your suitors, was wealthy enough to offer your father a staggering dowry. And I know that five years after your daughter's birth, rumours began to circulate of your unfaithfulness. Rumours that only increased ball after ball. Season after season. Rumours you claim your husband intentionally circulated.'

Olivia's back stiffened. 'I claim? You don't believe me?'

Philippa shrugged, her lavender frock wrinkling with the motion.

It gave Olivia a perverse thrill of satisfaction to see the glamorous duchess swathed in plain clothes. A petty thing to take pleasure from, but Olivia never claimed to be a saint.

'What reason have you given me to trust your words?' Philippa asked.

'What reason has Percival given you to trust his?'

The duchess sniffed.

One point to me.

'I told you. Percival found me with Daisy and became incensed. His rumours were just one more punishment. Not only did it ensure my humilia-tion amongst the beau monde, it made his decision to banish me so much easier for society to accept.' Olivia shook her head. 'Or rather, enthusiastically support. He was the victim. A loyal husband cuckolded by his beautiful wife. I can't say how many bored widows and unsatisfied wives offered comfort to Percival. That is the ultimate irony. While Daisy was my only affair, Percival fucked his way through most of the wives in the beau monde. Though that didn't stop his jealousy. His infidelity only increased his suspicions about my unfaithfulness. So, when I returned from exile, I egged him on with my behaviour. It was petty and cruel, but it was the only weapon I had to wield against him.'

Philippa raised an eyebrow. Her index finger rubbed in an endless circle against her thumb. It was a tell Olivia noticed after their second meeting. The duchess was irritated. 'And what of your time across the Channel? The stories of Marchioness Smithwick charming her way into some of the most scan-dalous bedrooms in Europe were featured in every gossip magazine in

London. *The Star of Venus* retained a monthly column devoted to your exploits.'

Olivia nearly choked on her bitter laugh. 'You claim to be a woman of high intelligence, Your Grace. Yet you glean your coveted, secret, quality information from *The Star of Venus*? What would the Queen say if she knew your sources were so suspect?'

A knock sounded, preventing Philippa from responding. She scowled and strode to the door. Her hand slipped into her pocket as she cracked it open. 'Oh. Thank you.' Pulling her hand free of the pocket, she opened the door wider, stepping back so a young lad could haul in their two carpet bags. His eyes went wide as dinner plates when Philippa pressed a shilling into his hand.

'Thank ye kindly, ma'am.'

With a nod of her head, the boy turned swiftly and exited.

'What exactly do you have in those pockets? Besides all that blunt? If you keep flashing gold and silver, no one will ever believe we are spinsters on holiday. For a woman who claims to be so smart, you're really quite stupid.'

Philippa's sharp glare could have cut through steel. Perhaps Olivia pushed too far. But something about the woman provoked her.

The duchess slipped her hand back into the pocket. 'I might be playing an inconsequential woman of no means, but never forget I am the Queen's Deadliest Damsel. To answer your question, I have weapons in my pocket. Because, unlike silly marchionesses who put themselves in dangerous situations and depend on those around them for rescue, I need no one but myself. One day, there won't be someone willing to save you, Lady Smithwick. And then what will you do?'

How dare *she accuse me of being helpless? I am* rather defenceless, *and she did come to my rescue, but that is hardly the point.*

In fact, acknowledging her own vulnerability only further incensed Olivia. 'You think your rage is more powerful than mine? That you can dismiss me as easily as one might step over a dead rat on the street? Just because you've heard stories of the wanton Marchioness of Smithwick and been thick enough to believe them doesn't mean anything you assume about me is true. You don't think I can defend myself? Come at me, all-powerful Duchess of Dorsett. Give me your worst and see how helpless I am. Because you'll find yourself flat on your back with a blade to your neck, I promise.'

She might not have the fighting skills of her opponent, but she had years of brewing rage and the desperation of a woman constantly underestimated. Philippa was no different from any other stuffed prig from the beau monde. Happy to be fed a six-course meal of lies depicting Olivia as nothing more than a brazen Jezebel. It was disgusting. And Olivia was sick of pretending it didn't matter. That *she* didn't matter just because her face was appealing and men – and some women – found her sexually desirable. She would no longer accept that her worth was only defined by how many people lusted after her.

Faster than Olivia could track, Philippa moved across the floor like wind through trees. Stumbling backwards, Olivia slammed into the wall by the small window. Philippa grabbed Olivia's shoulder, pinning her to the wall and wrapped her other hand around Olivia's throat. She didn't squeeze, but her fingers flexed over the delicate skin, lingering where Olivia's pulse thundered madly just below her jaw. It was an echo of the way Olivia had overcome Philippa in her ballroom, and there was no doubt the duchess did it intentionally.

'Strange. I don't feel like I'm flat on my back. And it isn't my pretty neck that is at risk this time.' She flexed her fingers, squeezing gently as she leaned close enough for Olivia to see the fine lines spanning around Philippa's eyes.

Frustration at Olivia's own ineptitude manifested in tears.

Bollocks to that! I will not cry in front of this woman. I will not show her weakness.

Olivia pressed her lips together and breathed deeply through her nose, but that only brought the scent of jasmine and frankincense into her lungs. A heady aroma tangling her thoughts and melting something low in her belly. 'You're nothing but a bully.' Her voice quavered, and she hated the duchess even more for highlighting Olivia's inferiority. Which made the strange tingling erupting where Philippa's fingers continued to stroke against her pulse even more baffling.

'You are full of insults this evening.'

'Only because you are so deserving.' Olivia willed her legs to transform back from pudding to flesh and bone. 'I spent ten years in the vilest pit of hell while you dined at the Queen's table.' Impotent rage rose like poison in her blood. 'And all the while, the beau monde gleefully tangled themselves in the web of lies my husband judiciously circulated. I became nothing more than a whore in the eyes of high society, but that couldn't be farther from the truth.

You think I should be punished for the crimes I've committed? Rest assured. I've been punished.'

Philippa's indigo gaze cut through all of Olivia's shields. 'I've read some people can taste a lie.' She leaned closer, her mouth only a breath away from Olivia's. 'I wonder if it's possible.'

'I dare you try. I've nothing to hide.' Rage coalesced into something just as hot, just as fierce, and far more dangerous.

Philippa's grip loosened, her fingers tracing up the side of Olivia's neck, sinking into her hair. 'Tell me to stop.'

'Why? Are you frightened?' A laughable question when Philippa was famous for her fearlessness. If Olivia hadn't been so lost in Philippa's gaze, she would have missed the flash.

My God. She is frightened. Of what? Kissing me?

It was enough to push Olivia past the fraction of space existing between them. Pressing her mouth against Philippa's sinfully stained lips, bursts of sweet, sharp sensation coalesced in her belly and exploded out like sparks.

Philippa's hand tightened in her hair, tugging just hard enough to feed the flames of Olivia's desire. Philippa moaned a throaty sound of pleasure that hummed over Olivia's lips.

Emboldened by Philippa's response, Olivia licked the seam of her mouth and thrilled as the duchess opened to her. She tasted of whiskey and wild winter wind.

Olivia gripped Philippa's hip, pulling her closer, hating the layers of skirts between them. Philippa pressed her thigh between Olivia's legs, a soft promise of sweet friction.

Perhaps Philippa was making good on her query, trying to taste Olivia's words. She slid her tongue over Olivia's in a velvet slide, exploring in languid sips and bold thrusts. Heat washed up Olivia's body, her heart thudding painfully in her chest. She wanted more. Needed the weight of Philippa's body holding her to earth, reminding her she was real and alive and still vital.

Diving intrepid fingers into Philippa's glorious hair, she broke the kiss and tugged Philippa's head back, exposing the elegant column of her throat. Olivia pressed her mouth just beneath Philippa's jaw in a gentle caress before nipping hard enough for Philippa to gasp. It was glorious to hold such a powerful woman in her arms and feel her body soften against Olivia.

A throat cleared, loud and shocking in the quiet room.

Philippa stumbled back as Olivia looked over her shoulder to the door. The innkeeper's wife stood with a tray in her hand.

'My 'usband really was sniffing up the wrong skirts. I 'ate to innerupt but I 'ave your supper.' She walked far enough into the room to deposit the tray on the desk next to the door.

'We were just, erm...' Olivia grasped for any plausible reason why she and Philippa would be in such a compromising position. The woman could call the guard. Accuse them of being inverts. Have them thrown from the inn for their immoral behaviour.

'I'm sure your friend 'ere had summink down 'er throat and you were jus' tryin' to 'elp 'er get it out. I'm no stranger to ladies 'aving passionate friend-ships 'ere abouts. 'oo doesn't need a chuckaboo to stay warm on cold nights like this?' The woman winked at Olivia. 'If I reported every person in this inn doing summink left of the moral centre, I wouldn't 'ave a customer to serve or a pot to piss in. You ladies 'ave a good night. But do yerselves a favour and make use of that lock.' She gave a hearty laugh and turned, shutting the door behind her.

Philippa walked to the door, doing just as the woman instructed. When she turned back to Olivia, her cheeks were flushed and her gaze focused on the window instead of Olivia's face. 'Well. That was... I'm not sure exactly. But it shouldn't have happened. And it won't happen again.'

Why shouldn't it have happened? Because I'm not worthy of the grand duchess? Just a weak woman who did terrible things out of panic and desperation?

Olivia pressed her lips together, refusing to voice her questions for fear of the answers. 'Fine. Good. I should hope not. Are you convinced at least that I'm not lying about Europe?'

Philippa refused to answer, instead shifting her focus to the tray. Lifting the linen cloth draped over their food, she inspected the two bowls of steaming stew as if they might contain the clues to eternal life. She sniffed. 'It smells edible.' Taking a bowl and spoon, she sat on the one chair available.

Olivia rolled her eyes at the ridiculousness of their situation. She strode to the tray, ripped a healthy chunk of bread from the loaf sitting next to her bowl, and plopped it into the rich stew. Philippa was wrong. It didn't smell edible. It smelled divine. Carrots, potatoes, onions, and chunks of mutton swam in a thick broth spiced with salt, pepper, rosemary, and thyme. Her mouth began to water. She took her food to the bed and perched on the edge.

It was an awkward meal, but the food tasted as delicious as Olivia imagined. Philippa opened the bottle of wine that the innkeeper provided and filled one of the two glasses.

'What fine manners you have. I would have thought a duchess with such esteemed friends as the Queen of bloody England would at least have the decency to offer me a glass of wine.'

Philippa raised a perfectly sculpted brow and sipped before answering. Olivia ignored the clench of her belly as the duchess licked a droplet of wine from her lips.

Damn the woman for being so...

Beautiful? Smug? Desirable? Dominant?

Yes. Exactly.

Olivia knew she was conducting a silent conversation with herself. But as the duchess refused to participate, she had little choice.

'You are not my guest. You are a suspect. If you want wine, come and pour it yourself.'

Olivia stood, placing her now empty bowl back on the tray and grabbing the bottle in jerky motions. She sloshed wine into her glass and took a hearty swallow. Philippa had to tilt her head up to watch Olivia, and Olivia saw the flare of her pupils as she wiped a droplet from her mouth with the back of her hand.

Good. I shouldn't be the only one damned by my desires.

'You have disliked me from the start, but it matters not.'

'I dislike you because you are shielding the leader of a nefarious group of men intent on harming innocent children for their own gain.'

The burst of tart and spicy grapes turned to vinegar on Olivia's tongue. Because Philippa was right. She turned and walked back to the bed. 'I'm not shielding him. I'm shielding another innocent child from harm. My daughter. He will take great pleasure in destroying her if I don't keep my promise.'

Philippa leaned forward. 'What promise?'

Olivia exhaled a shaky breath. Even sharing this much might prove disastrous. But if she could get the duchess to believe her, trust Olivia even the smallest way, she might aid Olivia in getting her daughter out of England. Far enough away from the Crow to ensure Hyacinth's safety. What happened after that mattered little.

'I promised to help Percival in securing orphans for the Crow.' Admitting her sins only increased her shame. 'And I swore no matter what, I would never reveal the Crow's identity.'

'Your brother told me he is willing to take your daughter into his custody and protect her. Isn't that a better fate for Hyacinth than living on the run with you?'

Olivia shook her head so violently, wine spilt from her glass and trickled down her hand. 'He can't protect her. No one can. Except me. You've no idea how powerful the Crow is or how far his influence extends.' How she wished she could pour out everything to Philippa. To divest herself of the burden and let someone else carry the weight of responsibility. But even if Philippa believed her, which was unlikely, if the Crow suspected her disloyalty, her daughter's life would be compromised. He would find a way to get to Hyacinth, and he would kill her. She was fairly certain her daughter's location was unknown to the Crow, but he had spies everywhere, and England was merely an island. It was only a matter of time before they were discovered.

'I can't help you if you don't tell me what you know.'

'And I can't tell you what I know until Hyacinth is safely away.'

Philippa tapped a finger against her lip, drawing Olivia's attention to the curve of her delectable mouth.

She's trying to distract me. Minx. That's my trick, and I won't be played by my own tactics.

Forcing her focus back to the woman, Olivia ignored the memory of Philippa's teeth scraping over her skin.

'Then we are at an impasse until we reach your daughter.'

Olivia nodded. 'Exactly.'

Philippa stood, placing her glass on the tray. She brushed her hand down the wrinkled skirt. 'I hate these clothes.'

Humour tilted Olivia's lips into a smile. 'I knew you would.'

The duchess picked up her carpet bag and hauled it to the other side of the bed, plunking it onto the mattress. Unclasping the leather strap, she rustled through the contents. Lifting her head, Olivia had to bite her cheek to stop the giggle from bursting free. The poor woman looked horrified. 'Is everything in here some variation of pink, lavender, or mint?' She pulled out a white lacy nightgown and shook it at Olivia. 'Are you jesting?'

She couldn't hold back the laughter any longer. It felt decadent to give herself over to an emotion so light and frothy, if even for a moment. Perhaps the wine was stronger than she thought. 'You might want to look in my bag.' It had been Ivy's idea to play a trick on the duchess, but Olivia was enjoying herself immensely. Even if her joy was temporary and aided by wine.

Philippa narrowed her gaze and stalked over to the other bag, not bothering to bring it to the bed. She crouched down and unclasped it, shoving the mouth open wide. 'These are my clothes.'

Olivia wiped away a tear of mirth. 'Ivy wanted to see you in a colour other than black. I didn't think you would agree to wear that.' She tipped her chin at Philippa's lavender gown. 'What lengths you'll go to in order to get your man. Or woman, I suppose.' Hopping off the bed, she snagged the nightgown from where Philippa had tossed it and swayed her hips slightly more than necessary as she made her way to the changing screen. 'I suppose we should get some sleep. I fear our coachman will want to make an early start.'

* * *

Philippa was going to kill Ivy. Right after she murdered Olivia. The woman was inflaming more than just her rage, and Philippa couldn't forgive herself for acting so recklessly.

I kissed her. What was I thinking? That I wanted to do far more than kiss her. And what does that make me? What would Liza say about my behaviour?

But for the life of Philippa, she couldn't conjure Liza's face or imagine her censure. That alone was enough reason to never again allow herself to be so weak with Olivia.

Lady Smithwick was guilty of aiding the Devil's Sons' leader in heinous crimes. Nothing about her should appeal to Philippa, yet even now, she watched the shadowy figure hidden behind the changing screen, and her body ached in places long forgotten.

Mayhap she isn't lying. We are all capable of doing terrible things to protect the ones we love.

No. She would not entertain such ideas. Her mind was trying to justify the needs of her body, and Philippa would not allow such hypocrisy.

But if her child's life is at risk, can I truly blame her for doing what she must to protect Hyacinth? Would I not do the same to ensure Hannah's safety? Or Millie's? Or Penny's? Or Ivy's... even if she did force me into this hideous dress?

Philippa shook her head. Olivia was a consummate liar. A seducer of men.

If not a member of the Devil's Sons, at least complicit in their crimes. Her motives did not justify the actions she took in helping Percival.

A soft sigh came from behind the screen as Olivia's corset flipped over the top of it and hung like a white flag of surrender. But Philippa was no fool. The woman wasn't surrendering anything.

Philippa needed to keep her focus on the case and secure Olivia's confession.

'The sooner the better,' Philippa murmured.

Olivia emerged from behind the screen in the frilled nightgown.

'Did you say something?'

The cotton hugging Olivia's form so closely was of fine quality. If the room had decent lighting, Philippa would have been able to discern the shape of Olivia's breasts. Mayhap even determine the colour of her nipples.

Not that I want to know.

Philippa blinked hard. 'No.' She turned back to her carpet bag and was relieved to find a silk set of pants and a sleeveless shirt. Her preferred nightclothes in comforting indigo blue so dark it looked black.

Olivia climbed into the bed they would be sharing, and Philippa slipped behind the dressing screen and twisted into a variety of embarrassing positions to reach the buttons running down the back of her dress. Once the wooden clasps were free, she quickly divested herself of the dreaded gown. Donning her nightclothes, she folded the dress and considered throwing it on the fire, but that seemed excessively wasteful.

'Will you blow out the candle on your side?' Olivia had already doused one of the flames. Her hair was loose, and it coiled around her face in wild disarray. Her bare arms peeked out of the blanket, pale and glowing in the dim light.

Philippa's pulse thudded at her wrists, behind her ears, in her chest where her heart stuttered.

It was going to be a long night.

Rubbing her finger against her thumb, Philippa approached the bed and willed her nerves to settle. This was ridiculous. She was just sharing a bed, nothing more. But tension tightened her limbs and made it difficult to take a deep breath.

'Goodnight, Philippa.' Olivia didn't smile. She didn't lick her lips or bat her eyes. She didn't coil her hair around a delicate finger. She just held Philippa's gaze with her own steady green one.

My God. What does she see? The duchess? The Queen's Deadliest Damsel? Or just me?

It was a terrifying thought. For while Philippa was used to garnering more than her fair share of attention as the infamous Duchess of Dorsett. The Queen's confidante. Winterbourne's untouchable widow. A striking femme fatale with sharp features and even sharper wit. Few people saw her as simply a woman. Flesh and blood. Fears and flaws. Desires and doubts.

But I think she sees all of it... all of me.

Troubling indeed.

7

Olivia nodded off in the carriage once again. She jerked awake and realised her boot had found its way between the duchess'. Again. Pulling her foot back, she glared at the duchess. It was her fault Olivia was so tired. She'd slept horribly the night before.

Because it is impossible to relax around this woman.

Every time Philippa had shifted in the bed, every sigh she'd made, even the scent of her, invaded Olivia's dreams. She had woken countless times throughout the night with an aching awareness. If she reached out her arm, her hand had brushed against Philippa's bare skin. If she turned her head, Philippa's hair had tickled her cheek. If she stretched her leg, Philippa's toes had bumped her calf. It was disconcerting. Unsettling.

Arousing.

And that was the crux of the issue. Olivia hadn't allowed arousal to play a part in her life for a very long time.

Not since Daisy was sent away.

There were limited opportunities, although even in the asylum, it wasn't unheard of for those lucky enough to share a cell to take comfort in each other's company. But Olivia had been kept in a solitary room for her sexual deviance. Her husband had insisted upon it. The only interaction she had with others was during mealtimes or when the doctors were administering her 'treatments'. The ice baths were the worst.

That thought chased away her fatigue. Even as Olivia shifted against the squabs to try and sit in a beam of autumn sunlight, she could feel the frigid water swallowing her. So cold it was like fire. Until everything went numb. Including her mind.

'Are you quite well, Lady Smithwick?' Philippa's sharp gaze missed nothing.

Olivia pulled herself from her memories and focused on the present. They had been travelling for hours and should be stopping at a posting inn for lunch soon, but the countryside flashing by was remote with no signs of even small villages, let alone a town large enough to boast accommodation. Just endless hills, rolling like a troubled sea. Fields were separated with stone walls, and every once in a while, fluffy sheep or scattered cows grazed lazily. She empathised with their fate. Sleep. Eat. Wait to be slaughtered.

'Do I not look well?' She raised her brows and cocked her head.

Why am I baiting her? She will think I'm flirting.

Because I'm flirting.

A terrible idea.

Philippa opened her mouth to answer, but Olivia interrupted, not sure she wanted to know how the duchess would respond. 'I was just lost in memory. Sometimes, it's a rather dismal place to find yourself.'

Philippa pressed her crimson lips together. It was impossible for Olivia not to admire the woman's physical beauty. Philippa was wearing a tailored travelling gown in green so dark it reminded Olivia of the ancient trees in the northern forest she'd visited on her honeymoon tour. It was one of the few pleasant experiences she had from that time. The dark hue set off Philippa's hair, which she had twisted into a simple chignon, and contrasted with her creamy skin. Olivia had never seen the duchess so simply attired in hair and cosmetics, although her lips were as red as ever. Certain beauty regimes could not be abandoned, no matter the circumstances.

She would never admit this to Philippa, but the simple gown and toilet only enhanced the woman's features. Large eyes, a strong nose, sharp cheekbones, elegant neck. No wonder the ladies of the beau monde hated Philippa, and the men battled fear and desire in equal measure.

'Are you thinking of your lost love? Daisy, wasn't that her name?'

Olivia hid her surprise at Philippa remembering what should be an inconsequential detail from Olivia's life. 'No. I wasn't. I mourned for Daisy, but that wound no longer bleeds. I loved her, but I wasn't in love with her. Does that make sense?'

Philippa blinked. 'It makes perfect sense.'

'I suspect the same is not true for you, Lady Winterbourne. You've the look of a woman still haunted by grief. You must have loved your friend very much indeed.'

'I still do.' Three words that revealed much.

Olivia's heart ached for her. She didn't love the woman in past tense. She loved her here and now, though she was no longer a part of Philippa's present. Such devotion was rare, and in the duchess' case, it seemed to be devastating. She fought the urge to offer comfort that would undoubtedly be rejected.

Philippa sniffed and turned her head to look out the window. 'It's funny. If it were my husband for whom I mourned, I would be able to speak of my loss openly with other women. They would extend their sympathy. Some might even be sincere. But because my love belonged to a woman, I'm denied even the comfort of sharing such grief with others. The only person I can speak to about this is her brother, and that is a complicated matter.'

'Did he know of your affair?'

'He discovered us. The idiot thought he was in love with me, and in a fit of jealousy, revealed us to his father.'

Olivia sat straighter on the padded bench of the carriage. 'Dear God. Did you kill him?' She only spoke half in jest. She could imagine Philippa cutting a man down for far less serious crimes.

Philippa's smile was small but genuine and Olivia felt strangely like she'd won some kind of prize. 'No. He still lives. You know him. He is the current Commissioner of Scotland Yard.'

Olivia's mouth fell open and she snapped it shut. 'Your love was Edward Worthington's sister?'

Philippa's smile sparked a small light in her eyes. 'So shocked? We grew up together, the three of us. Edward was young and foolish and thought he was in love with me. Idiot.'

Philippa's admission answered some lingering questions Olivia had about their interactions with each other when she'd observed them in the summer. Staying quiet, she hoped her silence would encourage Philippa to share more.

The duchess shifted in her seat. This time, it was her boot that found its way next to Olivia's. She twitched her foot, disturbing Olivia's skirts. 'He had no idea his father's fury would be so great, or his punishment so severe. Liza's father gave her two options. Marriage or bedlam. She chose the latter.'

A wave of nausea, unexpected and vicious, tore through Olivia. She knew intimately the torture of an asylum. Imagining Philippa's faceless love being exposed to such cruelty created an unexpected empathy in her for Liza.

Philippa rubbed her index finger against her thumb. A wisp of black hair streaked with silver fell from her chignon, but she didn't seem to notice. Though she looked out of the window, Olivia guessed it wasn't the bucolic countryside she watched so closely. 'She killed herself after six months.' Philippa blinked and turned to watch Olivia.

Olivia felt the tears spring to her eyes. She had seen the blank stares of fellow patients in the Home for Wayward Women. She remembered the sobbing cries in the middle of the night when the darkness seemed eternal. It wasn't uncommon for women to take matters into their own hands. To reclaim a small sense of control by choosing how they ended their lives, even if they couldn't control how they lived them. She could imagine it far too clearly, and it broke a piece of her heart away. No wonder Philippa kept herself so carefully separated from others.

'And you endured for ten years if your story is to be trusted.' Philippa spoke the last words like an accusation, but Olivia couldn't rise to the barb. Not this time.

'I couldn't die. My daughter needed me, and I knew one day, Percy would release me. At least, I hoped he would. His obsession was too great to let me linger there forever.' She never imagined speaking to anyone of her time in bedlam. She guessed Philippa felt the same about discussing her lost love. Yet here they were. Revealing secrets when there was still no trust between them. They were playing a dangerous game.

Acting without thought, Olivia leaned forward and took Philippa's hand into her own, squeezing it. 'Hope is a strange thing. It can give us the strength to survive the most hideous experiences, but it can also be a cruel master, twisting our choices in a desperate bid to gain what amounts to nothing but false promises in the end.'

A gunshot interrupted whatever Philippa had been about to say. She pulled her hand free and reached into her pocket.

'Bloody hell!' The coachman's gruff cry was the only warning they had before the carriage picked up speed and careened wildly over the rutted lane.

Fear sharpened Olivia's senses. She was acutely aware of the pounding hooves, the worn velvet squabs she gripped tightly to keep her seat, Philippa's face hardening into the lines of a fearsome warrior, and the sharp sting of adrenaline coursing through her veins.

'Highwaymen.' Philippa pulled out a pistol. 'Do you know how to use this?'

Olivia looked at the weapon as though it were a snake ready to strike. If she admitted her ignorance, the duchess would know Olivia had been bluffing when she threatened her in the ballroom. Not that it would matter if highwaymen killed them both.

'No.' She shook her head as they hit a bump, and the carriage tipped dangerously to the left before righting itself.

'You pointed a weapon at me that you had no idea how to use? You shot it at my butler!'

'I didn't mean to. I didn't even know it was loaded.'

Another gunshot sounded, and the unmistakable grunt of their driver caused fear to coalesce into panic. Olivia was quite certain she would toss up her accounts all over Philippa's smart travel ensemble.

Philippa grabbed her shoulders and shook her hard. 'The past doesn't matter. Forget it. Remain calm. Look at me. Right here. Focus on me.'

The stern command was impossible for Olivia to ignore. She stared into Philippa's calm blue eyes, and the panic ebbed.

'They are going to stop the carriage. When they open the door, we aren't going to wait for their demands. We are going to attack first. Take this gun.' Philippa released Olivia and picked the gun up from her lap. She shoved it into Olivia's shaking hands. 'I have another. All you need to do is pull back the hammer, here, and point and pull this trigger. Do you see?' Olivia lifted the heavy weapon and tentatively pulled back the hammer until it clicked. She was pointing the gun straight ahead, right at Philippa. The duchess shoved Olivia's hand to the left, so the gun pointed at the door. 'Bloody hell. Just don't shoot me. I'll never live down the embarrassment of being wounded with my own gun.'

'Right. Sorry. I won't.' Olivia shifted on her seat to gain better balance as the carriage slowed. There were no more sounds from the coachman, and she feared he might have been hit by one of the shots. Possibly both. 'I can't do this.' She swallowed bile rising in her throat. She wished her hands weren't trembling so terribly. No one would believe she could hit a target with the gun shaking like a leaf in a windstorm.

Philippa had pulled a second gun from her other pocket and glanced at Olivia. 'You can and you will. Because you must. If you don't, you will die. Didn't you tell me your daughter needs you alive?'

It was the exact harsh advice Olivia needed to hear. Pushing her fear down into the pit of her stomach, she thought of Hyacinth. She wasn't going to let some foolhardy highwayman rob her of a chance to save her daughter. Not after everything she'd endured. Taking a deep breath, her aim steadied as the carriage came to a stop. The sound of men shouting to each other, at least three different voices, and horses stomping near the carriage, had Philippa reaching into her magical pockets for a dagger.

'How many weapons do you have in there?' Olivia shifted her focus from the door to Philippa and then back again.

'Not enough if there are more than three men. These guns only have one shot, and then they must be reloaded.' She stopped speaking as the brass handle twisted.

The door opened, and just as a head appeared, there was a mighty bang. Sulphur and acrid smoke filled the carriage, making it difficult to see. The man now lay half in and half out of the door. He wasn't moving. He wasn't breathing. What parts of him Olivia could see were covered in blood.

'They're armed,' a deep voice shouted from outside the carriage.

'They killed Stewart!' another screamed.

'And we shan't hesitate to kill the rest of you if you don't depart immediately,' Philippa called, eerily calm. She took Olivia's gun from her hands and gave her the expended weapon. 'Get down,' she hissed. Olivia slid from her seat onto the floor, kicking to push the dead body out of the carriage. He landed on the ground with a wet thump. Philippa lay flat on her belly on the bench, her head peeking through the window next to the door. 'There's only two of them,' she whispered to Olivia. 'We might have a chance.'

We might have a chance. Marvellous. I might be sick all over myself.

Using the butt of the gun, Philippa broke the glass out. Olivia covered her head as shards rained down. She craned her neck to watch Philippa slide closer to the wall of the carriage. Olivia wanted to warn her to stay down, but she couldn't form words. Philippa sat up enough to aim her pistol out of the window. Another mighty bang had Olivia covering her ears as more smoke and the choking taste of sulphur made her gag.

'One left.' Philippa wasn't whispering any more.

'Fucking hell!' A high-pitched cry emanated from outside the carriage, followed by the sound of hooves pounding the ground. When the thundering became nothing more than a distant rumble, Philippa looked down at Olivia.

'He's gone.' The duchess calmly brushed glass from her skirt. 'Come on, then. Let's get out and see what kind of mess we're in.'

Olivia wasn't sure whether to burst into tears or start screaming.

She opted for the latter. 'What kind of mess we're in? Are you mad? You just killed two men!'

The duchess merely raised an eyebrow at Olivia. She'd seen the same look when Philippa had been served puffed cheese tartlets that didn't meet her standard at a ball. 'Would you rather I let them kill us?'

Damnation. She has a point.

Because while Olivia abhorred violence, she certainly didn't want to sit quietly while these men robbed, raped, and then murdered them. In the asylum, she had seen fights break out between the patients. Some of the orderlies liked to get rough when 'barmy bitches' wouldn't follow orders or kicked up a fuss about the treatments being administered. Olivia learned quickly the best way to avoid a smack across the face or fist in the gut was to comply. But that was its own form of torture. To submit when everything in her wanted to fight.

Philippa would never have let them steal her will. She would have found a way to crush them.

It was both inspiring and demoralising to know Philippa would have achieved what Olivia could only dream of accomplishing. Leaning closer, the infuriating woman reached out, and for a wild moment, Olivia thought she might try to kiss her.

Hardly the time! But...

Instead, she brushed her thumb over Olivia's cheek and looked at the crimson smear. 'You've cut yourself.'

Olivia reached up, pressing her palm against her skin and registering the sting. She was vain enough to wonder if it might scar. Anger reared, which was far preferable to the terrifying panic making her shake. 'Thanks to your work with the window.' She narrowed her eyes at the duchess and wrestled with her skirts. They had tangled around her legs, making it almost impossible to gain her feet in the small space between the two bench seats.

Philippa reached out to help her, but Olivia slapped her hand away.

'I don't need your help. You've done quite enough!' she hissed. Giving up on a dignified exit from the carriage, she crawled to the door but stalled at the body crumpled on the ground. Thankfully, the man landed on his face, so his features were hidden.

'He's just asleep,' Olivia whispered to herself.

'Dead asleep.'

Philippa's dry response had Olivia stiffening her spine.

Lifting her chin and refusing to grace Philippa with a response, she awkwardly jumped out of the carriage, landing next to his body. Philippa followed behind her.

'You are a terrible travelling companion.' Olivia turned to face Philippa, but her gaze caught on the driver. Unfortunately, he was *not* lying belly down. His face still stretched in lines of shock. His eyes stared sightlessly into the sky. His chest was a mess of flesh, ripped cloth, and blood.

Olivia bent forward and threw up the contents of her stomach onto her sensible leather boots.

* * *

'Blast.' Philippa's heart squeezed painfully. Not in fear, but something else. Something almost like regret. She hadn't meant to be so harsh with Olivia, but they hardly had time for anything else.

Striding over to her, she ignored the woman's attempt to wave her away with a flapping hand. Philippa gathered Olivia's wild curls that had escaped the coil she so carefully pinned before they left their rented room that morning as she retched once more.

One thing was blatantly clear. Olivia might have aligned herself with the Devil's Sons, but she was no hardened criminal. Philippa feared she might shatter as easily as the glass she knocked from the carriage window.

'Shh. It's going to be all right.' Philippa attempted to soften her voice, but the words came out closer to a terse command than a comforting murmur. She wasn't good at soothing. It was much easier to bully. Or scold. Or destroy.

Olivia straightened and spun to face her, forcing Philippa to release her glorious curls. 'How can you possibly say that? We're in the middle of nowhere. The coachman is dead.' She gestured to the poor man lying next to the wheel. 'Those two other men are dead.' She flung her hand at the highwayman by the carriage, then looked wildly around, not seeing the other victim of Philippa's keen aim. 'Where the bloody hell is the second one?'

Philippa looked down the road where they had travelled. 'His horse spooked when I shot him. Took off that way. He must have got caught in the stirrups.' She didn't elaborate. Olivia needn't picture the man being dragged along the roadside. 'The other horse no doubt followed him.' Which was a shame. The two beasts pulling the carriage looked to be decent horseflesh, but with no saddles, it would take some skill to ride them.

Pulling a flask from her pocket, she handed it to Olivia. 'Drink.'

Olivia eyed the flask, then squinted at Philippa's skirt. 'Truly. What else have you got in there? A magic carpet, mayhap? Some biscuits for afternoon tea? A lady's maid to manage your hair?'

She had to give Olivia credit. Despite everything they'd endured, despite her obvious horror at seeing three men killed in the space of as many minutes, and despite their dire situation, she certainly maintained a level of pluck that was admirable.

'Never you mind what's in my pockets. Drink this. It will help.'

Olivia unscrewed the flask and took a tentative sniff. She crinkled her nose. 'It certainly isn't sherry or French wine.'

'No. It's whiskey. It will fortify your nerves.'

Olivia took a small sip, swallowed, and sucked in a harsh breath. 'Or knock me out cold,' she wheezed before taking a second nip. 'No wonder you've nerves of steel.'

'I'm sorry. Was that a compliment?' Philippa couldn't stop the spark of humour from flashing in her eyes.

Olivia turned away from Philippa, carefully screwing the cap back on the flask. 'What should we do about them?' She nodded at the coachman.

With the men outweighing both women by at least ten stone each, there wasn't much they could do. Olivia wrestled the coachman out of his jacket, carefully placing it over his face to preserve a modicum of dignity. Philippa did the same for the highwayman, being careful to search his pockets for any clues before draping his much filthier coat over the upper half of his body.

'What's this?' Philippa found a purse of gold coins in one pocket. In the other was a folded note. The wax seal on the note had broken, and only half remained.

The body of a wolf. The tail of a snake.

'Damnation.' She didn't need to see the rest of the seal to know the identity of the sender. The Devil's Sons used a unique seal incorporating the body of a wolf, the tail of a snake, and the head of a crow. The same animals symbolised their leaders. Only now, the Crow was all that remained of the triad. Opening the missive, she scanned the instructions written with a neat hand. 'How well do you ride, Olivia?'

Olivia looked up from where she knelt next to the coachman.

Was she saying a prayer over the man?

Tears shone in her eyes as she sniffed, then turned to look at the horse. Her throat contracted, distracting Philippa. She had pressed her mouth just there, and licked the hollow, tasting the salt and spice of Olivia. More intoxicating than the strongest dram of whiskey.

Hardly the time! But...

'Percival never wanted me to ride. He said he worried about my safety, but I think it was the expense that frightened him. Or the independence.'

'Well, you're going to learn to ride today. We must make haste.' Philippa walked over to Olivia and extended her hand, helping her to rise. She handed her the note. 'These were not highwaymen. They were hired to find us. And if he knows where we are heading, then he likely knows where Hyacinth is hiding.'

Olivia's eyes widened as her gaze flew over the damning words.

Find the women on the Devon road south to Cornwall. Kill them, then go to Charlestown Port and collect the girl. You'll receive your final payment on delivery.

The Crow

'No, no, no! He can't possibly! How can he know she's there?' Olivia looked up to Philippa, her pupils blown wide with fear, her face pale. 'We must leave. Now. We have to get there first. We must.' A tear tracked down her face, streaking over the dried cut just below her cheekbone. Philippa's heart squeezed tighter.

Without thought, she pulled Olivia into a tight hug, holding her trembling body against hers. 'We will. I swear it.'

What the bloody hell is wrong with me? She's my enemy. I am sworn to hold her accountable for her crimes. Not hold her in my arms to promise all will be well.

But something about Olivia's desperation awakened Philippa's need to protect. It was a response as instinctual as breathing. Something she had never been allowed to do for Liza.

Liza. Dear God, what am I doing?

The memory hit her hard and unbidden. The week after Edward told his father of Philippa's affair with Liza, she had snuck out of her house, determined to see her love. To convince her to do the impossible and endure whatever trials lay ahead so they could find their forever.

Philippa had climbed the rose trellis outside Liza's room. It was a journey she had made countless times from when she was eleven until now, at twenty. First as girls to giggle over silly confidences, then as women to protect far more serious secrets.

Liza was at her writing desk. Her hair tumbled around her. Face puffy and red from crying. She had been beautiful even as she raged.

'I will not marry! I don't care what Father threatens to do. I would rather rot in an asylum than be forced to suffer a moment in the arms of the viscount. He's nearly as old as Father.'

'Then let us run away together. I have saved my pin money. We can leave tonight and start somewhere new. Where no one knows us.' Philippa was desperate. Tears flowed down her cheeks as she lurched across the room and sank down on her knees in front of Liza. She gripped her pale hands and squeezed, willing her stubborn love to listen for once.

'And how do you propose we live with no money? No connections? No men to provide for us? No protection.'

'I will protect us. I will teach myself how to keep us safe, darling.'

'It's impossible, Phil.'

'Living without you is impossible. I love you, Liza. I will love you forever, whether we are together or apart, but I can't let you go to bedlam. I won't allow it.'

Liza smiled, her face a heartbreaking contrast of love and fear, acceptance of the inevitable and seething rebellion. 'You don't have a choice, Phil. Neither of us does. This is the only option for me.'

Philippa rose up, framing Liza's face between her shaking hands. 'There is always a choice. *I will find a way to rescue you, Liza. I will make my fortune and get you out of there. I swear it. We will be together again. On my life, I promise you this.'*

But she hadn't kept her promise. And Liza died alone in the asylum.

I failed Liza, and now I'm betraying her.

But how can I turn away from Olivia when she needs my help?

Her situation was impossible. And lest she forget, three men had just died. Two at her hand. Olivia's daughter was being threatened by the Crow and might be in immediate danger. They were stranded on a deserted road, and the sky looked ominous. Philippa didn't have time to drown in past, present, or future regrets.

Releasing Olivia, she ignored the maelstrom in her mind and focused on the task at hand. She could complete this plan. She could protect Olivia and her daughter. She must. 'Come. There's much to be done.'

The next fifteen minutes were a flurry of unhitching the horses, packing what foodstuff they could find and the two flasks of water they'd brought with them into the coachman's leather satchel, and determining their location from the map the coachman kept in the front pocket of his bag.

'We can cut our journey down by several days if we take the coastline road here. It's far too difficult terrain for a carriage, but by horseback, we should be fine. If we ride hard, we'll get to Charlestown Port in three days. Four at the most.' Philippa kept her focus on the map, refusing to notice the sweet floral notes of Olivia's perfume or the way her cheeks turned from pale pink to deep rose in the cooling air. 'Put on your cloak. It will be much colder travelling this way.'

Olivia followed Philippa's orders, but when it came time to mount the smaller bay Philippa determined would be a better fit for Olivia, the woman pressed her lips together in a firm line and shook her head.

'I can't.' Olivia's eyes were wide as she stared at the horse the way many might stare down the barrel of a cannon.

'Don't be silly. It's just a horse. You simply sit on its back and squeeze your thighs tight.' The horse still wore part of the harness from the carriage, giving Olivia something to hold on to, though it would be almost impossible to guide the horse's head. Philippa planned to lead, using her legs to direct her slightly larger bay and trusting Olivia's mount to follow them.

'No. You will sit on its back and squeeze your thighs. I will sit behind you and hold on for my bloody life.'

Philippa frowned. Olivia's pleasantly low voice had become shrill. 'We've no time to waste, Olivia. Your daughter's life depends on our haste.'

'Exactly. So we should stop arguing.'

Philippa huffed out a sigh. 'You really don't think you can ride on your own?'

Olivia looked at the horse, then Philippa, then back at the bay. 'I know I can't. You must ride with me. It's the only way.'

'We'll lose time by riding together. One horse carrying two people can't travel as quickly as two horses carrying one person each.'

'But it can travel a damn sight faster than one horse dragging someone behind them. We can take both mounts and change frequently so they can each rest.' It was the tears shining in Olivia's eyes as she stared at the large animal that dismantled Philippa's arguments.

Olivia didn't cry, but the tears hovered there, making her green eyes burn even brighter in the autumn light. Somehow, that was more heartbreaking than if she had been sobbing.

Tsking, Philippa rolled her own eyes. 'Fine. We can ride together. But this is ridiculous. When this is all over, you need to take riding lessons.'

Olivia sniffed. 'When this is all over, you're sending me to Newgate prison or hell, so I shall hardly need to worry about riding down Rotten Row, will I?'

Philippa's heart squeezed again. It was shockingly painful. She instinctively rubbed her hand just above her left breast.

Stokes is right. I'm getting old. This must be some form of indigestion. Or perhaps it's the beginning stages of angina.

'Come on, then.' She hardened her voice and walked to the larger horse, linking her fingers together to make a cradle for Olivia's boot. 'Put your foot here and I'll boost you up.' She most certainly did not inhale deeply, trapping Olivia's scent in her lungs, as the beautiful woman put one hand on Philippa's shoulder. She awkwardly pulled back her skirts to fit her foot into Philippa's hands and then put her free hand on the horse's flank. Philippa also did not admire the delicate curve of Olivia's calf meeting her slim ankle or feel a rush of heat through her body as she imagined running her finger up Olivia's shapely leg to test the texture of her inner thigh. That would have been completely untoward. Hardly the behaviour of a proper duchess.

I've never been a proper duchess.

But she had always been a devoted duchess. And it frightened her to admit something was shifting in her heart.

Once Olivia was settled, Philippa led the horse to the carriage and used the step to help climb behind Olivia. The woman's soft curls tickled Philippa's nose. Her bottom fit perfectly between Philippa's thighs as she reached around Olivia to grip the harness.

'Hold his mane for balance. We'll start slow.' Her voice was rough as she spoke into Olivia's ear. She felt the quiver of apprehension or nerves running through the tense woman and wished she could ease Olivia's fears.

Nonsense. Fear is the only emotion I should hope to inspire in this woman.

But that was a lie.

This is going to be a long ride.

That was the truth.

8

Olivia's legs ached. Her body was sore in places she didn't wish to acknowledge. She longed to lean back against Philippa, close her eyes, and slip into unconsciousness, but then she would fall off the damn horse.

They had been riding over rough terrain for hours. The rolling hills shifted to rugged coastline as Philippa veered from the main road the carriage was following to take a quicker and far less travelled route southwest. When Olivia had questioned her about it, Philippa only urged the horse to move faster.

'The map was clear. This is the fastest path to Cornwall and your daughter. If the Crow sent those three after us, there's no reason why he hasn't already sent others in search of Hyacinth. The faster we find her, the better her chances are of escape.'

Olivia had pressed her lips together after that and focused on staying upright. Fear, fatigue, and the initial shock of their encounter with the highwaymen faded into a numb kind of trance as they traversed the many miles separating Olivia from her daughter.

Hyacinth. Hyacinth. Hyacinth.

She repeated her name silently. A mantra keeping Olivia focused on what was most important. She used the same trick when she was imprisoned in the asylum. Keeping Hyacinth in the forefront of her mind had been the only way to stay sane in a house designed for madness. Knowing she needed to survive, if only to hold her sweet girl one more time, empowered her to endure.

Of course, when Olivia had finally returned to England to be reunited with her daughter, the girl had stood with her father, their servants lined up on either side of the drive to receive the lady of the house, and each unfamiliar line of Hyacinth's face was hardened in hatred. She'd stiffened when Olivia tried to embrace her. Olivia barely recognised the angry young woman her child had become. It had been far more painful than any ice bath Olivia suffered at the asylum. More shocking than the brutal treatment of the orderlies. More devastating than the years of separation.

But no matter. If I can't earn her affection, I can at least ensure her safety.

Sending Hyacinth away would be the hardest thing Olivia had ever done, including riding pell-mell over the countryside with a dominating duchess at her back, but she would do it regardless. The girl already hated her. She would probably rejoice at a chance to be rid of her mother forever. And at least Olivia could face her fate knowing her daughter was safe. Because she wasn't lying when she told Philippa she would turn herself in if the duchess could ensure Hyacinth's escape from England. And more, she would make sure Philippa set Hyacinth up with all the contacts a young woman might wish from a duchess as powerful as Lady Winterbourne. Sacrificing her own life would be well worth knowing her daughter's future was bright. And part of her would finally be at peace. Knowing she would be punished for her crimes might actually help Olivia regain a modicum of respect for herself.

At some point during their journey, Philippa's left hand slid from the harness to rest around Olivia's waist. She felt the flex of Philippa's fingers and fought the urge to lean back against her. She would not allow the duchess to support her no matter how desperately her body wanted to sink into Philippa's warmth.

'Look. Just there.' Philippa let go of Olivia's waist and pointed in the distance. There was a dim grey shape in the waning light. A small cottage perched on the edge of the narrow path they were following.

'Do you think they'll let us stay for the night?' Olivia half-turned. Her nose nearly grazed Philippa's cheek. The woman's skin stretched tight over high cheekbones. For a wild moment, she was tempted to press her lips against the silky texture and watch Philippa's eyes widen in shock. Or perhaps darken with desire.

I really am going mad.

'We're going to find out.' Philippa turned her own head to look at Olivia.

Their lips were only a breath apart. Philippa's dark hair caught in the wind, tangling with Olivia's pale curls. If she leaned even a fraction forward, she could run her tongue over Philippa's full bottom lip. Nip her just there and swallow her gasp of need. She could take Philippa's longing and amalgamate it with her own. She could forget her desperation, just for a moment, and become lost in desire. Pretend she was just a normal woman in love.

No. Not in love. You can't love someone you also hate. Lust, certainly. But not love.

The duchess turned back to the cabin. Olivia felt Philippa's thighs tighten as the horse responded, moving into a rocking canter that forced Olivia to grip his mane tighter and focus once more on not falling. They had traded back and forth between the horses three times, and she imagined the animals were just as desperate to end their journey as the women who rode them. The larger bay certainly wasted no time in covering the short distance to the cottage. The smaller horse followed close behind, tethered to them by a strap from her harness.

The cabin was deserted. After dismounting – awkwardly for Olivia, and infuriatingly gracefully for the duchess – they carefully inspected the outside of the dwelling, peering through dusty windows, and knocking loudly on the front door. Olivia turned to Philippa and shrugged. 'Empty. At least for now. Do you think anyone will return?'

Philippa smudged a circle of clean glass on the windowpane and peered inside once more. 'Based on the dust covering the furniture, and the mouse I see sitting next to the hearth, my guess is, no.'

'Should we break a window?' Olivia looked around for a rock large enough to toss through the window. 'You're ever so good at it.' She turned to smirk at Philippa, who returned the expression with a far less amused twisting of her lips.

Philippa reached up into her half-assembled hair and removed a pin. Another jet-black lock fell free, brushing over her cheek. She held the small piece of metal up and raised her eyebrow. 'No need for such violence when we can just as easily pick the lock.'

'Too bad that doesn't work for carriage windows.' Olivia couldn't resist poking at her. She stepped aside and watched as Philippa bent the pin, inserted it into the lock, and twitched her wrist one way, then the other. She bit her lip in concentration. Olivia tried not to imagine her own teeth sinking into Philippa's plush crimson flesh.

Control yourself. You don't like her.

A click and Philippa's triumphant smile alerted Olivia to her enemy's success. Philippa twisted the handle and pushed open the door.

'Your luxurious accommodation awaits, my lady.' The glint of mischief flashing in Philippa's cobalt eyes warmed something tight and frozen in Olivia's chest.

Lifting her skirt, Olivia deliberately brushed past Philippa as she crossed the threshold. She didn't imagine the spark of *something* crackling between them, but she did back away from it. For her own protection. Philippa was not for her, and she had no desire to become like one of the drooling fools who followed Olivia around. She was the wanted, not the wanting. That position was far too powerless, and Olivia was already acutely aware of her limited autonomy.

She spent the next half hour exploring the one-room house for any food-stuffs in the cupboards, shaking out moth-eaten bedding, remaking the one bed tucked along the far left wall, and collecting kindling from a spider-infested pile of wood stacked in a sheltered alcove behind the cottage. She started a fire in the small hearth across from the bed. A water barrel stood near the woodpile and was overflowing with rainwater. Finding a dented pot in one of the cupboards, she filled it with water and hung it on the hook over the fire to boil.

While she kept herself busy turning the dusty room into a warm, clean, habitable space, Philippa handled the horses. There was a small stable at the back of the cottage, and she told Olivia she was going to bed down the horses, whatever that meant. The sun had set, and the temperature was dropping when Philippa entered the room carrying the driver's leather satchel. A strong wind picked up, wailing over the rocky cliffs and bringing with it briny ocean air and the call of gulls. Waves crashed against the cliff far below their little hideaway, but the walls were snug, and no draughts stirred the air inside the cottage.

After depositing the bag on a rickety table, Philippa did a slow turn, taking in the room. 'How cosy.' Her words should be complimentary, but her tone cut. Olivia was crouched by the fire, feeding the flames and waiting for the pot to boil. She stood, refusing to let Philippa's criticism hurt her feelings. What did she care if the pompous princess didn't appreciate her efforts?

'I'm so sorry it doesn't meet your standards, Duchess.'

'You have a way of turning my title into an insult.' Philippa's long legs ate the space between them.

'And you have a way of turning my attempts at compromise into an attack.' Olivia refused to back away. In part because fighting with Philippa was far preferable to admitting her attraction. And in part because she couldn't back away without stepping into the fireplace and catching alight. Though she already felt like she was burning from the inside. 'Why are you always at war with me, Duchess?'

Philippa reached out, pausing just before she brushed her fingers over Olivia's lips. She fisted her hand, stepped back, and turned away. 'I am at war with myself, a battle I fear I'm losing,' she whispered. Then louder: 'Did you find any food?'

Olivia wasn't sure how to respond. Why? Why was Philippa warring with herself? What about Olivia caused such conflict within a woman who never hesitated? Never doubted herself. Always knew the path she meant to walk.

Air rushed from her lungs as she focused on answering Philippa's question, because she had no answers for her own. 'It may have once been food. But not any more. I found a jar of something black and terrifying, a few cherry pits long since eaten by some creature, and another jar of weevil-infested flour. We'll just have to ration what we took from the carriage.'

She's hiding something. Why else would she retreat?

There was a reason Philippa preferred conflict over conversation. And Olivia was desperate to uncover exactly what the reason might be. The investigated becoming the investigator.

If she reveals her weakness, I might be able to use it to my advantage.

But that wasn't the real reason she wanted to pull away Philippa's shields and see the woman beneath the armour.

She does not fascinate me.

But it was no use. She couldn't deny her interest in Philippa. Nor could she stop herself from comparing the fierce attraction she felt for the duchess to the far softer flame she had once carried for her lady's maid over a decade ago. It was the difference between a crucible and a candle. Which troubled Olivia exceedingly.

Daisy had awakened Olivia to the joys of sexual pleasure between two people when attraction and respect combined to create magic. The few weeks they shared over a decade past had been a revelation. Olivia fell hard for the young woman with the passion of infatuation. At first, she thought her desires were an anomaly. That her maid held her in thrall like a witch. She thought she might only be attracted to another woman because that woman was Daisy. But during her years in the asylum, she had much time for reflection. She realised that, while Percival was a terrible match in every capacity, no man had ever sparked her interest. It mattered not if they were honourable, handsome, funny, or fascinating. She might enjoy their company, but she had never lusted after them the way she did with women. Not just Daisy, but other women as well, even though she never acted on her impulses. When fantasy was her only form of escape in the asylum, she didn't always imagine Daisy, but she always imagined women. Faceless, nameless, soft and strong female bodies that quickened her need in the dark nights.

Olivia would always hold Daisy in a sacred part of her heart, and she would never forgive Percival for sending her away to face a cruel world with no reference, no connection, and no hope of a safe future. But in the asylum, she grew to realise Daisy was her first love, but not the love of Olivia's life. Her guilt over Daisy's fate never eased, but her yearning for her faded like a painting left too long in the sun. And now, seeing Philippa's obvious grief over her lost love, it was clear Olivia had never experienced connection on such a deep level. She wondered if it was possible for someone who had loved so deeply as Philippa to ever love again.

This is not love. It is only lust. It means nothing. I can ignore my lust.

But she didn't want to ignore it. She wanted to indulge. A decidedly disastrous idea. It was a shame disaster always found her so easily.

* * *

Philippa cursed silently. It seemed no matter what she did to steel herself against Olivia, the fair-haired temptress refused to cooperate.

What right does she have to ask such impertinent questions? And why can't she stay on her side of this damnably small bed?

Olivia shifted on the mattress. Her thigh pressed against Philippa's, the honeysuckle and vanilla scent making it impossible for Philippa to focus. She was plotting her next step in taking down the last leader of the Devil's Sons, but her logical plans kept fizzing into mist every time Olivia moved next to her. The fire burned low, and the crackle and pop of logs was a sharp contrast to the constant crash of waves outside the window. Her wayward thoughts kept bouncing between faded memories of Liza and much more vivid images of her adventure with Olivia. Her earlier conversation with the marchioness repeated in her mind, like she was worrying a loose button until the damn thing fell off entirely.

'Why are you always at war with me, Duchess?'

'I'm not always at war, you know.' Philippa's voice was loud to her own ears. She immediately wanted to call the words back. The last thing she wished was for Olivia to think Philippa had been silently obsessing over her question for the past several hours.

I've been obsessing over many things. Her question is just one of them.

Olivia breathed in, and Philippa felt the sheet they shared shift. She refused to imagine Olivia's unbound breasts being the cause of the linen's movement.

'Truly? I can't imagine you at peace.' Olivia's husky voice played over Philippa's senses like someone plucking a cello string. Low vibrations resonating into the depths of her soul. 'Maybe I am the cause. You haven't liked me from the start.'

Philippa rolled her eyes. A useless expression as Olivia was staring at the ceiling, and it was too dark to make out much in the quiet room. 'It has nothing to do with whether or not I like you.'

'But you don't. At least admit that.'

Tapping her finger on the sheet, Philippa contemplated her answer. 'I don't like the way you make me feel.' It was far more honest than she wanted to be, and once more, she regretted her words.

'Angry?' Olivia asked.

'No, anger is something I'm used to feeling. I like anger. It's far better than fear.'

Olivia shifted on her side, bending her elbow to rest her head on her hand so she could face Philippa. They had no pillows and were using their coats. She used her free hand to re-bunch the material beneath her elbow. Her blonde curls shone in the sliver of moonlight peeking between wind-chased clouds. One curl fell over Olivia's cheek, and Philippa resisted the urge to reach out and tuck the silky strand behind her delicate ear. An ear she desperately wanted to nibble, if only to hear what sounds the woman might make.

'What is the Duchess of Dorsett possibly frightened of? The Queen's Deadliest Damsel. A fearsome creature with pistols in her pocket and daggers in her boots. Men tremble in terror of you.'

'It isn't men who worry me.'

Doing what Philippa could not, Olivia reached out and let her finger follow a strand of Philippa's hair from her forehead down to where it lay on her shoulder.

'Who is it then? Certainly not me.'

Philippa twisted to mirror Olivia's pose. Their faces were only inches apart, and the fire was warm on her back. 'It's me. I'm frightened of myself.'

Olivia's brow furrowed. 'I don't understand.'

Because I hardly understand. So how can I possibly explain the thoughts racing in my head?

She never spoke of Liza. At least, not to anyone but Liza's brother, Edward. But for reasons she refused to examine, she wanted to speak of her now. To Olivia. And why not? The marchioness already hated Philippa. Confessing her darkest crimes wouldn't change Olivia's opinion of Philippa one whit, nor did she care.

Liar.

Pressing her lips together, she breathed deeply through her nose and savoured the scent of Olivia. 'Control is something I prize as it is something women are rarely given. Control of my choices. My future. My feelings. I'm sure you understand.' She waited for Olivia's nod. 'I think every woman does. It was the one thing I despised about loving Liza.' Even saying the words aloud shattered a wall she'd built deep within. A barrier to contain the blackness of her soul.

Olivia didn't say anything. She just held Philippa's gaze with her own. Steady and true. The silence allowed Philippa to continue.

'Loving her was the most beautiful thing I've ever experienced.'

'Tell me what you love most about me.' Liza scrunched her face, her hair haloed on the green grass as a bee buzzed lazily nearby.

Philippa rolled over and stroked her fingers over Liza's soft cheek. They had shared their first passionate kiss only a few weeks prior, but already she knew this was it. This was forever.

'I love everything I know about you, and everything I've yet to learn.'

Liza giggled and shook her head. 'You're supposed to say you love my eyes. Or my mouth. Or my hair, silly.'

Philippa rubbed her thumb along Liza's jaw. 'Those are just things on the outside. I like those things. But I love what's inside you.'

Liza popped up and grabbed Philippa's hand, pressing it against her chest. 'Like my heart?'

Philippa leaned forward, hovering a moment away from Liza's mouth. 'Yes. I love your heart.'

She pulled herself from the memory. If they had known how things would end, would they have altered how they loved each other? It was a question Philippa would never be able to answer.

She cleared her throat. 'And loving Liza was the most devastating thing I've ever experienced. Losing her nearly broke me. I vowed to love her forever. And I do. But I also swore to never let myself be so vulnerable again. To never give my love to another. Because I had no control when she died.'

Philippa blinked, remembering when Edward told her what had happened. It was the single worst day of her life. 'I had no control over the choice she made. Or my emotions because of that choice. Or my thoughts. They would take me back to some of our most beautiful moments and make everything within me hurt. Even my own decisions seemed out of my control. My body went places without asking my mind for permission. Wandering to our haunts in the middle of the night. Not sleeping. Not eating. I was paralysed for months. Unable to go back to the time when we were together. Unable to move forward. It was as though I died with her and was just a shell. The smallest tap might shatter me, and sometimes, I wanted to shatter. I wanted to join her, wherever she was.'

'Philippa.' Olivia's soft murmur brushed gently over her raw nerves. Her warm hand stroked down Philippa's arm in a gesture of comfort.

'I couldn't share my grief with anyone. I wasn't supposed to be in love with a woman. Certainly not my childhood best friend. The only people who knew were those punishing me for loving her. They would likely take pleasure in knowing I suffered. Except Edward. But I was too angry to speak with him. So I kept the pain inside like a secret that grew fierce and feral in the dark.' Philippa didn't realise she was crying until Olivia cupped Philippa's face in her soft hand. She brushed her thumb over Philippa's cheek, catching her tears. Philippa pulled back and sniffed, unwilling to accept kindness.

'You mourn her still. Such devotion is something few people show.'

Shaking her head, Philippa shoved her hair away from her face. 'You don't understand. I am not some romantic woman pining after my one true love. I love Liza, but I hate her too, for what she did. To herself. To me. To any chance we might have had to reunite. I was so angry with her for not choosing life. Was our love not worth living for? I swore I would find her. That we would be together. Did she not have faith that I would keep my promise? Because I would have moved heaven and earth to rescue her.' Philippa's voice shook with her emotion.

'I don't doubt that you would have torn the sky apart to save your love.' Olivia's words soothed something bleeding in Philippa's soul just as they caused a thrill of panic to run through her. Why did this woman see her so clearly? The woman she was. The woman she hoped to become. The woman she hated within herself. Olivia seemed to see them all. 'But you can't know how terrible it must have been for Liza. Sometimes, death seems far gentler than life.'

Philippa shook her head. 'No. Where there is life, there is always hope. She took that hope with her when she died. I hate her for that.'

'Your anger is understandable. But is it standing in front of your pain? Protecting you? Is hating Liza easier than grieving for her?'

An unbearable ache stretched inside Philippa's chest, threatening to shatter her ribs. But Olivia kept talking.

'I think, until you feel that anguish, the anger will never leave.' She ran her delicate hand up and down Philippa's arm as tears trailed down Philippa's face unchecked, plopping onto her coat. She probably looked a complete fright. The duchess. Totally undone. It was horrifying to think about. But easier than accepting Olivia's words. Yet even as she tried to pull away, the pain seeped from the darkest corner of her heart, desperate to flow as free as her tears.

'Let it run through you, Philippa. Don't be afraid.'

Ridiculous. I'm never afraid. Except any time I think of Liza. And every time I look at Olivia. And now. Right now, I'm bloody terrified.

Because the grief was too large. Too heavy. Too sharp. Like the waves crashing far beneath them and the jagged rocks upon which they crashed. Grief was both of those things. And she wasn't strong enough to feel all of that without exploding into a million tiny pieces. So, she called forth her rage to push back the sorrow.

'What could you possibly know of my pain?' Lashing out seemed far wiser than letting Olivia see her with no shields. 'You don't know me, Marchioness. And you never will.'

Olivia pulled her hand back. Her green eyes flashed with hurt before they hardened like emeralds. She nodded her head in agreement, but it didn't feel like a triumph. 'No. You are going to make sure of that, aren't you? Because you don't want anyone to see behind your carefully curated image of the powerful, fearless Duchess of Dorsett. Always right. Always in control. You wouldn't want people to discover the broken, terrified, lost woman you really are, Philippa Winterbourne.' She flipped over, punched her coat and flomped back down, giving Philippa her back. 'But I see you. And you can't frighten me away by shaking your stupid sword and telling me I don't know you or your pain. I know you better than you think.' Flipping back, she pointed a finger at Philippa's face. 'And you can't force me to fight you because that's the only thing you know how to do when your feelings get too scary. Perhaps we're both cowards, but at least I'm trying to change.' Olivia turned away again, her hair slapping Philippa's cheek. 'Goodnight, Duchess.'

Philippa wanted to reach out, pull Olivia's shoulder down so she could see her face, and apologise for being a total arse. But the duchess did not apologise because she was never wrong. It was a thought that usually brought her great comfort. But she didn't want to be right. Not about this.

'Goodnight, Marchioness.'

Nothing about this night was good. Olivia was right. Philippa was a coward. She didn't have the strength to stay true to her oath to Liza and walk away from Olivia, but neither did she have the courage to reach out and pull Olivia into the cradle of her arms. She could feel the heat of Olivia's body, but couldn't let the warmth sink past her own skin and melt the ice freezing her soul. Olivia offered comfort and understanding, but Philippa couldn't accept it without betraying a woman she loved and hated in equal measure. There was always a choice. Hers was just an impossible one.

9

Three days of riding from sunrise to sunset answered three questions Olivia never thought to ask. Was sleeping outside charming? Decidedly not. Would she ever be comfortable on horseback? Surprisingly so. Did the Duchess of Dorsett have any human emotions at all outside of anger? A resounding yes, but they were a tangled mess. And with good reason. The woman had gone through hell, and she was still reeling from Liza's death. It was a fearsome blow.

After their night in the cliffside cottage, Olivia expected the duchess to resume her snarky attitude. Philippa certainly made it clear the last thing she wanted was Olivia's comfort or concern. But the following morning, she had gone out of her way to make tea for Olivia. Her hand had lingered on Olivia's waist when she helped her mount. Throughout their three-day journey, she had taken care to stop more often and travel at an easier pace. But the true shock came on their last night. Most of their food was gone, but they had been hoarding a shortbread cookie. When Philippa had handed the prized treat to Olivia with a ridiculous excuse about not liking shortbread, Olivia knew the woman was trying to apologise.

I won't let you off so easy, Duchess. If you want my forgiveness, you'll need to ask for it outright. After you help me get Hyacinth to safety, and before you lock me in Newgate.

Olivia shook her head at her own stupidity. She knew Philippa had more feelings than she wanted to admit, but she wasn't sure if any of them included friendliness toward Olivia. Even if they did, it wouldn't stop the duchess from accomplishing her goal of ensuring Olivia faced judgement for her crimes. And how could Olivia argue with her? She was guilty of being willing to sacrifice children she didn't know for the child she did. A child she was going to see in mere moments. Hope and fear battled within her. Hope that Hyacinth might be grateful for her return. Fear that she wouldn't.

They plodded along the gravel lane leading to the small farmer's cottage made entirely of stone. It perched next to a green field ending in a rocky cliff. A path of steps cut from the stones led down to a cove where sand sparkled in the autumn sunlight.

A young man emerged from the door and squinted against the sun as he watched them approach. Well-worn breeches, a homespun shirt, and a battered waistcoat declared his station in life.

'Callum! It's good to see you,' Olivia called from the horse's back, not wanting to alarm the young man.

His stern face softened in recognition, though he did not smile. Light-brown hair curled into his grey eyes. He crossed thick arms over his chest and rocked back on his heels. 'Lady Smithwick. I'm hoping you've come to collect your daughter and get her far away from here. She's a terror right and true, she is.'

Philippa shifted behind her, and the horse slowed to a stop in front of Callum.

'And who is your travelling companion?' Callum stepped forward to assist Olivia in dismounting.

'Just a friend.' Philippa spoke before Olivia could. Looking at Callum's outstretched hand as though it were a rotten limb infested with the plague, she easily swung her leg over the horse and slid nimbly to her feet. Callum took a step back, his eyes assessing the duchess.

'And do you have a name, or shall I call you "friend", though I must admit you don't seem very friendly.'

'I'm not.'

The hostility sparking between them was neither necessary nor helpful.

Olivia stepped between Philippa and Callum. 'This is, er...' She'd forgotten the blasted name they'd given Philippa. Gertrude? Edna? No, it was something with an 'H'.

Philippa's derisive snort created a hot blush to creep up Olivia's neck. 'You can call me Winters.' Not a bad pseudonym, as she was currently projecting about as much heat as that frigid season. And since it was so close to Philippa's actual name of Winterbourne, Olivia was sure to remember it.

'Um. Yes. Miss Winters is an old chum from finishing school. She knows of our situation and has offered to help.'

Making no move to take them into the house, Callum kept his sharp gaze on Philippa. 'Isn't that so very generous of her?' But his tone implied no compliment. Indeed, he seemed much like a bear guarding his den. 'I'll have a word with you in private, Olivia.' His eyes never left Philippa as he spoke.

'You'll do no such thing. Wherever she goes, I go.' Philippa raised her eyebrow like a guillotine blade ready to claim its next victim.

'Is that because you don't trust me, or you don't trust her?' Callum tipped his chin in Olivia's direction.

'I don't trust anyone, save myself.' Philippa strode forward and stopped toe to toe with Callum. 'Now, take us to Hyacinth so we can collect her and be on our way.'

'I shall not do a blasted thing until I speak with Lady Smithwick.' Callum fisted his hands by his side. His jaw muscles clenched, and he held his ground against the duchess.

Satisfaction that at least she had made a good choice in leaving Hyacinth with Callum filled Olivia with some comfort. He might not like her daughter, but he was willing to put himself in harm's way to protect her. Few men had the courage to stand against Philippa. Even less would do so on behalf of a girl they hardly knew.

Philippa narrowed her eyes. 'Fine. But be quick about it. We were attacked by highwaymen on our journey here. They carried with them a note outlining our route, so someone is working against us. The same person might have sent others here if they have even a hint of suspicion as to Hyacinth's whereabouts.'

Callum held his ground for another moment, no doubt digesting the information. Glancing at Olivia, he tipped his head toward the house.

'Come inside. You, stay out here.' He jabbed his finger at Philippa, and Olivia couldn't stop the smug smile curling her lips. Finally, a man was willing to stand up to the beautiful woman instead of shrinking back in fear. Philippa caught her gaze. Her eyes darkened. She threw her shoulders back and jutted out her chin, a warrior holding back her charge, but not for long.

Olivia sailed by a fuming Philippa and entered the sparse, but meticulously clean cottage. She had spent a few days there with Hyacinth when they first fled London, making sure her daughter was settled and that she would be safe before Olivia returned to town to collect her prize. The snug home was designed with the front door opening right into a small parlour. Beyond that was a hallway leading to the back of the house, where the kitchen and larder could be found facing the sea. On her right was a staircase leading up to the bedrooms. The parlour was empty, and there were no sounds of voices in the rest of the house.

'Where is Hyacinth? Is she well?' The words came out in a rush. Olivia wanted to grab his arm and shake the information free.

'She is as well as a spoiled, selfish, spiteful girl could be expected. If I'd known how much trouble she'd be, I wouldn't have agreed to this, no matter how much my mother esteems you.'

'You didn't agree. She did.' Mrs Hughes was once Olivia's nanny. She had been young Olivia's favourite person for all her childhood, and that affection only grew as she transitioned from girl to woman. 'Where is she, by the by?'

Callum's dark eyebrows lowered over his grey eyes. 'With your daughter. They're thick as thieves, those two. Miss Hyacinth has Mam convinced she should be taking more walks. They've gone down to the shore. Mam'll probably fall on the rocks and twist her ankle following that wild hellion.'

The news of her daughter forming some kind of connection with Mrs Hughes when she had no interest in Olivia struck a chord of jealousy within her that twanged painfully. But she pushed away the disloyal feeling and chose instead to focus on defending Hyacinth's honour. 'She's hardly a hellion. The child had to make do without a mother for ten years. It's no wonder she's formed such a connection with yours. She was always so kind to me when I was a child.'

Mrs Hughes had been a part of Olivia's life from the moment she was born until a few weeks before Olivia's marriage. Mrs Hughes found a sweetheart of her own. A handsome farmer with a young lad of four who needed the kind of help Mrs Hughes was ready to give. She married and made the move to the Cornish coast. While saying her goodbyes, she promised to always be there if Olivia needed anything. Even then, Olivia imagined Mrs Hughes knew Olivia's future would not be easy. Her nursemaid never liked Percival, though she wouldn't say a word about it to Olivia's father.

Olivia wrote to Mrs Hughes during the first few years of her marriage, and the sage woman shared advice, encouragement, and understanding. She became Olivia's anchor in a troubled sea until Percy dragged her kicking and screaming across the Channel to an asylum in Germany.

The Home for Wayward Women believed in horrific treatments to cure their patients, but they weren't as strict as some of the asylums in England. They allowed patients to write and receive letters if they showed exemplary behaviour, though they also used this as a tool to ensure obedience. When Olivia received her first letter from Mrs Hughes, she thought it was a cruel joke. How could she possibly know where Olivia had been sent? Percy was adamant no one find out where he'd imprisoned her, reminding her when he left the asylum that she was completely alone. But the informational network of the servant class was second to none. Mrs Hughes kept in touch with several of the maids in Olivia's house, and they had informed her of the gossip surrounding Olivia's sudden disappearance. No doubt one of them had seen the correspondence between Percy and the lead physician of the asylum and put the pieces together.

Mrs Hughes was the only person who wrote to Olivia in the asylum. Her letters came once a month without fail, though Olivia wasn't always allowed to receive them. At times, the doctors and nurses would withhold the missives until Olivia submitted to whatever treatment they deemed necessary to cure her of the sexual depravity raging through her system. Once, a particularly nasty orderly burned Mrs Hughes' letter in front of Olivia before she could read it. Punishment for refusing to voluntarily enter the ice baths.

But every time she was allowed to read the precious words from her nursemaid, she felt hope stir in her chest. Mrs Hughes made sure to fill her letters with silly details that brought tears and smiles in equal measure. The normal beauty of life captured by ink on parchment reminded Olivia of everything she fought to regain and everything she was missing. The bees buzzing over Mrs Hughes' roses. The cat who curled up on her lap when she was trying to knit. Callum, the child of her heart, if not her body, who grew into a man as Olivia read letter after letter in her solitary cell. Even the tragedy Mrs Hughes experienced when her husband passed from acute angina after only nine years together was a reminder to Olivia that life was always changing and nothing would last forever, neither sorrow nor joy. Mrs Hughes' grief at the loss of her husband, and ability to heal from that grief to a place of gratitude for the love they shared filled Olivia with longing for something *more*. And on the rarest occasion, Mrs Hughes would hear word of Hyacinth. Those letters were the hardest to read. The ink would run with Olivia's tears.

Mrs Hughes' correspondence reminded Olivia there was an entire world outside her four walls where the sun shone. The rain fell. The wind blew. And people lived. Even after experiencing tragedy. They didn't just survive. They savoured honey on fresh bread. Walked through frothy waves on a sandy shore. Hummed melodies and tapped their toe to the rhythm of life. Olivia refused to believe she wouldn't one day rejoin the living because Mrs Hughes ended every letter with the same message of hope: *Until we see each other again, I hold you in my heart.*

The first letter Olivia wrote upon being released from the asylum was addressed to Mrs Hughes in her little stone cottage on the Cornish coast. And she was the only person Olivia trusted to offer sanctuary when she needed it most.

Callum crossed his arms over his chest again. 'She is the kindest woman I know. And I won't be exposing her to any danger. Not for you nor your daughter. So, tell me, who is this Winters? Can we trust her?'

'We can trust her to fight for her interests. And right now, it is in her interest to get Hyacinth to safety.'

'Why might that be?' Callum's hard stare dared Olivia to lie.

Because then I'll tell her the identity of the Crow. And she will make sure to hold me accountable for my crimes.

'I have something she needs.' It wasn't the full truth, but neither was it a lie.

Callum exhaled through his nose. For a man of only twenty, he carried himself with the weariness of a much older person. 'Fine. The sooner you leave, the sooner things will return to normal. I haven't had a moment's peace since your daughter walked through that door.'

And as if his words conjured her from thin air, the lilting sound of Hyacinth's laughter carried above the distant crashing waves. A door in the back of the house creaked open and slammed shut.

'And that is why mermaids always steal a lock of their lover's hair.' Hyacinth was looking at Mrs Hughes as they walked into the parlour together. Her cheeks, already pink from the sea air, darkened to a rose when her gaze stalled on Callum. 'Oh. I didn't think you were…' Her musical voice trailed off when she saw Olivia.

'You're back! And sooner than we expected.' Mrs Hughes strode forward, pulling Olivia into a strong hug. 'I'm so glad you're safe.'

Hyacinth pressed her bee-stung lips together and crossed her arms in a defensive pose. 'Really? I didn't expect her for at least another ten years. Isn't that your preferred time between visits?'

Olivia pulled free of Mrs Hughes to face her daughter, but before she could reply to Hyacinth's cutting remark, Philippa burst through the front door with a pistol in her hand. 'What the Devil is going on?'

Eyes going wide at the sight of a weapon, Hyacinth froze. Olivia instinctively stepped in front of Philippa to block her shot while Callum moved in front of Hyacinth.

'Everything is fine.' Olivia had her hands stretched out in front of her.

Because I can certainly catch the bloody bullet before it tears through my body.

Philippa's pupils dilated. She immediately lowered the pistol, allowing Olivia's chest to loosen a fraction. Staring down the barrel of a gun Philippa held was no easy feat. Clearing her throat and willing her heart to slow to a normal speed, Olivia clasped her hands together in front of her waist. 'Philippa, allow me to introduce you to Mrs Hughes, the woman who raised me.'

Mrs Hughes looked from Philippa's pistol now resting by her skirts to the woman herself, and Olivia tried to see her nursemaid through Philippa's eyes. Her hair was once a rich brown, but only a few streaks of mahogany remained amongst the various shades of silver and white. Her eyes were brown as well, but there were striations of green, turning them hazel in the sunlight. Wrinkles creased around the corners of her eyes and mouth, put there by endless moments of laughter and endless moments of worry. She had always been a sturdy woman, but in her older years, she was leaning toward stout, and Olivia was glad for it. Stout meant food was not scarce. The farm must be doing well for Mrs Hughes and Callum.

Her nursemaid's lips twitched in an expression Olivia knew as well as the veins tracing over her hand. She was trying not to smile. 'It would seem Olivia has found herself a protector. Finally.'

I shan't ruin her opinion by pointing out Philippa is a predator who is hunting me, not a protector who is saving me.

Philippa raised her perfectly sculpted brow. 'It would appear she's always had one.'

Mrs Hughes' cheeks became pink, and her eyes sparkled in the afternoon sunlight streaming through the parlour window. 'How lovely of you to say. Thank you.'

Philippa merely inclined her head in a regal nod.

Taking courage from the interaction, Olivia turned to her daughter. 'And this is Hyacinth, my daughter.'

Hyacinth looked from her mother to Philippa. 'Why do you carry a gun? Do you know how to shoot it? Would you have shot my mother?'

Philippa blinked at the girl's rapid-fire questions. 'I carry a gun for protection. And one shouldn't handle a weapon if they don't know how to shoot it.' She gave Olivia a meaningful look and pointedly left the last question unanswered.

Hyacinth turned back to Olivia. 'She could have shot me. What kind of mother introduces a murderous, mad woman to her daughter? Father was right. I'm better off without you. I wish you'd stayed away. Forever.'

The words did more damage to Olivia's soul than Philippa's bullet would have done to her body. But she absorbed them because her daughter wasn't wrong. She most likely would be better off without Olivia. And soon, she would get her wish. It would be the best gift she could give Hyacinth.

Philippa tucked her pistol in her pocket and shrank the space separating her from the girl. Olivia and Callum both moved to intercept her, but Philippa had Hyacinth backed up to the wall before anyone could stop her.

Hyacinth's pink cheeks whitened to chalk as Philippa stared at her like one might stare at a bug on the dinner table. 'Your father was right about very little. Know this: your mother has endured much to get back to you. If nothing else, she deserves your respect.'

Hyacinth swallowed. She broke eye contact with Philippa, instead staring at her feet.

Olivia grabbed Philippa's arm and pulled her back. 'Don't.' It was a harsh command.

Philippa turned, her fierce gaze capturing Olivia. A message flashed in her eyes, one Olivia couldn't decipher but desperately wanted to understand. 'She will not speak ill of you in my presence.'

'She's a child.'

Both Philippa and Hyacinth gave twin sounds of disgust.

'I'm old enough to marry.'

'She's old enough to hang for her crimes.'

'Hard to know which is worse,' Mrs Hughes chimed in, cracking the tension with a hearty laugh. 'Why don't we all take a breath? Callum, have you offered these ladies any refreshments? They look well to worn out from their travels. I shall put the kettle on. Hyacinth, come and help me in the kitchen while these two get settled. I've only one spare room, so you'll have to share.' Mrs Hughes winked at Olivia.

Dear God. Does she know?

Olivia never spoke of the reason she was imprisoned in the asylum, but if Mrs Hughes had been able to extract her location from the wagging tongues of her family's servants, then it wasn't a stretch to imagine she'd also discovered the cause of Olivia's punishment.

And now she's putting me in the same room as Philippa.

Mrs Hughes had always been progressive in her views on women, but this beat them all.

Olivia turned to Philippa. 'Well. I suppose we should go and freshen up before afternoon tea.'

* * *

Philippa couldn't decide what infuriated her more. Seeing the disdain with which Hyacinth held her mother after everything Olivia had been through to get to the cottage, or knowing at the end of this nightmare, she would once more be holding Olivia at gunpoint – only then it would be with the intent of pulling the trigger or securing her in a cell to await her fate with the House of Lords. Because while Philippa had no faith in the justice system to hold their brethren accountable, she was quite sure they wouldn't hesitate to castigate a woman for her crimes.

But the idea of punishing the marchioness was becoming less and less appealing. When Olivia had stepped in front of her gun, Philippa's whole body recoiled. Not since her first assignment had she felt nauseous at pointing her pistol at an assailant. But she did today.

I must simply remember the reasons Olivia is guilty. She joined with her husband to help kidnap young orphans. Orphans who would have been sold into the flesh market. Then she refused to protect Ivy when her life was being threatened. She is an evil, horrifying, malicious woman.

Except she wasn't. During their time together, it had become clear Olivia was a desperate woman with few choices. She was also courageous in times of peril. She was kind in times of cruelty. She was thoughtful, and funny, and wonderfully sarcastic. She would damn her own soul to protect a daughter who showed her no love and little dignity. Hardly the work of a vile fiend.

'Please excuse Hyacinth's behaviour today. She has been through many difficulties. I'm sure she was acting out of shock.' Olivia's usual bravado was deflated, and her words sounded hollow as she shut the door of their shared room. Philippa eyed another single bed, though this one was a vast improvement over their last. The linens were crisp, the pillows fluffed, and she doubted the mattress had any creatures living within it. It was also much larger than their last bed, which gave Philippa a twinge of regret.

'We've all experienced difficulties. It's no excuse for her to treat you with such disdain. I'm not sure why you tolerate it.'

Philippa took in the rest of the room. There was a dressing table with a porcelain bowl, a jug of water, and a cake of soap at the ready. An armoire – scarred, but well-polished – stood in the far corner of the room with a vase of flowers sitting atop. Pictures of ocean scenes and sunsets decorated the walls. While the signature gracing the artwork was not a recognisable name, the skill of the painter was evident. Walking closer, Philippa squinted at a squiggle in the left corner and made out a clear C and H. It was an easy bet these paintings were created by young Callum. A farmer hiding an artist's soul.

'I tolerate it because I deserve her enmity. I abandoned her for ten years to the cruel will of her father. And her feelings about me are not likely to improve when she realises I am going to banish her to a foreign country with no friends, no family, and no connections. Whatever love she might have once held for me will be totally destroyed when she understands her fate, so yes. I accept her disrespect because I deserve far worse. I deserve her utter contempt, and I'm quite sure I shall receive it.' Olivia's voice shook, and her eyes, greener than a northern forest, flashed with rage and grief. Two emotions Philippa knew well.

'Where are you sending her?' She wanted to cross the small space separating them and pull Olivia into her embrace. Not to seduce, but to comfort.

Highly alarming. The Duchess of Dorsett did not comfort criminals. And yet, her chest ached to see such anguish on Olivia's features erased.

'Percival has a distant cousin who took his wife to the Americas to see what fortune he might find in the new lands. He's done rather well for himself there, according to the letters he would send. Percival never liked him, which is all the recommendation he needs in my eyes.'

Philippa couldn't stop the sharp laugh. 'A sound measure for a man.'

'His letters always sent poor Percy into a snit. I wrote to him of our need to find sanctuary for Hyacinth in August after everything... transpired. He has welcomed her into their home for as long as necessary. He and his wife live in Baltimore. They were not blessed with children, so mayhap there is some room in their hearts to care for a child, though she's hardly that any more. It is not ideal, but she will be safe, and that is what matters.'

Not whether she loves her mother. Or is able to spend any time with her.

'Whatever happens, I want you to know I am sorry for what you've lost with your daughter.' The words ripped free from Philippa, and she was shocked at the pain of it. Pain she felt for Olivia's suffering. She never felt empathy for her enemies.

Is she still my enemy?

Olivia tipped up her chin and swiped at a single tear trailing down her cheek. 'Thank you.'

Tension pulled between them, tightening like a corset and making it diffi-cult to breathe. Philippa took a step closer, and when Olivia did not retreat, she took another, then another. She stopped when Olivia was within arm's reach.

'You are not what I expected, Lady Smithwick.'

'Olivia. I think we are past using titles, don't you, Philippa?'

Hearing her name on Olivia's lips shifted something elemental within Philippa. Few people earned the right to be so intimate with her. But Philippa yearned to hear her name once more. 'Say it again.'

'Philippa.' Olivia's voice was raw with either pain from Hyacinth's earlier rejection or something quite different but no less vital. Desire.

Reaching for her, Philippa took her hand and pulled her closer until their bodies met, but she didn't press her mouth against Olivia's sweet lips. Instead, she indulged in her own need to comfort the woman. Wrapping Olivia in her arms, she held her tight. Olivia's breasts pressed against her own, her trim waist was designed for Philippa's hand to rest on the flare of her hip. Her body was stiff, but after a moment, Olivia softened, melting into Philippa like honey in the sunlight.

They stood that way for moments, or maybe millennia. Philippa rubbed her hand up and down the bumps of Olivia's spine. Their breaths aligned. Her heart thumped in rhythm with the woman in her arms. Peace, an elusive and fleeting thing, descended.

Olivia pulled back first. 'We should return to the others.'

'Of course,' Philippa replied. But her body ached at the loss, and she fought the urge to pull Olivia back.

She belongs in my arms.

Clenching her jaw, she spun toward the door. It was an impossible desire. The last place Olivia belonged was in the arms of the Queen's Deadliest Damsel. A woman who long ago accepted she lost her heart when she lost Liza. So why now did it beat so painfully within her breast?

10

Callum was proving himself to be an accomplished cook. Afternoon tea had been a delightful affair with buttery shortbread, spicy Banbury cake, and tangy blackberry tarts. Mrs Hughes suggested an afternoon walk to rebuild their appetite before supper. They rambled over the fields to the cliff's edge, Hyacinth striding ahead, refusing to converse with the group. Watching Olivia trail after her daughter, her gaze never once straying from the girl, her expression a mixture of hope and resignation, Philippa determined to find some time alone with the young woman. Someone needed to explain to her the sacrifices her mother had made to ensure Hyacinth's safety.

Philippa let the sea air whip around her, wishing it could clear away the confusing emotions roiling within her breast. She rarely questioned her own actions. Her course was set, and she followed it without hesitation. But this case confounded her. Her initial estimation of Olivia being nothing more than a deceitful and manipulative woman was not entirely right.

Not right at all.

Doubt crept into her mind. Philippa was questioning her own judgement. Something she had never done in the past. But she'd never felt a sense of dread like she did when imagining Olivia facing the Queen's consequences.

Later that evening, the party of five sat around a snug table in the parlour with a warm fire dispelling the autumn chill. Dishes of steamed peas, honeyed carrots, boiled parsnips, and late-summer salad were placed on the table for easy serving. A golden-crusted pie took pride of place at the centre, steam coiling up and emitting the buttery aroma of delicate pastry.

'This looks divine. I rarely meet a man of the house who is also king of the kitchen.' Olivia winked at Callum, who glanced at Hyacinth and blushed a furious crimson before ducking his head.

'It's just fisherman's pie. Mam isn't fond of cooking, and I don't mind taking my turn in front of the stove.'

'He's being modest. Callum here is quite the chef. During the summer markets, people come from miles around to buy one of his pies. Leave some space for his plum pudding and custard.' Mrs Hughes nodded sagely.

'One wonders where he finds the time when he is so busy sticking his nose where it doesn't belong.' Hyacinth held her plate out to Callum, her lips curled in a sharp smile, her eyes flashing with challenge.

Interesting. Hyacinth seems awfully committed to hating young Callum.

A tickle of recognition stroked along her senses, but Philippa focused on her own slice of pie instead. It was filled with some kind of flaky white fish with dill, leeks, and onions in a creamy sauce. Topped with seasoned mashed potatoes and melted cheese, her French chef would be hard pressed to create a more delicious meal. Her mouth watered as she took a delicate forkful.

Callum gripped the knife he held, his knuckles turning white as he exhaled through his nose. He roughly grabbed Hyacinth's plate, cut a large slice of pie, and slapped it down. 'This is my property. My farm.' His eyes darted to his mother. 'Mine and me mam's. Anything that happens on this land is my business. Including letters you might be sending to a sweetheart.'

Hyacinth took back her plate, the pie nearly sliding off from the force she used to grab it from Callum's hands.

'My letters have nothing to do with you. And if I do have a sweetheart, that is my prerogative.'

Philippa's ears pricked as Olivia turned her full focus onto her daughter.

'You are writing letters? To a sweetheart?' The marchioness' green eyes grew alarmed. 'If he were to share your location, Hyacinth, we are in grave danger. I explicitly forbade you to contact anyone.' Her voice rose in fear. Philippa saw the slight tremor in Olivia's hand as she scooped peas and carrots onto her plate.

Hyacinth turned the focus of her ire to her mother. 'Why? So you can keep me isolated forever? I'm no better than a prisoner here.' She spat the words as if they were poison in her mouth.

'Enough.' Mrs Hughes' soft voice hardened as she slapped her hand on the table. 'I will not allow you to speak of your mother so. Callum, you should have told me. Olivia is right. Hyacinth's safety is threatened by anyone who knows she's here. This young man may have already told people of your whereabouts.'

Hyacinth's eyes widened, and her mouth fell open. 'I thought you were on my side.' Her trembling chin reminded Philippa of just how young the girl was despite her attempts to convince them otherwise.

Reaching out to cover Hyacinth's small hand with her own, Mrs Hughes squeezed. 'I am, dear. And so is your mother. You must understand, you are not safe.'

Hyacinth pulled her hand free, stood, and threw down her napkin. She fairly shook with rage. 'No one here thinks I'm capable of making my own choices, but I'm not some stupid child! I'm going to bed. I suddenly feel very ill.' She turned and walked from the dining room.

'That went well.' Olivia's smile was so brittle, a breath of air would probably shatter it.

Mrs Hughes turned to Olivia. 'You need to tell her what Percival did to you, Olivia. She's only ever heard his version of events. The bastard. She doesn't know the truth or how hard you have fought to return to her. Or what danger she is in right now. If she knew, she would feel differently. And she might act with more caution.'

Philippa's opinion of Mrs Hughes was growing by the minute.

'As for you.' Mrs Hughes shook her fork at Callum like a chiding finger. 'Next time you see letters from her going anywhere, you tell me right away.'

Callum's cheeks reddened. 'I didn't think it were any of my business.'

'Her safety is all of our concern,' Mrs Hughes huffed. 'She's barely more than a child. Stubborn and impetuous, just like her mother. But don't be hard-headed now, Olivia. Speak to your daughter.'

It was Olivia's turn to blush. 'Even if she would sit long enough to listen, I doubt she would believe me.'

'Give her the opportunity to try. She might surprise you.' Mrs Hughes glanced again at her son, though her expression softened. 'Judging someone too quickly steals from us the joy of discovery. Sometimes, realising you are wrong about a person can be the most liberating experience.'

The woman's words hit too close to home. Philippa wiped her mouth. 'I believe I shall follow Hyacinth's example and also seek my bed.'

Olivia nodded. 'Yes. We have much to do on the morrow if we hope to secure passage for Hyacinth to the Americas.'

Callum turned his head sharply, directing his words to Olivia. 'You are taking her to the Americas?'

'I am *sending* her to the Americas. Unfortunately, I will not be able to join her on her journey.' Though Philippa watched her closely, Olivia kept her gaze on Callum. 'I have other duties to fulfil here.'

A tight sensation wrapped around Philippa's chest as her ribs refused to expand.

What is wrong with me?

'She can't travel so far alone.' Callum's voice grew hoarse. 'Mam just said she is barely grown. Certainly not ready to go on such a journey by herself. Vulnerable to all manner of rogues who might take advantage. You can't be serious.'

Olivia looked at her plate and pushed peas around with her fork. 'I intended to go with her, but circumstances changed. I have no other choice. It is not safe for her to remain here, nor is it possible for me to accompany her.'

'Nothing is impossible,' Philippa spoke quietly, carefully placing her cutlery onto her plate. 'Perhaps a bargain can be struck with whoever is keeping you here.' While she didn't look at Olivia, she could feel the woman's gaze drilling into her.

'The person to whom I made my promise is known to be stubborn. Once a deal has been made, they never falter from their course.'

Philippa shrugged. 'Then you shall have to convince them to make an exception.'

Olivia shifted in her seat to face Philippa. 'And how, pray tell, do you recommend I do that?'

Philippa couldn't stop the rush of heat pulsing through her. 'Use your skills at negotiation. I'm sure you have something they want. Offer that in return for your freedom.'

'Something they want?' Olivia arched her brow, her tongue darting out to test the corner of her mouth.

Philippa met Olivia's gaze and leaned infinitesimally closer. 'Discover what they truly desire, and you will have a powerful bargaining tool.'

'What if they only desire revenge?'

Slowly shaking her head, Philippa slid her foot silently across the floor until it bumped into Olivia's. She was making a choice. One her body committed to before her mind could catch up, but it was too late to withdraw.

And I don't want to. If I am going to let a guilty woman walk free, and sell my soul to the Devil to indulge my own needs, then I will at least enjoy my damnation. One night. Surely Liza can forgive me for one indiscretion after all these years. And then Olivia will be gone forever. It is a worthy bargain.

A pang of something sharp and painful cut through her desire. But if Philippa was not going to deliver her usual brand of justice to the marchioness, then she needed Olivia to leave England. Banishment, while not as fitting a punishment as originally planned, would still be acceptable to the Queen as justice for Olivia's crimes.

'You are a convincing woman, Lady Smithwick. I'm sure you can sway them to want more than mere revenge.'

'Look at the time.' Mrs Hughes broke into their discussion, reminding Philippa she wasn't alone at the table with Olivia. 'We must be off to bed, Callum. There are cows to milk in the morning.'

Philippa ripped her attention from Olivia to refocus on the two others at the table. Callum's eyes were wide as he bounced from Philippa to Olivia, then back again. 'R-right you are, Mam.' He stood abruptly, clearing plates from the table that were still full. 'I'll just pop into the kitchen and do the washing up.'

Mrs Hughes rose a little more slowly, her hand pushing into her lower back as she arched. 'I'll help you, love. You two must be exhausted. Go on to bed. I'm sure a path forward will be much clearer in the morning. It's always a wonder to me what a good night of sleep will do for a body.' She glanced at Olivia, then Philippa. 'I hope you're comfortable tonight.'

Philippa lowered her chin in a nod she'd perfected during her visits with the Queen, the only person to whom she showed deference. Until now. 'I'm sure we will be more than content. You have been most kind.' Standing, she looked at Callum. 'Thank you for a delicious meal. Your mother is blessed to have such a talented man in her house.'

Once more, Callum's face burned crimson. 'It weren't nothing.'

Philippa smiled. 'No, it was not. It was quite something. Shall we retire?' She stepped back, giving Olivia space to rise. The fair beauty's cheeks were also suspiciously pink.

'Thank you, Mrs Hughes. For everything.' Olivia held her nursemaid's gaze for a beat, then turned to Callum. 'And to you, Callum. Goodnight.' Brushing past Philippa, the duchess felt the feather-soft whisper of Olivia's fingers as they trailed over her hand.

Let the negotiations begin.

* * *

Olivia's heart raced as she pushed the door open to her room with Philippa close behind. The day had been a chaotic frenzy of emotion, and she felt the evening had only just begun. As soon as Philippa closed the door behind them, granting privacy, Olivia turned to face the woman who should be her nemesis. The woman who was becoming so much more.

'Are you serious? Would you actually consider freeing me?' If Philippa was toying with her, Olivia was quite certain she would explode and take the duchess with her.

Philippa tapped a finger to her sinfully stained lips. 'I'm always serious.'

'What are your terms?'

Raising a single eyebrow in an expression that heated Olivia's desire and anger in equal measure, Philippa smiled. 'A name. Who is the Crow?'

Blinking, Olivia crossed her arms over her chest. Exhaling, she struggled with a strange sense of deflation. 'I thought, after our conversation in the dining room...'

'That I would demand rights to your body in return for your freedom?'

Well, when she puts it that way, it does sound quite sordid.

Olivia pretended an intense interest in a mark on the wall just over Philippa's right shoulder. 'Erm, it just appeared that perhaps you might... well... be interested in a trade. Of sorts.'

Philippa stepped closer, her hand tracing a loose curl that tickled Olivia's cheek. 'I'm very interested in *you*, Olivia. I won't deny my attraction, nor will I pretend to ignore yours.' She leaned closer as her fingers dove into Olivia's hair, holding her head steady. When Olivia expected Philippa to press her mouth against hers, she surprised her, changing directions until her breath whispered over the delicate skin just below Olivia's ear. 'Make no mistake. I want you. Desperately. And I am never desperate.'

Olivia tried to breathe normally as her body ignited with sparks and fire. But she didn't miss the hint of frustration in Philippa's statement. No doubt, the duchess hated being so needy. Olivia certainly did. 'I'm sure that infuriates you.'

Philippa sucked Olivia's lobe into her mouth, her teeth scraping deliciously over the sensitive flesh as Olivia's nipples tightened. Warm, wet need bloomed low in her belly, dripping along her channel, her intimate muscles clenching in aching glory.

Dear God. I might climax right here. From nothing more than this.

'It does.' Philippa's words echoed in the shell of Olivia's ear. The duchess moved her head lower, kissing a trail across Olivia's clavicles, sucking on the delicate skin where her pulse beat madly. 'But I won't bargain with your body. If you give me the Crow's name, I will let you leave with Hyacinth, never again returning to these shores.' Philippa gripped Olivia's waist, squeezed, then traced up her ribs until she palmed her breast. Olivia moaned.

Thankfully, Olivia had left some of her clothes at the cottage before her trip to London. She had lent Philippa a dress and changed out of her travel-worn clothes into a simple gown for dinner. It was a far cry from the glamorous ensembles she wore when attending balls in London, but the eggshell colour complemented Olivia's fair skin, and the neckline scooped low enough to reveal the tops of her breasts. Philippa's clever fingers peeled back the silk. Olivia's corset was also cut low, her rose-pink nipple peeking out, puckered and sensitive to the cool night air. Philippa bent forward, licking the ruched tip like it was a lemon drop. Another rush of liquid need flooded through Olivia.

Fingers sinking into Philippa's hair, she pulled her closer, needing more pressure. More friction. Philippa understood her wordless plea. She sucked Olivia's nipple, swirling her tongue around the sensitive nub, nibbling and nipping until Olivia worried she might melt into a puddle at the duchess' feet. It would be so easy to let go. Fall deeper into the haze of desire. Drown in sensation until she was nothing but tingling sparks of splendour. Her thoughts wanted to scatter to the wind, but she pulled them together with intense focus.

'Are you trying to seduce his name from me?' Her words came out as a gasp.

Philippa pulled back far enough to capture Olivia's gaze. Her eyes were deep blue. The colour of a sapphire, or the sky as day darkened to night, or a pool so unfathomable, Olivia could sink forever and never find the bottom.

'Yes. I am trying to seduce you. And I want his name. Both are true. Neither depends on the other. You can give me his name and nothing more, knowing you have won your freedom. You can deny me his name but give me your body as I will give you mine, but I won't be able to let you leave with your daughter. Or you can tell me the Crow's identity, we can indulge in this madness together, and you can walk away tomorrow and never look back. For someone who has had few choices in life, I give you a bounty of options. What do you choose, Olivia?'

The things she says.

Olivia's heart cracked a little. Because Philippa was giving her more than most, but still, it wasn't enough.

If I take my night with her, give her the Crow's identity, and leave with Hyacinth on the next departing ship, what more could I really want?

The answer drifted, just out of reach.

As Olivia leaned closer, the Crow's true identity on the tip of her tongue, another name whispered at the edges of her mind.

Liza. When the night is over, Philippa will hate me for seducing her into betraying her true love.

After what Philippa shared with Olivia in the little cottage on the cliffs, it was clear she hadn't stopped loving Liza. And Philippa wasn't the kind of woman who could love one woman and sleep with another without hating herself in the process. Olivia might be able to weather Philippa's disdain, but she knew the duchess couldn't continue her life despising herself on such a deep level. It would destroy her. And Olivia didn't want to destroy Philippa. She wanted the very opposite, in fact.

'What about Liza?'

Philippa froze, and Olivia's heart plummeted.

But she would rather deny herself the burning pleasure of Philippa's crimson lips, her clever fingers, her stunning body, than watch Philippa implode.

Stepping back, Philippa broke all physical contact with Olivia. Grief darkened her eyes further, anger flamed bright, and desire still blew her pupils wide. How she held so much within her without letting any of it spill forth was a mystery to Olivia.

'What about Liza?' She spoke each word like a slap.

'You love her. How can you spend tonight with me and still hold true to your promise to her?'

'Must you be so cruel?' Philippa's voice was a dark rasp.

Olivia swallowed. Horrifically, tears threatened as she struggled to set her dress back to rights. 'I am not trying to be cruel. I'm trying to protect us. Both of us. I want you so much my bones ache. But I won't take what you are offering until I know I'm not also crushing a piece of your soul by having it. Can you tell me honestly that you won't loathe me tomorrow for what we do here tonight? That you won't also hate yourself?'

Philippa valued honesty, honour, and loyalty. She would never forgive herself if she believed this night with Olivia was a betrayal of her dedication to Liza. And she would never forgive Olivia. She didn't expect to win the duchess' undying love, or even her tacit approval, but she would like to part as something more than mortal enemies.

'I already inspire your ire just by existing. How much more will your hatred grow if you fear you've betrayed your love to spend a night with me? I can accept that you dislike me, but I won't be the reason you despise yourself.'

Because she didn't want anything, even the memory of Philippa's lost love, to poison what could be a beautiful experience between them.

Philippa rubbed her thumb and index finger together in an endless circle. 'Don't presume to understand me, Marchioness.'

'Don't pretend I'm not right in this, Duchess.'

And we're back to titles. What did I expect?

Nothing more than this. But her heart squeezed painfully in her chest because she had hoped for more.

Turning, Philippa walked to the door. Before she could turn the handle, Olivia lunged forward, grabbing her arm and spinning her back. 'Where are you going?'

Wrenching her arm free, Philippa's nostrils flared and her eyes hardened. 'Out. You are so desperate for freedom. Well. You have it. Keep your name. I shall find the Crow on my own. I work best that way. Seek your bed, Marchioness. You and your daughter have travel arrangements to make on the morrow. And I have a devil to hunt.'

This time, when Philippa opened the door, Olivia let her go. Yet again, she had no other choice.

* * *

A wild wind kicked up as Philippa followed the trail they took earlier in the day. It pulled her hair free, tossing it around her shoulders in disarray, tugging at her skirts and tangling them between her legs. Artemis' moon battled with the clouds, providing Philippa with enough light to navigate the uneven terrain. She revelled in the violent weather. It called to a feral part of her soul, clawing to be free.

'How dare she?' Philippa raged, her words swept away in the howl of the wind. A howl that echoed the grief in her soul. 'Accusing me of disloyalty.'

But she didn't. She accused me of hating myself. And she's right. Damn her.

'The unmitigated gall! For her to think she knows me. Knows my love for Liza,' she fumed.

But she does. And she knows I blame myself for Liza's death as much as I blame Liza. Because I couldn't save her. Not from her father. Not from the asylum. And not from herself.

'One night with Olivia would mean nothing!' The venom spilt from her, caustic and scathing.

It would mean everything. More than I can hold in my heart. And I would hate myself for betraying Liza, but I would also hate myself for not giving Olivia what she deserves.

'I want to be alone. I deserve it. It's easier!' she cried out into the darkness, daring the gods to refute her. A raw sob burst free. She crested the hill and didn't stop until her toes touched the edge of the world. Below her, a stormy sea tossed froth and foam against the cliff wall. Rain fell, joining the tears coursing down her cheeks.

'Why? Why did you leave me, Liza? Why didn't you wait for me to find you? I would have found you. I would have saved you.' Head tipped to the boiling sky, Philippa screamed her questions into the abyss.

'It isn't your job to save me, Phil. I need to save myself. And whether I do or don't, my fate is no longer tied to yours. Nor is your fate tied to mine. I will always carry a piece of you with me. Wherever I go. I love you. And I release you from our promises.'

Liza's soft voice echoed in Philippa's mind as the words she wrote in the last letter Philippa received so many years ago came back to her. Anger gave way to grief. Collapsing on the ground, Philippa let the pain course through her. 'I can't let you go, Liza. I promised. My devotion to you is forever. I couldn't keep my promise to protect you. But I must keep my oath to be devoted to you, no matter if we are together or apart.'

Then you shall never be free. Nor will I. Release me, Phil, as I released you. Love me, and let me go. Live the life you deserve.

Liza's voice filled her mind, and she felt her soul strain. The mystics believed celestial disturbances could portend a thinning between the veil of life and death. Philippa had no faith in such nonsense, and yet, roses and rosemary danced on the wind. Liza's scent.

Philippa had never fully given herself to grief. Because to do so would be admitting it was really over. But it swept through her, as powerful and overwhelming as the sea. As cleansing and cold as the rain. As wild and reckless as the wind. She rocked on her knees, her wails blending with the storm's cry.

'I miss you, Liza. How can I move forward in this life without you?'

You already have. The girl I loved is no more. In her place is a fearsome woman. You move forward because you are strong, and relentless, and you must.

Liza always knew how to sway Philippa to her way of thinking. Some things even death couldn't change. But not this time.

Moments or millennia passed as sorrow seeped from Philippa, sinking into the ground, salting the earth with her pain. Dress sodden, fingers and toes numb, heart empty and echoing, she shook her head, refusing to acquiesce. 'I can't. I won't.'

A crack of lightning split the air.

'I control my choices. And I won't let you go, Liza.'

Then you will never be free.

'I don't want to be free if that means you are truly gone.'

Yes, she was screaming into a storm. Yes, she was arguing with a woman who died twenty years ago. And yes, the dead woman was right. But Philippa would be damned if she admitted it.

Standing, Philippa staggered back down the hill. She was chilled to her bones, and her dress was ruined from the muddy field, but something had changed. Admitting her refusal to move forward – if only to the storm that raged on the edge of the Cornwall sea, and to the imagined ghost of her lover – shifted her anger from Liza to herself. Where it belonged. Because she was the only person responsible for her misery. And the only one capable of changing it.

Desperate for warm, dry clothes and a soft bed, Philippa almost missed the flickering yellow of a lantern bobbing along the road leading to the stone house.

A thrill of adrenaline rushed through her veins, blessedly distracting her from personal revelations.

Was Olivia looking for her? Or was this an intruder? Another one of the Devil's Sons intent on finishing what the highwaymen were unable to accomplish?

Using speed and stealth developed from countless hours of training, Philippa dropped low, gliding over the fields with the grace of a predator. Her rate of speed would bring her to the house almost simultaneously with the intruder. The stranger was approaching the front of the house from the road, and she would reach the back from the field. She could sneak around the edge and determine if this nocturnal guest was friend or foe. But just as she approached the cobblestone courtyard between the small stable and house, the lantern shifted abruptly, slowly illuminating a wide arc around the left side of the cottage.

He is coming to the back. To the bedrooms.

Philippa adjusted her course. Pressing herself against the stable wall, she kept to the shadows. If the fickle moon came out from the clouds at the right time, it might just allow her enough light to identify the mysterious intruder. Of course, it might also allow him to see her, if he was looking in the right direction.

But great risk brings with it great reward.

And sometimes even greater defeat. The thrill of the hunt drowned out any hint of fear.

A nicker and huff from the stable, followed by a stomp of hooves, made it clear at least one creature marked her presence.

The lantern halted abruptly. The cloaked figure stood near the door leading to the kitchen, frozen like a rabbit in the fox's sights. Philippa ducked into a darkened alcove used to store hay. Inching closer to the corner of the stable, she crouched low – hopefully lower than his sight lines – and peeked out, thankful for her dark hair and dress.

Olivia's curls would be blazing even in the blackest of shadows.

A stupid thought to have, Philippa pushed it aside and focused on the lantern. Wind rushed through the courtyard, granting Philippa two favours.

The moon finally broke free of the clouds.

The man's hood blew free, exposing his features to the silver moonlight.

Damn. Not a man at all. It's Hyacinth. What the Devil is she up to?

As if she could hear Philippa's thoughts, Hyacinth looked from right to left before pulling her hood back over her hair. Dousing the lantern, she snuck to the kitchen door and slowly twisted the handle. With a final glance that had Philippa ducking back behind the alcove, the stubborn girl slipped into the house.

Perhaps Callum was right. Mayhap Hyacinth was exchanging more than just letters with a sweetheart. Was she sneaking out in the middle of the night to see a man?

Philippa tapped a finger against her lips. Olivia's daughter was as stubborn and headstrong as her mother. Confronting her about this would only have the girl dig her heels in deeper. Putting Hyacinth on a ship sailing to America and getting her away from whatever young man she had snuck out to see might protect her from more than just the Devil's Sons. It might protect her from her own silly choices.

Philippa couldn't believe she had granted Olivia her freedom without first extracting the name of the Crow. But in the moment, the words escaped before she could think better of it. Sending Hyacinth into the wilds of America alone seemed just as horrific a crime as letting Olivia escape justice.

But what kind of justice has she experienced? Ten years in an asylum. Separated from her daughter. Her reputation destroyed by a husband intent on controlling her completely. Is that not penance enough for her actions?

An errant image of Olivia and Hyacinth on the deck of a ship, pulling away from the harbour, Olivia's untameable curls blowing free in the wind, brought another sharp pain to Philippa's chest.

Why do I care if she leaves? I want her to go and take this incessant need with her.

If Olivia left, Philippa wouldn't have to examine her heart. She wouldn't have to face the uncertainty that her life might take an unexpected turn. She wouldn't have to contend with her desire for another woman when for so long she believed her chance for love died with Liza.

This is not love. I do not love Olivia. I hardly know her.

But the words rang hollow in her heart. Because with every moment they spent together, Philippa was discovering more about Olivia. And each revelation contradicted her preconceived opinions. What if she had been wrong about Olivia all along?

The infallible duchess finally makes a mistake? Impossible.

Her own thoughts mocked her, and Philippa shook her head, though no one could appreciate her disdain as she stood up alone in the darkness. How arrogant she had become. No better than the men she railed against. Wouldn't Edward revel in triumph to see his childhood friend finally on the wrong side of the truth?

'This is ridiculous,' Philippa muttered to herself. 'Right or wrong, I'm going to catch my death standing out here contemplating my own failings like a complete idiot.' Following Hyacinth's example, she let herself in through the kitchen and dripped down the hall and up the stairs to her room.

The door creaked as she carefully pushed it open and stepped inside. Olivia had left a candle burning for her. Something soft and sweet unfurled in her chest even as she tried to push it down. But the feeling refused to obey, blooming bigger and squeezing her already battered heart. It was a thoughtful gesture in the midst of a bitter fight.

She began the arduous task of unbuttoning her borrowed gown, a job made infinitely more difficult with numb fingers. Wishing desperately for Delacroix to help, or even Stokes to come and take the mud-soaked dress away, Philippa tried her best to hang the thing over a chair in hopes it might dry within the next year or two. Stripping off her wet and icy shift, she stood naked in the centre of the room. Her skin tightened from the cold, her nipples contracting as a shudder ran through her. If she were not sharing a bed with Olivia, she would have dove under the covers naked and waited for the heavy blankets to warm her frigid body. Instead, she grabbed the cotton nightgown Olivia had left out for her, donned it with shaky hands, and carefully pulled back the blanket to slip into bed.

Olivia was turned away from her, but as Philippa's body sank into the feather mattress, she felt the woman behind her shift and turn. A warm arm snaked over Philippa's waist and pulled her close, cocooning Philippa's body within Olivia's sweet, soft embrace. Philippa stiffened, holding her breath, wondering if Olivia was awake. But the woman mumbled something unintelligible, her breath puffing evenly against the small hairs tickling Philippa's neck.

Breathing a sigh of relief, Philippa knew she needed to extricate herself from Olivia's hold. And she would. Soon. The blonde beauty would be mortified if she woke with Philippa in her arms. But Philippa was so cold, and so tired, and so sore in places that couldn't be seen or touched. Olivia's heat seeped through her numb skin, thawing nerve endings, melting the ice that had so long encased her heart. One particle at a time, she dissolved into Olivia's unknowing embrace and drifted to sleep.

11

Philippa woke to the scent of fried kippers and the cheerful sound of voices chattering. It took a moment for her thoughts to assemble.

Dear Lord. I slept the night in Olivia's arms.

She turned, but the bed was empty. Olivia must have risen while Philippa still slumbered. The idea of the marchioness watching Philippa sleep, knowing she had cradled her body throughout the night, awoke a vulnerability within Philippa she rarely felt.

What if I was drooling?

Embarrassment swept in as she wiped her hand over her lips, grateful to find no evidence of dried saliva.

Of course I wasn't drooling. The Duchess of Dorsett does not slaver in her sleep like some wild beast.

Although she wasn't certain that was true. Pulling the covers aside, she made haste in dressing for the day. Her gown from the night before had mysteriously disappeared from the chair. When she made her way to the parlour, a cozy scene greeted her.

Olivia sat at one end of the table. Her hair was loose around her shoulders, shining bright in the gloomy morning like a beacon. Pink cheeks darkened to rose as her gaze refused to settle on Philippa.

'Well, good morning to ye.' Callum stood from the table, his brown curls falling into his eyes as he brushed them away. He pulled a chair free next to

Olivia. A plate sat waiting for Philippa to fill it with any number of delicious items piled in the centre of the table. Her meals were never quite so informal at Belgrave Square, but she was growing to like the casual ease of it.

As she settled in her chair, Mrs Hughes eyed her with a twinkle of mischief. 'You must have been right worn out. I hope you slept well.' She winked at Philippa, and the duchess was shocked to feel heat rushing to her cheeks.

Am I blushing? The Duchess of Dorsett does not blush.

It would seem she was breaking her rules of decorum willy-nilly. Resisting the urge to press cool hands over her warm cheeks, she distracted herself by scooping a spoonful of clotted eggs onto her plate, followed by crispy kippers, and a slice of toast. Yellow butter sat in a dish next to a pot of blackcurrant jam. She spread both liberally onto her toast.

'Where is Hyacinth this morning?' Philippa tried to keep her voice light as she made the not-so-innocent inquiry. No doubt the young woman was catching up on lost sleep.

'She hasn't risen yet.' Olivia studied her over a cup of steaming tea. 'You are looking well. A night of rest did much to restore colour to your cheeks.'

The minx's lips twitched. She was teasing Philippa. No one teased the Duchess of Dorsett.

Except Olivia, apparently.

'I have a strong constitution.' Philippa arched a brow and licked jam from her thumb, noticing how Olivia's eyes shifted to her tongue, her pupils expanding.

'Hyacinth's usually up with the starlings. I'll just pop into her room and check on her.' Mrs Hughes pushed her chair back to rise, but Olivia scrambled to her feet.

'Don't. I'll do it. I can't remember the last time I woke her.'

Mrs Hughes' cheeks creased, and her eyes softened. 'Right you are, Ollie.'

'Ollie?' Philippa raised both brows, looking from Mrs Hughes to Olivia.

Olivia was the one hiding her blush now by turning quickly to rush down the hall.

Mrs Hughes speared a kipper with her fork. 'A pet name I used when she was just a girl. Always getting into scrapes, that one. Fearless. She kept me on my toes, that is certain.'

Philippa desperately wished for a splash of whiskey in her tea. 'A trait her daughter seems to have inherited.' She turned to ask Callum about the letters he'd intercepted, but a scream had her pushing free from the table and racing down the hall and up the stairs instead.

'She's gone! Hyacinth is gone! Someone must have broken in and taken her. Oh my God. What can we do? We must find her. Now. Immediately.' Olivia was tearing apart her daughter's very empty room. Her face had paled considerably since she left the table, and her green eyes were wide and wild.

Philippa intercepted Olivia as she lunged for the chest of drawers snugged under a window. She wasn't sure if the frantic woman hoped her daughter was hiding in one of the drawers, or if she was going to scale the dresser and try to squeeze out of the window and jump to the ground in pursuit of the girl. Holding Olivia's shoulders in a firm grip, she used her best duchess voice. 'What we must do is remain calm, Olivia. And you must breathe. Slowly.'

Olivia shook her head, tears spilling from her eyes. 'I can't. She's gone. They took her.' Her words were strangled by obvious panic.

Philippa ran one hand up her shoulder and gripped Olivia's neck, squeezing gently. Commanding her hadn't worked. Perhaps she should try a different tactic. 'I need you to breathe, darling. In through your nose, hold it, then out through your mouth. One deep breath.' She had softened her voice to a soothing hum. Olivia blinked rapidly, but she dipped her chin in assent. Philippa saw the woman's chest expand, freeze for a moment, and then slowly contract. 'Good. That's excellent. Now again.'

Olivia repeated the deep breath.

'Good. Once more.' As Olivia complied, Philippa applied gentle pressure on the back of her neck, rubbing the tight tendons. 'Well done. Just focus on your breath.'

Sniffing, Olivia reached up and used the back of her hand to swipe at her wet cheeks. Her bottom lip quivered. Philippa glimpsed what she must have looked like as a young girl, but it was Olivia the woman who straightened her spine, pulled back her shoulders and pressed those lips together in a determined line. 'What should we do, Philippa?'

My God, she is brave. And fierce. And fantastic. And she's asking for my help. I will not fail her.

'Let's search her room. Carefully. Mayhap we can find a clue as to her whereabouts.' Turning her head, she spoke to Mrs Hughes who stood in the narrow hall with Callum behind her. 'Will you help? Callum, can you check the stables and see if any of the horses are missing? Look for clues about which direction they might have gone: carriage wheel tracks, anything that could give us an indication of what time they left and where they might have been heading.'

Callum looked ill. His cheeks had gone terribly pale, and his Adam's apple bobbed sporadically as he swallowed. 'Yes, of course.' Spinning, he rushed to follow her orders.

She returned her focus to Olivia. 'We're going to find her. I promise you that. And when we do, we'll get her safely away from here.'

It was a promise Philippa intended to keep.

* * *

Olivia couldn't believe the number of things she didn't know about her daughter. She had an affinity for Gothic horrors. She collected seashells, most particularly any blue ones she could find. Her drawers were messy, but her desk was tidy. She had a folder of poetry hidden beneath her mattress. Rather good poetry, though Olivia would never claim to be an expert in such a subject. And Hyacinth was a prolific writer and receiver of letters. Countless letters were secreted away in a leather satchel tucked under a loose board next to her bed.

'Money under your floorboards. Letters under hers. You two are far more similar than either of you thinks.' The small curl in Philippa's lip invited Olivia to join her in a moment of levity.

'You might be right.'

'I usually am.'

Ah. There was the proud duchess Olivia had seen striding across every great ballroom in the beau monde. Stealing her breath. Invading her thoughts. Wreaking havoc on any attempt to remain unaffected. But instead of infuriating her, she found comfort in Philippa's confidence. Surely with such a powerful ally, she would find Hyacinth.

But aren't we supposed to be enemies?

It didn't feel that way. Not any more.

'Here.' She gave half of the letters to Philippa, sat on her daughter's bed, and began sifting through her pile.

Mrs Hughes emerged from the closet, her hair dishevelled, her face suspiciously blotchy. It was clear the woman had been crying. 'You two look through those letters. I'll put the kettle on. Tea never hurts in these situations.'

'Tea with whiskey often helps in these situations,' Philippa murmured.

'I'll see what I can rustle up.' Mrs Hughes' gaze lingered on Olivia for a moment. 'Hyacinth is so like you, Olivia. Stubborn and headstrong. Courageous and brave. Resilient and resourceful. Whatever has happened, she will be smart. She will endure. She will survive to come home, just like her mother. I know it.'

Olivia's heart wrenched painfully. 'Thank you, Mrs Hughes.' She spoke the words with a harsh rasp.

Mrs Hughes cleared her throat. 'Right. Tea.' She walked down the hall, her feet clipping sharply on the wood.

For several minutes, Olivia and Philippa sat next to each other on Hyacinth's bed and flipped through their separate piles.

Most of the letters Olivia had were from an old chum of Hyacinth's. A young girl named Polly, who seemed frightfully obsessed with lace and crinoline.

'I had no idea Hyacinth was so close to your brother.'

The blood in Olivia's veins froze. 'P-pardon?'

Philippa looked up from her pile, her cobalt eyes creasing with concern at whatever she saw on Olivia's face. 'Lord Hardgrave. He must have written her over twenty letters. The first one dates back to when she would have only been seven or eight. He was obviously concerned for her when the two of you disappeared in August, but I didn't realise they were so close.'

'Give me those.' Olivia snatched the letters from Philippa's hands, recognising the heavy swipe of her brother's penmanship. Quickly scanning through each letter, first glance would make it seem the relationship had started harmlessly enough. A doting uncle and his devoted niece. But something black and bitter rose in Olivia. 'He wouldn't dare,' she hissed. But as she found the more recent letters, the last one dated only a week ago, it became glaringly obvious that he would.

'Olivia, your hands are shaking.'

Lifting her eyes from the parchment, Olivia knew she must seem unhinged, but she didn't care. 'He has my daughter.'

'Your brother?'

'The Crow.'

* * *

As soon as she spoke the words, fear rushed in. Cedric Hardgrave, Lord High Chancellor to the Queen, Duke of Blackmore, and leader of the Devil's Sons had her daughter. It played like a litany in her head.

The Crow has Hyacinth. I failed. The Crow has Hyacinth. I failed.

And each time it repeated, madness crept closer.

Philippa stood and pulled her fan from a deep pocket. 'Lord High Chancellor Hardgrave is the leader of the Devil's Sons?' She thwacked it against her leg. 'He is the Crow? The name you refused to give me? Impossible.' She thwacked it again. 'He is the advisor to the Queen.' *Thwack!* 'Second only to her in power over all the bloody British empire.' *Thwack!* 'If this is true, I would have known.' *Thwack, thwack, thwack.*

'This isn't helping, Philippa.'

Philippa pressed her perfect lips together and stared at Olivia. 'If you truly believe this, why didn't you tell me from the start?'

'Because I didn't trust you!' Needing movement, Olivia pushed up from the bed and paced in a tight line to the window and back. 'You were threatening to throw me in Newgate. You thought I was a deceitful, evil creature. I had no hope you would believe me. And what would have happened to Hyacinth if I wasn't there to protect her? Cedric would have had unfettered access to her.'

'Cedric?'

'My brother. The Lord High Chancellor.'

'His name is Cedric?'

'That isn't the point. I needed to make sure Hyacinth was safe from him. Don't you see? That is why I did those awful things. Why I was willing to risk those poor orphans. Even if it meant condemning my soul to hell for all eternity. Because I had to do everything in my power to save her from him. He's a monster.'

Philippa blocked her path to the window, holding Olivia's gaze. 'I am used to vanquishing monsters. And we will do everything we can to free her. But I can't believe Lord Hardgrave is truly as evil as you say.'

'He is my brother, Philippa. I've known him my whole life. And my whole life, I've watched him grow darker, more twisted.' Olivia shut her eyes, wanting to push away the long-buried memories clawing up from the graveyard of her mind. But she needed to convince Philippa of the truth, and facts were the only way to sway the duchess. 'When I was only three or four, we were in the gardens. I loved seeing the butterflies dancing on the flowers. Cedric caught one, brought it to me, and made me watch as he ripped the wings from its body.'

Philippa stepped closer, but Olivia held out her hand. If the duchess offered comfort, she wouldn't be able to continue. And she needed her to understand the depths of depravity to which her brother sank. 'Have you ever heard a cat scream?'

Philippa shook her head, her skin paling.

'I have. Mother gave me a kitten. On my tenth birthday. A sweet ginger ball of fluff. A week after I got him, Cedric lit his tail on fire because I refused to give him my lemon drop sweets. He laughed as the terrified creature raced through the house. He promised he would drown my cat the next time I defied him. I found the kitten later that night hiding beneath my bed, bound his tail, and made Mother give him to one of the servants.'

'Olivia—'

But she wasn't done. 'When I was thirteen, he lied about one of our maids. The same one who Mother gave the kitten to, and sometimes, I wonder if that's why he chose her. Cedric could hold a grudge for decades. Nursing it like a coal, feeding it bits of kindling to stay alive until he was ready to fan the flames into an inferno. He said she was stealing from his room. He demanded she be beaten for her crimes and would have done it himself if Father had allowed him to. Instead, he watched as she was whipped, his face like a child on the morn of Yuletide. Not just excited, but joyful. It doesn't stop there, Philippa. I could tell you ten more stories just like that. Twenty. Thirty. How many do you need to hear before you believe me? He is not well. And he is dangerous.' Olivia had been accused of madness, but it was her brother who was insane. He hid it behind a calm veneer, beautifully tailored suits, the right words spoken in a genteel tone. But underneath his polished exterior beat the heart of a monster who derived pleasure from inflicting pain on others and watching them suffer. 'You must believe me.'

Philippa rubbed her index finger against her thumb in an endless circle. Tipping her chin in an abrupt nod, she appeared to make a decision. 'I do believe you.'

The measure of relief washing through Olivia nearly felled her. She stumbled a step back, sitting hard on the bed. Tears welled in her eyes, but she refused to let them fall. For if she allowed one to escape, she would drown in a sea of emotions she had held at bay for so long. 'Thank you.' Finally, she didn't feel alone.

Philippa sat next to her, took her hand and held it in her own, her slender fingers intertwining with Olivia's. She squeezed gently. 'Take heart. We will come up with a plan. Together.'

Olivia allowed herself to rest her head on Philippa's shoulder, hoping to absorb some of her strength. 'Thank you.'

The sun shifted higher in the sky, gulls called, the waves crashed against the cliff, but they stayed still and silent. Philippa ran her thumb up and down Olivia's finger as she breathed in salt air, jasmine, and frankincense.

Philippa moved first. Giving Olivia's hand a final squeeze, she rose from the bed. 'We must return to London. Hardgrave holds far more power than I ever guessed, and your stories shed light on a disturbing picture. If he is mad, he will be unpredictable. Most men are motivated by self-preservation, but with your brother, I'm not so sure.'

Roused from her window of peace, Olivia also stood. 'No. He wants to win. He believes he deserves to win, and he also thinks he's far too clever to ever get caught. Because he is. How are we going to do this, Philippa? What if the Queen is aware of his actions? The Prime Minister?'

Philippa shook her head. 'The Queen would never condone such actions.'

'Are you certain?'

Philippa's silence spoke volumes. For whom was ever completely safe from corruption? Those with great power could so easily be seduced by the promise of more. Or the need to protect what they had already amassed. 'No. I'm not. I am certain of Hannah, Millicent, Penny, and Ivy. I'm reasonably confident about their men. As confident as any woman can be about a man.'

Olivia shared a look with Philippa. In the midst of her panic and fear, it was glorious to have common ground with the duchess. Philippa was strong, powerful, clever, and dangerous. Olivia respected her as an enemy, but having her as an ally brought more comfort than she would ever have guessed. And something else. A warmth sparking in her belly and rolling through her body like a wave. The glimmer of hope that terrible wrongs might be righted.

Philippa spoke with calm determination. 'We should leave immediately. Hardgrave will have taken her to his home in Mayfair. He knows you will come for her, and he wants you back on his ground. Where he can control you.'

Olivia nodded. It would be just like her brother to force her back to his home. A cruel reminder she had no choice. No power. No freedom.

Philippa's eyes flashed. 'But he is forgetting, London is the battlefield of the Queen's Deadly Damsels. And we will meet him blow for blow.'

'He'll use Hyacinth as leverage. He won't hesitate to hurt her, Philippa. She is just another kitten to torture, maid to punish, insect to crush. It makes no difference to him that she's his niece.' Fear re-emerged, dousing Olivia's newfound courage.

'We won't let him. We must make haste. I shall send a message ahead of us to the Damsels.' Taking Olivia's shoulders in her hands, she shook her gently, forcing her to meet Philippa's gaze. 'We will fight, and we will win, Olivia. I promise.'

Olivia bit her lip, noting the flare in Philippa's eyes. 'What if you can't keep your promise? What if it's impossible?'

Philippa blinked. 'You asked me to trust you; now I'm asking the same. Trust me. Something is only impossible because it hasn't been accomplished yet. We can do this. The Deadly Damsels, their men, you and me. Together. We will save Hyacinth and take down the Crow. I swear it on my life.'

Her confidence was so potent, her passion so evident, Olivia couldn't help but get caught in the current of Philippa's sheer will. If anyone could save her daughter and defeat her brother, it was the duchess. 'All right. Together then.'

Philippa leaned forward and pressed her lips against Olivia's.

Needing to feel something other than fear, Olivia opened her mouth, welcoming Philippa's questing tongue. Philippa nibbled on Olivia's lower lip, her teeth scraping with the hint of something sharp and decadent. But worry for Hyacinth pulled Olivia from the moment. She leaned back, pressing her forehead against Philippa's, sharing her breath. 'Our timing is rather dreadful.'

Philippa grew serious. '*You* are rather dreadful for my concentration. And also, rather right. There is much to be done. But, dear God, Olivia. You make me wish things were different. You tempt me beyond all reason.'

Olivia couldn't decipher exactly what Philippa wished was different. Had she resolved any of her feelings? Likely not, but hope bloomed regardless. Heat flared, rushing from the apex of Olivia's thighs – a pinpoint of aching need – up her chest, over her neck, and into her doubtlessly crimson cheeks. 'The things you say.'

'The things you make me ache to do.' Philippa brushed her thumb over Olivia's lower lip. 'But as you said, this is hardly the time.'

Olivia covered Philippa's hand with her own, stopping her from pulling back. 'But if it ever is the right time, I will be more than ready.'

Philippa's pupils blew wide, and Olivia took a measure of satisfaction from knowing she wasn't the only one needy and raw. If only things were so simple. But trouble had found Olivia once more.

Dropping her hand, she stepped back, needing distance if she were going to focus on what mattered most. Getting her daughter back and defeating the Crow. 'How are we going to get back to London in time?'

Philippa took a moment, and Olivia could almost see her collecting each thought in her mind and organising them into order. When she curled her lips in a wicked smile, Olivia remembered all the reasons she was once so intimidated by the duchess.

I'm still intimidated.

But that wasn't quite true. Impressed? Certainly. Intrigued? Most definitely. In love?

Not possible. But infatuation sometimes feels like love.

Philippa's eyes flashed dangerously. 'Oh, darling. We are going to return to London with the speed and style a duchess demands. There's nothing wealth and power can't influence. Including travel arrangements.'

Philippa was as good as her word. Within the space of three hours, she organised a hired carriage and driver to arrive at the seaside cottage, had their few belongings packed and ready, and wrote messages to the Deadly Damsels. The carriage would take them to the Great Western Railway station in Exeter and from there to Paddington Station.

'Callum, can you take these notes to a messenger and see he gets them into the hands of these ladies as quickly as possible?'

Callum shook his head. 'There's no one in town who can get to London faster than me. I'll ride ahead, get your notes where they need to be, then be ready to help you when you arrive.'

Mrs Hughes stepped forward. 'Callum.' Her voice held fear and pride in equal measure.

Callum turned and faced his mother. 'I'll be all right, Mam. I've got to do this. I can't stay here knowing someone has Miss Hyacinth. That she might be hurt. Not if there's something I can do to help.'

Putting her callused palm on Callum's cheek, she patted him. 'Just make sure you keep yourself in one piece and come back to me, hale and hearty. You hear me, my boy?'

Ducking his head, Olivia could imagine what he must have looked like as a young lad. 'Yes, Mam. Course I will.'

But there were no guarantees when entering a battle. And that is what they were doing. Still, Olivia found comfort in knowing Callum would be with them to help. She only hoped he didn't hold a flame for her daughter. As soon as they found Hyacinth and freed her from the Crow, she and her daughter would be getting on a ship and leaving England forever. If the Queen was involved in this madness, escape might be the only option for all of the Damsels. Trying to imagine Philippa carving out a new life for herself far from Belgrave Square seemed nearly impossible.

God. If the Queen is involved, how can we possibly win?

Olivia shook her head and refocused on climbing into the carriage. One step at a time. Even if every step led them closer to a cliff from which they must jump.

12

The driver was possibly a demon in disguise. He blazed a trail from Cornwall to Exeter in record time, stopping only to change horses and allow the women scant minutes to manage their private needs. His focus and determination were nearly a match for her own. Philippa considered offering the man a position on her staff, but after depositing them at the railway station, he took his payment and disappeared into the busy street traffic with nary a backward glance.

The train ride to London was immensely faster and more comfortable than their journey to Cornwall, and Philippa's carriage was waiting outside Paddington Station to take them home.

Philippa led Olivia up the impressive stone staircase, between the marble columns, and to the ornately carved door large enough to accommodate three men standing astride. Taking stock of her dreadfully wrinkled gown, she stiffened her spine in preparation for whatever caustic remarks Stokes might make. Without a hint of hesitation, she pushed open the door and strode into her entrance.

'Stokes. Where are you? Napping, no doubt,' she called out into the marble foyer and waited, tapping her toe.

Olivia's eyes widened as the butler emerged from a hidden panel in the hallway.

Philippa had directed Callum to return to her house once his messages had been delivered. No doubt Stokes had loved hosting an uninvited guest. Her lips twitched just imagining the butler answering the door only to be given a note from Callum in her hand instructing Stokes to make up a bed in one of the guest chambers for the dirty, bedraggled, uncombed lad. She imagined the butler had been waiting for her arrival from that moment forward. Plotting his petty revenge. Ghastly man.

'Ah. You've returned. I very nearly called the guard, thinking the house was beset upon by street toughs. How marvellous to find that it is merely the lady of the house. What an interesting choice of clothing you selected for your travels.' The portly man had a spine so straight Philippa often wondered if he strapped a plank to it beneath his perfectly pressed coat.

'We were attacked by highwaymen early into our journey. Certain standards had to slip while endeavouring to maintain our lives. Don't work yourself into a lather; I can see how upsetting it is for you to imagine such peril besetting us.'

'Indeed.' He wrinkled his prodigious nose as though he smelled something foul. 'As instructed, a room has been made ready for the...' His brow rose ominously. 'Messenger boy.' The title might have been a euphemism for pile of rotting shit. 'Are we starting a new custom? Housing servants in the guest wing? I must say, the maids will be thrilled.' He flicked his gaze to Olivia before looking back at Philippa.

'Callum is a friend who was kind enough to help me deliver some very important notes. But don't fret. I'll never confuse the role of friend and servant with you, Stokes. A man with such deep respect for the class system need never worry that I might breach your stalwart boundaries.'

Stokes lifted a heavy brow. 'What a relief, Your Grace.'

'Make up the room next to mine for Olivia.' Philippa had taken over the duke's rooms a year after his death. The lady's chambers were connected to her suite of rooms and had remained empty ever since she moved out. Even when Hannah Simmons had moved into the house, Philippa didn't feel right about giving Hannah her old rooms. It had less to do with propriety and more a desire to keep some space between herself and anyone else living in her house. Even someone she came to think of as a daughter. But for reasons she suspected were far more complex than she wished to admit, she wanted Olivia close.

'Certainly you can't mean—'

'I meant exactly what I said.' Philippa enjoyed sparring with her butler, but she would be damned if he would censure her behaviour in her own house. He could disapprove of her all he wished, but no one was going to tell her how to live her life in the privacy of her own home.

'Perhaps I should just...' Olivia's voice trailed off as her gaze bounced between Philippa and the butler.

Philippa turned. Olivia was pale. She had lost weight during their journey. Her usually glowing complexion was dull, and there were bruises beneath her emerald eyes. Worry, an emotion Philippa rarely felt, washed over her like a cold wave.

A footman stood to attention by the front door. Bypassing Stokes completely, she turned to him. 'Brown, isn't it?'

The young man's mouth fell open, and he nearly swallowed his tongue. 'B-Baker, Your Grace,' he stuttered, his face darkening to crimson.

'Ah. Yes. Baker. Of course. Please escort Lady Smithwick to my private sitting room and see a tray is brought with afternoon tea. We are famished.'

'Y-yes, Your Grace.' He jumped from his spot on the wall. 'This way, Lady Smithwick.'

Olivia frowned. 'I can wait until you are ready to go up.'

'I need a private word with my butler.' Philippa returned her gaze to Stokes, who had the gall to lift his chin a degree higher. 'I shall join you shortly. A cup of tea and some sandwiches will do both of us a world of good.' Philippa didn't look away from her quarry. She would eviscerate her butler and hang him by his entrails.

'All right.' Olivia spoke quietly, and Philippa waited until the sound of her feet on the stairs disappeared.

'I know you blame me for the duke's death, Stokes.' As she spoke, she strode closer to the butler. 'I know you think I was a terrible choice for him as a wife. And I know you wished he hadn't left me everything when he passed.'

Stokes clasped his hands behind his back, his chest puffing out. 'It is not my place to have opinions about such things, Your Grace.'

Philippa snorted. 'Please. You have more opinions than a priest on Sunday.'

The obstinate butler pressed his lips together in a tight line.

Taking another step closer, she noticed a small strip of stubble he'd missed in his daily shave. It gave her a perverse sense of satisfaction to identify such a glaring imperfection. 'I don't mind that you dislike me, Stokes. Your disapproval of my work with the Queen, your muttered reprimands about desecrating the ballroom by turning it into a training space for the Deadly Damsels, your disdain for my habit of taking whiskey with my tea. None of that matters to me. I actually enjoy our little battle of wits, in large part because I usually win. I tolerate your disrespect and derision because in the decades we've spent together, you've shown the one trait I do care about. The characteristic I hold of utmost importance. Loyalty. Perhaps it is because of my connection with the Queen, or perhaps it's because you know I could skewer you like a pig at a Yuletide feast. Whatever the reason, I appreciate your dedication to keeping my secrets just that. Secret. If you cannot maintain this level of trust with *all* my secrets, then it might benefit us both to consider a change in staff. You served the duke with admirable discretion. Despite your obvious dislike for me, you have shown the same faithfulness, for which I am grateful. I would, of course, offer you a generous pension if you feel you can no longer continue your service here.'

Stokes blinked. His back remained straight. His gaze averted. His hands clasped behind his back. He was the perfect example of a proper butler. 'I have been in service since I was a lad of six and ten. I served the Duke of Dorsett for over four decades before he took you as his wife. His secrets were far darker than your own, Your Grace. And yet, I kept them. Just as I will keep yours. I don't need to like my employers to be an excellent employee.'

Philippa narrowed her eyes. Was he referring to his late employer or his present one? It was impossible to tell.

Probably both.

She wondered exactly what hidden horrors the man had witnessed in his time with Lord Winterbourne. She hated to give Stokes any credit, but he truly was a superb butler. 'Wonderful. As an excellent employee, I expect you to extend your services to Lady Smithwick in the same manner in which you do for me. Only, perhaps you could actually show *her* some respect.'

'Of course, Your Grace.'

'We'll both need baths brought up to our rooms. And inform Delacroix, I'm in desperate need of her skills. We shall be having visitors tonight, and I would like to look less like a... what was the term you used?' Philippa raised her brow at him as he flushed.

'A street tough, Your Grace.'

She sniffed. 'Yes. Exactly. Do let the cook know we'll need dinner for twelve tonight.' She had asked all of the Deadly Damsels and their partners to convene for a planning session. Her invitation also extended to Commissioner Worthington's secretary, Mr Reading. The man had proven invaluable in their last investigation. Turning to take the stairs to her suite of rooms and find Olivia, she caught Stokes muttering something about the uncouth nature of spontaneous dinner parties and couldn't stop the small smile.

'What?' She turned on the stairs.

Stokes straightened his spine even further, his eyes focused on a point over her shoulder. 'I was just calculating how many bottles of whiskey I should bring up now that you have returned, Your Grace. Although perhaps it would be best to stick with something less potent. I've read women of advancing years should refrain from consuming such large quantities of strong spirits. It can affect all manner of things. Wit being one, the waistline being another.'

'Your concern for my health is gratifying. As I am equally worried about yours, I would remind you of the dangers inherent in men expressing opinions about subjects to which they have no knowledge. Wouldn't the world be a much more peaceful place if the male species only spoke when they had something meaningful to say?'

'Of course, Your Grace.'

'Oh, and do make sure the tea is made with an extra dram of whiskey, won't you, Stokes?'

Snapping his heels together, he turned toward the kitchens while she resumed her regal march up the stairs.

13

Olivia was past the point of exhaustion and facing delirium. The footman led her up a winding staircase, down a long passageway lined with portraits of what she could only assume to be Winterbournes of old, until they reached the third-to-last door in the corridor. The footman opened it to a large space with windows on the far wall looking out to the gardens.

'Her Grace's sitting room, Lady Smithwick.' He stepped back, allowing Olivia to walk into the sumptuously decorated room. The walls were painted a soothing toasted biscuit, creating the perfect neutral canvas for jewel-toned furniture that managed to be both strong and feminine.

The perfect description for Philippa.

Choosing the deep-purple settee, Olivia sank onto the velvet cushion and sighed. If only she could loosen her corset, slip into her favourite and most worn nightgown, and fall into a dreamless sleep. Forget everything for a few blessed hours. She leaned her head against the back of the couch, but just as her eyes were falling closed, a maid pushed open the door. She carried a large tray covered in all manner of delightful treats. Cucumber sandwiches with soft cheese and dill, savoury tartlets stuffed with chicken and caramelised onions, tea cakes with lacy pink icing, cleverly shaped marzipan sweets, and Olivia couldn't manage to feign interest in any of it.

How can I possibly eat when I've no idea if Hyacinth is hungry or cold? Scared and alone?

Though it was far more likely her daughter was happily ensconced in her uncle's home, oblivious to the horror Cedric could unleash at any moment. It was the one comfort Olivia could take. He would want her to feel safe and pampered to ensure her loyalty remained with him until Olivia either followed his orders or defied him. Only if she didn't bend to her brother's will would he exert his punishment on Hyacinth. She knew him well. Waiting to exact his cruelty while he lavished his niece with attention, presents, and treats only increased her brother's pleasure when he would finally be able to put his plan into action. Hyacinth's feeling of betrayal would enhance her pain and suffering, which in turn would deepen his enjoyment.

'Thank you.' Olivia tried to smile at the maid who placed the tray on a low table in front of the settee, curtseyed, and quickly exited. A cheerful fire crackled in the large hearth that took up most of the wall Olivia faced. She might not be hungry, but tea was always welcome. Nothing bolstered the spirits quite like a strong cup of tea.

Olivia poured a dish for herself, adding a dollop of cream and a spoonful of sugar. Stirring, she absently wondered how long Philippa might take. After so many days of constant movement and companionship, it seemed strange to sit silently, alone, in a clean room.

She's hardly been gone a few moments, and I'm already missing her.

She shook her head.

'Don't get used to her company, Olivia.' Speaking out loud in the quiet room only highlighted her solitude.

She should have learned her lesson with Daisy. Opening her heart to someone like Philippa would end in shattered hopes. And besides, she had more important things to focus on than whatever stupid parts of her heart ached for Philippa.

'Useless organ that it is.' She sipped her tea and almost spat the mouthful onto the lush Aubusson rug. Gasping at the whiskey masking itself as tea, Olivia didn't notice the woman who entered from a door behind her until a firm hand was patting her back. She stood abruptly, shrieking and nearly spilling the cup. 'Who in the blazes are you?'

A woman with a prominent nose and a quizzical brow, hair slicked into a perfect chignon, wearing an expertly tailored black uniform with a crisp white apron, took Olivia's measure. She might be dressed as a servant, but she carried herself like a queen. 'I am Miss Delacroix. Lady's maid to the duchess.

'oo are you?' She wielded her French accent like a weapon, establishing her superiority.

'I am Lady Olivia Smithwick. The duchess' guest.' Olivia pulled her shoulder blades together, widening her narrow frame like a peacock preparing to battle.

'What are you doing in 'er personal chambers?' Delacroix pursed her full lips in a perfect pout. Ever so French.

'I was invited here. What are *you* doing in her personal chambers?'

'My lady will be wanting me to 'elp 'er prepare for dinner.'

Something hot, ugly, and tight gripped Olivia's chest.

Exactly how does this French maid prepare Philippa for dinner?

'Well, she doesn't need your help tonight.' Olivia put her hands on her hips and remembered that she was not some wilting wallflower. She was a marchioness. She had survived ten years of bedlam only to return to the beau monde and inspire jealousy in every lusty widow, instigate fear in every innocent debutante, and command the attention of every man under the age of eighty. She intimidated others. She was not intimidated by them. Including French maids who seemed to have a rather intimate relationship with their mistress.

Not that it matters to me with whom Philippa chooses to be intimate.

Except it did matter. Quite a lot. And realising that made things even more complicated. Still, her confusion was no reason to allow some curvy woman with a sultry accent to help Philippa undress.

Exactly.

Delacroix crossed her arms over her chest, tapping long fingernails against her black sleeve. 'I see.' She raised her eyebrows knowingly, a smile curling at the corner of her stupidly perfect mouth. A mouth Olivia was certain had pressed against Philippa's. The image flashing through her mind transformed jealousy into rage.

The nerve of her!

Although Olivia wasn't sure if she was angry at Philippa for dallying with her maid, or Delacroix for seducing her mistress. A small part of her mind suggested she had no place being mad at either of them. There was no understanding between her and Philippa. Nor would there ever be, as Philippa was in love with a ghost. A woman impossible to be with in the present. A marvellous way to keep her heart insulated from life's greatest hurts.

And its greatest joys.

It was all madness, probably brought on by Olivia's fear, fatigue, and severe lack of food.

None of this matters. I'm leaving. Whatever I might want from Philippa could never last longer than a few moments. I have no right to place any expectations on her.

A fact which struck her like a well-placed blow.

'Never mind. You know your mistress far better than I do. Stay if you like. It matters not to me.' Olivia walked to the fire to warm her hands. She felt suddenly rather cold.

'I do know 'er. And if she 'as invited you into her rooms, then I imagine she will 'ave no need of my 'elp until later.'

Olivia turned sharply. What was this woman about? Was she mocking her? But the maid's dark eyes softened.

'Rest easy, my lady. You 'ave nothing to worry about with me. 'er Grace is an incredibly good woman. Proud and stubborn, *oui*. But also courageous, generous – though she would never admit to such. She doesn't dally with 'er servants, even if they wish she did.'

Olivia's face reddened. 'I wasn't implying... that is to say, whatever Philippa does or doesn't do... you misunderstood me.'

The maid's eyes twinkled with a certain smug satisfaction. 'Perhaps. But I 'ope you will not misunderstand me when I tell you, she is not as strong as she thinks. 'er Grace needs another warrior 'oo will fight for 'er. Fight with 'er, *oui*?'

Olivia struggled to hold Delacroix's frank stare. Was she suggesting Olivia might be that woman? She was a survivor, certainly, but enduring hardship was very different from hurtling oneself into battle.

Still, the idea of standing beside Philippa as an equal in strength, determination, and skill, fighting together to protect girls like her daughter instead of running from the danger, was a dream she wasn't sure she could imagine.

Delacroix blinked long lashes. 'If you are not that woman, don't play with 'er affections.'

'I doubt Philippa holds much affection for me.'

'You do not doubt 'er. You doubt yourself.'

Goodness. I'm being summarily dismantled by a lady's maid.

And why not? A maid's entire job was to watch and understand her employer. They were more adept at determining the inner workings of a person's mind than the most skilled psychologist.

All cracked men who love cocaine, opium, and have an unnatural fascination with their mothers.

'What woman is without doubt? You might be correct, but so am I. Your mistress holds no interest in me other than how I can help her succeed with this mission.'

'We shall see. Tell 'er I will be back to get 'er ready for dinner.' With a saucy wink, the maid turned and flounced out of the room the way she came. Olivia assumed the door led to Philippa's bedchambers. She was desperately tempted to follow the smug little woman into the duchess' room and poke about, see what hidden truths she might uncover, but Delacroix was probably lingering there, and Olivia would be mortified if she were discovered seeking secrets about Philippa. *Like some lovestruck ninny.*

Not lovestruck. That was a ridiculous notion.

Before she could tell herself any more lies, Philippa entered.

'Did I hear Delacroix? Where did she disappear to? Ah, tea. Lovely.' Philippa walked directly to the table, poured a cup of whiskey-pretending-to-be-tea, and sat where Olivia had just been on the settee.

'Careful. It's quite strong.' Olivia turned her back to the fire and allowed herself a moment to watch the duchess.

'I certainly hope so.' Philippa flicked her gaze to Olivia, catching her staring.

There was no denying, while Olivia was decried amongst the beau monde as a beauty, Philippa was equally striking. Her dark colouring was the perfect foil to Olivia's fair, delicate features.

Without intending to move, she stepped away from the fire behind her to draw nearer to the flame burning so brightly within Philippa. The light seduced her like she was a fluttering night creature, inexorably pulled out of the darkness toward certain conflagration.

'I've always found strong things to be irresistible.' Philippa took a sip, her double meaning clear. She raised her perfectly sculpted eyebrow at Olivia. 'Is something amiss?'

It was a dare, and Olivia could imagine the woman's thoughts.

Advance or retreat, Olivia. The choice is yours, but do something.

Olivia took another step closer. With the shock of Hyacinth's disappearance wearing off and realising Cedric wouldn't hurt Hyacinth until he knew it would have the most impact on her, Olivia's panic had receded to a level of constant anxiousness. She desperately needed to escape her worries for a few moments. Philippa was giving her a chance to seek comfort and respite before re-entering the fray. Olivia wanted a second of beauty and pleasure before her world flew into chaos.

'You are breathtaking, Philippa. Sometimes, when I look at you, my thoughts simply scatter. So yes. Something is amiss. My wits, and I'm doing my best to collect them.'

Well, that was certainly more honest than I intended to be. What will you do with my unabashed attraction?

She had shocked the duchess, who no doubt expected her to retreat. Philippa opened her mouth to say something, but no words emerged.

Right. Well. In for a penny...

Olivia dove deeper into dangerous waters to say what was racing through her mind before she lost her nerve.

'I want you. I know you don't love me, and that is not what this is about. If all we engage in is physical intimacy, your heart will still be devoted to Liza. You won't be breaking your oath. It's terribly selfish of me, and you'll probably hate me later. But as long as you don't hate yourself when this is through, I can withstand your anger. At least I'll have a beautiful memory with you. There are a million things to fret about. A million things I should be doing. We could easily fail in this mission, but right now, I just want to hold you.' Olivia bit her lip, desperate for comfort, no matter the consequences.

'We won't fail, Olivia. And while I feel far more than I'd like, hatred for you is not what plagues me. The Damsels are coming for dinner in a few hours. We shall make a plan and execute it. Together. Until then, there is nothing more to do.'

'I can think of several things we could do that might keep me from crawling out of my skin.' She thrust her chin out and refused to let the guilt keep her alone and terrified. Didn't she deserve a small escape? To lose herself in desire just once, just for a blessed moment after so many years of complete isolation? To seek physical comfort when her emotions were so troubled? 'I am wildly attracted to you, Philippa. Even in the midst of this nightmare. Perhaps because of it. Moments are precious. Is it so wrong to steal a few of them to feel something other than this fear threatening to swallow me whole?' Her words cracked on emotions too large to contain, like an exposed nerve shrieking through her system. She shook her head. 'I'm sure I'm the worst woman in all of England, but I'm also so tired of pretending that I don't want you.'

There. She said it. Now that it was in the open, Philippa could reject her, and Olivia could slink into the shadows and dissolve into a useless puddle of worry and fear.

'If the beau monde were to ever hear you say those words, you'd be sent back to bedlam.' Philippa's pleasantly low voice rose a notch.

It was a painful reminder of what she'd already endured, and a deft refusal.

Fine. That's just fine.

She was accustomed to enduring hardship alone. She could hold her worries and fears for Hyacinth without seeking support from a woman so intent on disliking her. 'I expect that would bring you great satisfaction. Me locked in a cell. What difference does it make if that cell is in Newgate or back to the Home for Wayward Women?'

Philippa tapped her fingernail against her teacup before sipping again. When she brought the porcelain away from her lips, Olivia noted how they glistened. 'I don't want you in a cell. Seeing as we are speaking truths tonight, I must admit I'm not sure what I want, and I *always* know what I want.' She shook her head slowly from side to side. 'With you, I'm flummoxed.'

A small sense of satisfaction bloomed in Olivia's belly, spreading through her veins like warm honey. 'Well, at the very least, I can take comfort in knowing I confounded the Duchess of Dorsett. That thought shall keep me warm wherever I find myself.'

Philippa set down her teacup. 'Our mission has changed. I was pursuing you to find the Crow. We've found him. He is our new target.'

'So, I am no longer your enemy?' Olivia stepped closer. Only a few feet separated them.

'I'm not sure what you are, Olivia.'

Olivia exhaled a shaky breath. 'I know exactly what I am. Terrified. Of losing Hyacinth. Of leaving England for an unknown future. Of confronting my brother and being defeated once again. The only time I forget to be afraid is when you are near.' *Will I still feel this pull for you across an ocean?*

Philippa rose and closed the gap between them. 'What do you feel when I am near?'

Olivia licked her lips, tasting the words before she spoke them. 'Hope. Power, even if it's only because I'm borrowing yours. Desire. Like a fever burning me from the inside.'

Burying her hand in Olivia's hair, Philippa tugged gently. Olivia turned so her cheek brushed against Philippa's wrist. She closed her eyes and savoured the sensation of Philippa's soft skin against her face.

'You are right to hope, Olivia. The Damsels will help, and together, we do not fail. You don't need to borrow my power because you have more than enough of your own. Tomorrow, I am going to start training you. A woman who knows her own strength is a dangerous creature indeed.'

'And what of my desire? Am I wrong to need your touch? To crave your mouth against mine?'

Philippa's pupils dilated, the black nearly eclipsing the blue. 'No more wrong than I am to obsess about burying my hands in all of this hair. To want to lick you right here.' She brushed a thumb over the delicate skin where Olivia's earlobe met her jaw. 'I don't remember need ever feeling this vital.'

Olivia swallowed. *Not even for Liza?* She couldn't ask the question. Nor would it be fair. Philippa's love for Liza was a precious thing. A secret treasure that belonged to Philippa and Liza alone. No matter if Olivia and Philippa shared a wild tumble or an endless fall, she vowed to never try to replace Liza in Philippa's heart.

And besides, I don't want her heart. This isn't about love. It's about hunger and heat. Distraction and desire. Comfort in times of trouble. That is all.

But could the heart expand enough to hold past love while making room for someone new? Someone living in the present? It was a question Olivia wasn't brave enough to ask because she didn't want to know the answer. But she wanted this now. So she would claim it and damn the consequences.

Leaning forward, Olivia took Philippa's mouth in a desperate assault. Plunging her tongue into the duchess' depths, she tasted whiskey, tea, and a hint of aniseed. When Philippa's nails scraped against her scalp, Olivia grabbed her waist and pulled her hips flush against her own. Philippa thrust her thigh between Olivia's legs. She wished her layers of silk, crinoline, and cotton would magically disappear. But the fabric created delicious friction as Philippa pressed her leg harder into Olivia's cleft.

Nibbling along Philippa's jaw to her neck, the scent of jasmine and frankincense filled Olivia's lungs, and her heart hitched. She sucked Philippa's skin into her mouth, biting hard enough to make the duchess hiss. Philippa palmed her breast.

'Vicious,' Philippa murmured, throwing her head back to give Olivia better access.

'Just trying to match you, my lady.' Olivia couldn't stop the smile curving her lips as Philippa traced the neckline of Olivia's dress, dipping her finger below the silk and finding the hardened, sensitive bud where pleasure sparked like fire.

'Ride me. Let me watch you fly apart.' Philippa dropped her hands to Olivia's hips, sliding her thigh back, then forward again as she ground Olivia against her. She hit the cluster of nerves at the apex of Olivia's slit. Olivia couldn't stop the moan of need as she caught the rhythm, chasing the sweet promise shimmering just out of reach. Philippa watched her like a hungry predator, and something about her gaze made Olivia come alive. She pulled down the front of her dress, exposing her breasts and revelling in the flare of unfiltered need in Philippa's eyes.

'Touch yourself. Show me what you like,' Philippa demanded. Her fingers dug into Olivia's hips as she dragged her harder against her strong thigh. Olivia lifted her hands, cupping her breasts and kneading them, imagining Philippa's hands instead of her own. She pinched each nipple, rolling one, then the other, gasping at the sharp, sweet pleasure that pulsed in her clitoris and rode Philippa with barely controlled frenzy. Looking down at the erotic display, her pink nipples turning dark rose as she tortured herself for her own pleasure, Olivia felt alive and free and so powerful.

'My turn with those pretty nipples.' Philippa brushed Olivia's hand aside and bent her head, her crimson lips pressing a soft kiss against the tightened tip of Olivia's breast before she sucked the bud into her wet depths, using her teeth and tongue to push Olivia over the precipice of pleasure and pain. A small orgasm rippled through her, but it wasn't enough. She wanted more. She wanted everything.

'You make me wild.' Olivia struggled to keep her voice low.

'I want to taste you as you come. Will you let me?' Philippa's voice, husky with need, created a resonating shiver through Olivia. The images her words conjured made Olivia drunk with desire.

Pulling back, Olivia wanted to memorise Philippa's raw expression. She doubted many had seen her quite so undone. Lifting her chin, imperious as a queen, she gathered her courage. 'On your knees, Duchess.'

Philippa didn't move, but her eyes touched every inch of Olivia's exposed skin. Where her gaze landed, heat bloomed as flames licked over Olivia. 'I don't remember the last time someone dared to command me.'

Olivia tightened her hands to stop the trembling. Had she gone too far?

Or perhaps, not nearly far enough.

'You will always remember me, Philippa.'

14

Philippa was burning. Between her thighs, the tips of her breasts, her lungs, her heart. Everything was aflame, and she didn't know whether to flee from the fire or pour oil onto the conflagration and let it incinerate everything she knew until she emerged like a phoenix from the ashes, renewed.

'Come.' She took Olivia's hand and led her to the settee. Pushing her down onto the cushions, Philippa bent to grab a pillow and drop it on the floor between Olivia's slippered feet. Olivia's eyes widened, and the wild wish to possess the talent of a painter swept through Philippa. To capture the beauty of Olivia's flushed skin, her long legs, her pale breasts tipped with nipples reddened by Philippa's mouth. To find the exact shade that might match the shine of Olivia's wild curls glowing in firelight, the right line to trace the arc of her neck, the brushstroke that would immortalise the emerald depths of her eyes. But her talents lay in destruction, not creation.

So I will destroy her for any other woman.

It was a brutal sentiment, but Philippa was feeling ruthless. Something about Olivia's demand called to the uncontainable heat simmering in Philippa's blood. She wanted to take Olivia to heights neither of them had ever reached. Claim the woman who infiltrated her mind like a cunning criminal. Stole her thoughts like a skilled thief. Whittled away her control over desires Philippa long since buried.

It is only fair Olivia should feel the sharp edge of my need.

Philippa kept her eyes locked onto Olivia as she slowly lowered herself to her knees. Olivia's unbound breasts rose and fell with each inhalation. The impetuous marchioness bit her lower lip.

Ah. Not as confident as you pretend to be.

They hadn't discussed their past experiences. She didn't know how far Olivia had taken things with her maid. What paths they had wandered down in their quest for pleasure. Olivia had only been with one other woman, but that told Philippa nothing.

I have only been with Liza.

Guilt rippled, but it was eclipsed by something else. Didn't Olivia deserve a moment of softness? Didn't Philippa? That is what this was between them. Two women finding strength within each other. It wasn't anything like her sweet discoveries with Liza. They had been the best of friends, slipping from laughter into love like spring warms into summer. Learning how to pleasure each other through fumbled explorations and breathless experiments. What they lacked in sophistication and knowledge, they gained in the joy of experiencing physical bliss with total trust and deep connection.

But I am no longer a young girl on the cusp of sexual awakening.

She was a woman grown and confident in her desires. She had read widely and imagined all manner of wicked pleasure to be had between the thighs of a willing partner, even though she remained celibate after losing Liza. But tonight, she gave herself permission to play. Because this wasn't love. It wasn't betrayal. She didn't know what it was, but she knew she wanted Olivia with a fierceness that defied logic.

'Lift your skirts.' Philippa could have helped, but instead, she rocked back on her heels and watched as Olivia gathered the layers of cloth, dragging them up her calves, exposing stockings tied at her knees in little blue bows. The hemline riveted Philippa as it moved slowly higher. She couldn't decide if Olivia was being intentionally coy or if the woman who so casually commanded the attention of dukes, viscounts, and barons alike was suddenly shy. Flicking her gaze up, she saw the tremble in Olivia's lips. 'Are you frightened?'

Olivia shook her head quickly. Too quickly.

'Exactly how much experience have you had with another woman?'

Olivia's blush told Philippa all she needed to know. 'There was kissing. And touching, of course. She was quite skilled with her hands. But... we never. I mean to say, she spoke about how good it could be when one used their mouth and tongue, but Percy discovered us before we could ever progress to... umm. Yes. Well.'

Philippa raised a brow. With all of Olivia's charm and sophistication, her practised flirting at balls, her confidence while twirling on the dance floor in the arms of any number of men, she never would have guessed the woman to be so inexperienced. But then, mayhap that was Olivia's game. To keep everyone at arm's length by making them believe she was far too experienced to ever dally with a bed partner unmatched to her in sophistication.

It bloody well worked.

Until now.

'I doubt your husband was very generous in his lovemaking.'

Olivia's snort of laughter broke some of the tension pulling tight between them. 'My pleasure was never his concern.'

'It is mine, tonight.' The thrill of showing Olivia what her body could feel both humbled and aroused Philippa. 'Your pleasure is my singular concern.'

Olivia froze with her skirts just cresting her thighs.

That won't do.

Philippa held Olivia's gaze. 'Your skirts, I want them around your waist.'

'So demanding, Duchess.' But Olivia complied.

She couldn't stop herself from tracing her fingers up Olivia's shapely calf, toying with the ribbon before she rubbed her thumb in a rhythmic circle on the inside of Olivia's knee. She kept her eyes on Olivia's face, drawing out the moment before she let her gaze fall.

Olivia's maidenhair was dark gold, hiding pink lips glistening with the evidence of her desire. Philippa's mouth watered for a single taste. 'Perfect everywhere. I can't decide if I'm envious or enamoured.'

'Would it be too bold of me to hope for both?'

The comment caught Philippa off guard. She smiled. Not a calculated stretch of her lips, nor a sharp curl of her mouth designed to expose her teeth like fangs, but a genuine expression of surprised mirth. 'Are you not always bold? You swan onto any dance floor in the beau monde with as much confidence as the Queen.'

Olivia shrugged, the movement doing fascinating things to her breasts. She looked at Philippa's eyebrows instead of meeting her gaze. 'When it doesn't matter, it's easy to pretend.'

'Ah.'

But this matters.

And that revelation was far too complicated to examine. Philippa had been grieving Liza for so long, she'd long ago accepted that the remainder of her life would be spent in solitude. The danger inherent in starting a love affair with another woman hardly seemed worth the effort when her heart would never be involved, and taking a new husband was never an option.

But then she met Olivia.

Somewhere along the way, mayhap it began on a storm-tossed cliff above the Cornish sea, her long-accepted future fate, which had been so clear, became opaque. It was a problem she couldn't untangle now with the distraction of Olivia's luscious body laid out before her. Philippa focused instead on discovering Olivia's pleasure and spinning it out until they both shattered. Because that was something she could control.

Leaning forward, she pressed a kiss just above Olivia's knee. 'I remember the first time I saw you. At Lord Renquist's ball. You wore a white gown with purple feathers.'

'You remember that night?'

Philippa gently pulled Olivia's legs further apart. Her thumb grazed higher on the delicate skin of Olivia's inner thigh. The woman jerked, pulling her legs together and caging Philippa between them for a moment before she relaxed.

'I remember everything about you. Your skin glowed. You were laughing at something someone said, and I nearly lost my breath.'

'I thought you hated me from the start.'

Sliding both hands higher up Olivia's legs, Philippa hunkered down between them and swiped her tongue where Olivia's hip jutted out. She was a cat lapping cream. Olivia cried out, shifting her pelvis, making more space for Philippa's body.

'I hated how quickly I lost control of my desires. I hadn't felt that way about another woman in too long to remember. But I've discovered the perfect revenge.' Philippa sucked hard enough to leave a love bite high on Olivia's inner thigh. The feeling of triumph, knowing Olivia would see evidence of what she did to her for days to come, shocked Philippa. But not enough to stop her as she turned her head to give equal attention to Olivia's right leg.

'Dare I ask?' Olivia threw her head back, eyes closed as her breasts quivered with every laboured breath.

Accepting the unspoken invitation, Philippa reached up and squeezed the firm, hot flesh. When she pinched Olivia's nipple and rolled it between her fingers, the woman's body tightened like a sail in the wind. Olivia pressed a hand over her own mouth, muffling her cry.

Before she answered Olivia's question, Philippa blew on her core, watching as pink petals parted like a flower opening for the sun. 'Making you want me as much as I want you. When this is over, you'll never feel pleasure without thinking of me.' She nuzzled into Olivia's maidenhair before swiping her tongue between Olivia's lips. A rush of sweet liquid heat burst on her palate.

'You are a tyrant, Philippa.' Olivia gasped.

'And you are a siren singing me into the depths.' Philippa let her words vibrate over Olivia's slick inner flesh before she licked again, savouring the salty tang. She nudged and nibbled, sucked and plunged, teased and tormented, toying with the tight bud of need as it swelled, but never lingering long enough to grant Olivia satisfaction. Each time she brought her close to the edge, she retreated.

But Olivia didn't suffer alone. Philippa's clitoris pulsed with every heartbeat, screaming for pressure and friction. Her nipples tingled, demanding the same attention Philippa had lavished on Olivia. Pressing her legs together tightly, she was tempted to slip her hand from where it kneaded Olivia's luscious arse and rub herself to climax. But she couldn't let Olivia go. Instead, she accepted the ache as she focused on her mission.

Slipping her hand down Olivia's sweet hollows and soft curves, she slipped a finger into the tight channel, then another as her tongue danced circles over Olivia's bud. Soft, hard, tight, sweet. When she pushed her third finger in and curled them upward, coaxing Olivia's climax closer while sucking the sweet cluster of nerves at her centre, Olivia screamed again, her hand not able to contain the hoarse explosion. Satisfaction and something else filled Philippa. Something soft and warm and soothing, like honey on a ravaged throat.

Philippa flattened her tongue, lapping Olivia's orgasm, desperate to ensure she missed nothing. When Olivia finally pushed Philippa's head away, she reluctantly relented.

Olivia's pale skin was flushed a beautiful pink. Her nipples, dark and swollen, were still deliciously exposed. Philippa leaned forward to kiss one, then the other. Olivia caught her before she could retreat, pulling Philippa's head against her chest where she could hear the comforting rhythm of Olivia's heart. She should push back, get up, create some distance. But Philippa's skin was still buzzing with desire, her tongue was still drenched with Olivia's flavour, and a strange peace stole through her, making her limbs heavy even without reaching her own climax. It was lovely to rest in the soft cradle of Olivia's body.

'I never knew how good it could be.' Olivia's soft words brushed over Philippa like a caress.

'Oral pleasure is one of life's greatest gifts, and so rarely enjoyed by women.'

'That's not... I mean, yes. It was quite a revelation, but that isn't what I meant.'

Fear thrilled through Philippa at the open yearning in Olivia's voice. She knew that tone. She'd used it herself with Liza. But this wasn't anything like that. It *couldn't* be anything like that.

'I don't think—'

'Let me finish.' Olivia's voice lost its breathless quality and took on a note of command that did strange things to Philippa, stoking both her angst and arousal. 'I had a great tendre for Daisy. She was sweet and kind and gentle. Nothing like you.'

Ouch! Well played, Olivia.

Philippa pulled free of Olivia's arms and stood. She couldn't have this conversation while still nuzzling in the sanctuary of Olivia's body. After all, this was going to become a battle. It had to be. Fighting was the only way to distract her from the fact that this might have been more than two women seeking comfort in each other's arms. 'She sounds rather insipid.'

Olivia's lips pressed together in a white line. She breathed out through her nose and fisted her hands. 'She wasn't. She taught me not to fear my attraction to women. She helped me understand it wasn't something shameful or disgusting, but actually rather beautiful. Far more natural than being forced to marry a man I neither knew nor liked, who inspired fear and revulsion within me with his constant physical and mental brutality.'

Philippa couldn't use snark against such an earnest truth. Especially when she wholeheartedly agreed. Which was incredibly inconvenient, as they were meant to be fighting. She needed this to be an argument. 'Fine. So not insipid, but clearly far too soft for a woman like you.'

'A woman like me? What kind of woman am I, exactly?'

* * *

Adrenaline fuelled Olivia and she wasn't sure if she wanted Philippa to turn and leave, kiss her senseless, or demand a duel to the death. What she actually wanted was Philippa back in her arms, skin against skin, soaking in the warm afterglow of her climax, giving comfort and seeking some in return instead of continuing this asinine argument.

Philippa turned and walked to the hearth, rubbing an imaginary smudge from the well-polished wood. 'The kind who needs an equal partner. Someone as strong, and smart, and clever as you are to keep you from running riot over them.'

'An insult wearing the clothes of a compliment. Well done, Your Grace.' Olivia stood from the couch, righting her dress to cover herself. One did not enter the battlefield with their breasts jostling about willy-nilly. 'I wonder if you learned such tactics from the Prime Minister. Such skilled duality belongs in parliament.' Before Philippa could let more verbal arrows fly, Olivia let loose her own volley. 'Is that why you're pulling back? Because you're worried I might run riot over you? That you might not match me in strength and intelligence?' Olivia stepped closer, crossing her arms over her now-covered chest and wishing for a weapon.

'I'm pulling back because there is no way to move forward.' Philippa bit out the words, her hair loose from Olivia's fingers, her cheeks flushed with arousal or anger, the crimson stain on her lips gone to reveal her natural shell pink. It felt glorious to knock the stoic lady from her horse of detached indifference.

Olivia leaned into her advantage, refusing to acknowledge how Philippa's dishevelled appearance only transformed her beauty from fierce to fragile: a devastating contrast. 'You presume to know what I want. Because the duchess is always right, is she not? I should no longer be surprised at such arrogance.'

'It isn't arrogance, it's confidence. Because I *am* right in this.'

Olivia threw her head back and laughed. 'Please. You sound like the men you despise.'

'I don't despise men, but neither do I blindly respect them.'

'At least on that point, we can agree. Tell me, oh wise and infallible Duchess, what is it I want?'

'You want to rescue your daughter.'

'Earth-shattering insight, Your Grace. One I believe I've told you about three hundred times on this journey.'

Philippa stepped closer, her hand lifting to slap or caress, Olivia couldn't decide. Nor could she determine which she would prefer. Philippa dropped her hand to her side before Olivia could find out. She rubbed her index finger in circles against her thumb. 'You want to be free. Have control of your choices and your destiny.'

'Every person wants that.'

'But don't you see? Any entanglement with me would ruin that freedom for you. The beau monde would thrill to catch us together. Whatever autonomy you seek would be stripped from you forever. And what of me? I could lose my fortune. My property. My place with the Queen. My work with the Damsels. Everything.'

Philippa's words sucked the fight from Olivia's blood. Because she was right. Which was infuriating. But they should be willing to face those dangers together. If Philippa cared as much for Olivia as she feared she did for Philippa. Because Olivia was willing to face the dragons of their day and fight for their right to love each other.

Olivia clenched her jaw tight before speaking. 'Mayhap I wanted a woman courageous enough to battle those insurmountable odds with me and beat them. Didn't you say something is only impossible because it hasn't been accomplished yet? Or have I finally proven you wrong?'

Philippa stepped back as though she'd been struck. 'You have no idea what you are asking. I thought that way once. With Liza. And then she was taken from me and chose death over the reality she faced. Loving someone the way I love her is not a gift. It is a curse that strips everything from you. Your strength. Your choice. Your power. I would never wish that on you, and I certainly won't subject myself to such torture ever again. I can give you pleasure. I can give you physical intimacy in the short time we have together. I can give you comfort, because you deserve that at the very least. But that is all. I cannot give you love or lifelong companionship. If you seek that from me, you will only be disappointed.'

Olivia felt her heart stretch and snap. Pain poured forth like poison from a wound. She realised, in her stupidity, that that was exactly what she wanted from Philippa. Even if she knew it was impossible. 'Disappointment is something I'm used to. I just didn't expect to be disappointed in you.' She watched each word strike Philippa like arrows.

Good. I shouldn't have to suffer alone.

Brushing a hand down her tragically wrinkled travelling gown, Philippa pulled her shoulders back, her face hardening into the mask of the duchess. 'Baths have been brought to our rooms. I'm sure you are weary from our travels. I suggest we each retire and refresh ourselves before dinner. We will have much to discuss with the others if we hope to rescue your daughter, catch the Crow, and grant you the freedom you desire.'

Ah. Back to the mission. Because tracking down an insidious murderer is far easier than arguing with me. Fine. Wonderful.

Olivia executed a dramatic curtsey. 'Of course, Your Grace. I wouldn't dare disagree with the duchess. Except for one point, that is.'

Philippa pressed her lips together. Olivia should have guessed she wouldn't rise to the bait. No matter. She would speak her mind whether or not Philippa wished to hear it.

'I'm sorry you lost Liza. I wish I could heal that pain, protect you from the sorrow. Truly, I do. But love is not a curse. It is a gift. If one is courageous enough to accept it.'

'That isn't fair.' Philippa's mask slipped. Raw grief shone in her eyes.

Once more, Olivia's fight faltered, making way for soul-aching empathy. For what Philippa had lost. What Liza – a woman she had never met, yet someone she felt a certain kinship with – had suffered. But she wouldn't back down. 'No. Life isn't fair. What happened to Liza wasn't fair. Losing your first love wasn't fair. But shutting yourself off from life's beauty for fear of its cruelty isn't fair either. To you. To Liza. Or to me. You are stronger than this, Philippa.' Olivia turned and walked away because she couldn't stay.

15

Olivia leaned back in her chair, the plush padding pressing pleasantly against her lower back, and wished her corset weren't quite so tight. Philippa's cook must be a sorceress for each course delivered to the massive dining table by a bevy of servants eclipsed the last in splendour.

She let her spoon rest in the remaining drizzle of caramel sauce on her plate from a crème brûlée that gods and goddesses might trade their ambrosia to eat.

'That was delightful!' Millicent Drake, a copper-haired temptress with a figure as full as her personality, sighed in satisfaction. Her forest-green gown was cut low and highlighted a figure better suited to a Valkyrie than a mere mortal. Her husband sat next to her at Philippa's impressive dinner table. Major General Beaufort Drake was a mountain of muscle and scars. His closely cropped hair glinted nearly white in the light cast from the two chandeliers hanging above them. Drake watched his wife with the smouldering gaze of a man who seemed more intent on savouring Millie than any dessert. A scar cut diagonally across his face, making once austere features quite savage. Millie didn't seem to notice as he leaned close, whispering something in her ear that had her freckled skin flaming like a torch.

'Beau!'

The dragon of a man let out a low chuckle, nearer to a growl than laughter, as she playfully slapped his arm.

'Shall we retire to the parlour? Brandy, whiskey, port, and plotting are in order, I believe.' Lady Hannah Killian, once Philippa's ward and now the Duchess of Covington, placed her small hand on her husband's much larger one. Lieutenant General Robert Killian was the perfect opposite of his best friend, Drake. Dark hair, fine features, and an athletic frame, which perfectly fit his tailored suit. But the same heated blend of love and desire Drake displayed when looking at Millie filled Killian's gaze when he turned to Hannah.

'An excellent suggestion, darling. If I can manage to stand after stuffing myself to bursting. Lady Philippa, you really must share your chef's secrets.'

Philippa raised a signature brow at Lieutenant General Killian. 'I have no desire to be poisoned, Killian. A fate sure to befall me if I betray the cook. Shall we?' She stood, leading the way out of the dining room and pointedly avoided Olivia's gaze.

Grand. I don't want to look at you either. I might fly from my seat and attack if you give me the least provocation.

The idea sent satisfaction thrilling through Olivia, although she wasn't sure if she would pummel Philippa or offer some quid pro quo for her earlier ministrations. Either way, it would be explosive.

Callum, who had seemed a bit overwhelmed at the grandeur of the dinner and its guests, excused himself from joining the others. Olivia gave him an understanding smile before he disappeared to his guest room. A small part of her wished she could slink away to the safety of her own bed, but battle plans wouldn't make themselves.

'How are you getting on?' Lady Ivy Worthington sidled up to Olivia on their way to the parlour after giving her husband's arm a gentle squeeze. Commissioner Edward Worthington's face transformed from the serious leader of Scotland Yard to a smitten suitor as he watched Ivy glide across the floor, her arm entwined in Olivia's.

'I'll feel better when we have a plan. I hate knowing that Cedric has Hyacinth.'

Ivy's fair brow, a few shades lighter than Olivia's, pulled down over crystal eyes. 'Do you fear he's mistreating her?'

Olivia shook her head. 'No. I'm sure she is being spoiled silly in his bid to gain her loyalty. Though I know he won't hesitate to devise all manner of torture for her if I don't comply with his requests. Hurting Hyacinth after gaining her trust is one more tool in his arsenal. He knows his betrayal will make whatever fate he plans for her even more devastating.'

Ivy shook her head, a silky strand of sleek hair escaping her simple twist. 'Monster.'

Olivia nodded her agreement.

'We will find a way forward, Olivia. I swear it. Philippa has defeated far worse foes than your brother, and we are all here to help.'

Olivia slipped her arm around Ivy's lean waist and squeezed in gratitude as they entered the parlour. Philippa's sharp gaze flicked to them, and Olivia noted the woman tighten.

Jealous? Good.

Olivia had no intention of trying to seduce Ivy. The woman was clearly enamoured with her handsome husband and showed no interest in the fairer sex, and Olivia had only ever felt friendship for Ivy. But if her closeness with the woman inspired any envy in Philippa, then Olivia was glad for it. The duchess wanted a physical relationship with her, excluding any other bonds, but that was meaningless. She would seek out friendship and comfort where it was offered, manage her own pleasure in the solitude of her rooms, and Philippa could go hang.

'Thank you, Ivy. I hope you know how much your friendship means to me. I know I apologised for my betrayal, but I shall never forgive myself for deceiving you last summer.'

Ivy batted away Olivia's guilt with a gloved hand. 'Pish. You made an impossible choice to protect your daughter. Any one of us would have done the same thing in your position. You had no one to help you but yourself. But that isn't true any more.'

Tears filled Olivia's eyes, and she swallowed past a lump threatening to choke her. 'Thank you, Ivy. You've no idea what your forgiveness means.' She had been fighting alone for so long. To know she had allies – women and men who would join with her against her brother – was an impossible dream. A dream being realised.

If only the impossible dream of being with Philippa could also be realised.

But that would mean the stubborn woman would have to admit she's wrong. That loving again after losing someone so dear is possible.

And Olivia wasn't sure herself if that was true.

As they settled next to each other on a well-padded settee swathed in brocaded upholstery as deep blue as Philippa's eyes, Ivy leaned close to Olivia. 'How are things with you and Philippa? I hoped the journey might bring you to a more convivial place, but it seems you are still at odds.'

Olivia narrowed her eyes as she watched Philippa pour herself a snifter of whiskey. 'We would find common ground. If the arrogant, smug, stubborn woman would ever deign to admit someone else might be right once in a while. That she doesn't need to be some bloody martyr on her pyre of lost love, smouldering forever alone. Never being willing to light a new fire.'

Blast. I've said too much. And muddled a metaphor, I'm quite certain.

Ivy's gaze bounced back and forth from Olivia to Philippa. Before she could voice a response, Philippa called the group to order.

'After chasing the Devil's Sons for nearly a year, finally, thanks to Olivia, we have the identity of the Crow.' Philippa kept her gaze on every face but Olivia's. 'But now we know the Lord High Chancellor is our target, we must proceed with even more caution.'

Penny Renquist, former maid who recently married the Marquess of Stoneway in a scandalous union, leaned on the armrest of the wingback chair where she perched. Liam Renquist, her golden-haired husband, stood beside her, his hand resting on her shoulder. 'This is dire news, Philippa. If the Lord High Chancellor is the mastermind behind this flesh trade, how deep does the infection spread? Can we trust the Queen? The Prime Minister? Could they all be part of this, or at least complicit?'

Liam squeezed his wife's shoulder and shook his head. 'I can't imagine the Queen would ever sanction such behaviour. Why ask us to investigate these crimes if she knew the leader all along?'

'I would make the same argument for the Prime Minister,' Killian interjected. While Killian and Drake worked for the Prime Minister with the mission of bringing corrupt peers to the House of Lords to be tried for their crimes, Liam, Philippa, Hannah, and the other Damsels were covert operators for the Queen who held little confidence in England's lords to hold their brethren accountable. It was a divide that once kept the group on opposite sides, but this new information changed things.

'I think it would behove us to assume nothing. We can't say with total certainty who is on our side except for us.' Reading, Commissioner Worthington's secretary and a new member of the group sat on a hardback chair, a ledger perched on his lap and a quill clasped between his elegant hands. One was distracted from focusing on his finely featured face by the presence of a nearly non-existent moustache struggling to make an appearance.

Edward Worthington brought a cup of brandy to Ivy then turned to face the group. 'Much as I hate to admit it, I think Reading makes a good point.'

'A brilliant point, some might say.' Reading kept his eyes on his ledger, a small smile playing on his lips.

Edward rolled his eyes.

'So, we trust each other, and no one else?' Drake's rough voice filled the space like thunder.

Philippa, resplendent in a deep-purple gown only a few shades lighter than black, tapped her finger against her glass. Olivia begrudgingly admitted Philippa's lady's maid, Delacroix, was incredibly talented. She must have magic fingers to create the intricately coiled braids and curled twists in Philippa's elaborate coiffure.

Philippa had sent a maid to assist Olivia, who did her best with the wild tangle of Olivia's curls. In the end, they determined a loose braid cascading over her shoulder was the best option. And it was glorious to be wearing a clean and freshly pressed gown. A pale-green confection of frothy lace that enhanced Olivia's eyes and complemented her fair skin. It was cut low enough to reveal her décolletage, and while she would like to pretend she didn't choose the dress to intentionally torture Philippa, she couldn't deny the flush of pleasure when the duchess' eyes had stalled on her silhouette as she descended the stairs before dinner, nor the several times during their meal she'd caught her host's gaze trapped just below Olivia's chin before quickly darting away.

Returning her focus to the discussion, she tried to keep up with the plans bouncing back and forth between their assembled party. A heated debate was ensuing, with Killian and Drake on one side, Hannah, Millie, and Penny on the other. Liam was wisely staying quiet.

'He must meet with his men at some point. If we follow him long enough, he's sure to betray himself.' Drake's voice was carefully controlled, though his hand fisted at his side convulsively.

'That could take weeks, Drake. Or even months. With Hyacinth in his clutches, we don't have that kind of time. We need to strike quickly. Decisively,' Millie argued, her ample bosom jostling with each word, which seemed to momentarily distract her husband, much to his chagrin.

'What we need is evidence. Something tangible and concrete to tie the Chancellor to these crimes,' Killian interjected, avoiding the glare of his wife.

'What kind of evidence do you imagine the man keeps? He is far too smart to leave a paper trail, Killian.' Hannah stood, stepping away from her husband and plunging her hand into a cleverly sewn pocket in her dress. Killian's eyes dipped to that pocket, then back to his wife's face.

'Darling, I certainly hope you aren't planning on throwing that dagger at me.'

Just as he said the words, Hannah pulled free a muff pistol. 'I'll leave the daggers to Millie.' She glanced at the redhead and winked before returning her focus to Killian. 'My aim is better with a pistol at any rate.' The flash of challenge in her eyes prompted a flush high on her husband's cheek.

Dear God. Are they flirting or fighting? It's impossible to tell.

But something in Killian's earlier statement tickled at Olivia's memories. She closed her eyes, trying to ignore the cacophony around her and chase the thought hovering on the edges of her mind. A black leather book. Embossed with her brother's initials. He kept it in his pocket and, as a boy, was always scribbling in it. Once, she found it left out in the parlour. In a fit of rebellion, she dared to open it. The carefully printed words scrawled over page after page chilled her blood and caused bile to rise in her throat.

It was a list of her brother's achievements. Some crimes she knew, and some were far worse than she ever would have guessed. Mementoes were pressed between the pages. Hair that matched the exact colour of the maid's. A ribbon Olivia tied around her cat's neck as a jaunty collar. A swatch of clothing stained with something rusty and brown. A human tooth. She had hastily shut the book and dropped it back on the table before her brother returned to the room. When he did return, he'd snatched it up, his cold gaze raking over Olivia as she pretended to ignore him and play with her doll. But she could never escape his notice.

He'd put the notebook in his pocket, walked over to her, and tried to rip the doll from her hands. When she'd fought him, he pinched her so hard on her arm, she had carried the bruise for a week. She had let go of the doll, and he pulled the head off. She never forgot his words, because he proved them true over and over again.

'There is nothing you have I can't take away.'

And then he had thrown the decapitated doll into the flames. She'd pressed her lips together, knowing to show him her pain would only embolden him. He'd turned and walked out of the parlour, whistling a nursery song as he went.

'His journal!' Olivia pulled herself from the chilling memory and jumped to her feet.

The entire group stopped talking at once and turned to face her.

Philippa cocked her head. The movement highlighted the dip of her clavicle, and Olivia imagined pressing a kiss in that sweet little hollow. 'What?'

Olivia forced herself to look at the other faces in the room, landing on Ivy's pale countenance. The lithe woman, who was as slender as she was strong, wore a dress of icy blue and shone like a beacon. She was Olivia's closest ally. If she could convince Ivy, the others would follow. 'Cedric had a journal as a child. He would write down all of the terrible things he did. Sometimes, he would press keepsakes between the pages like some terror-filled memory book.'

Commissioner Worthington put down his glass and stepped closer to Olivia. 'How do you know this?'

Olivia shrugged under the intense stare of the serious Commissioner, feeling like a child caught stealing sweets. His dark hair and piercing eyes made sweat break out on her upper lip. She had no idea how Ivy fell in love with the man after suffering through one of his interrogations. 'H-he left it out once. When we were children.'

'And you opened it?' Commissioner Worthington's face was hard lines and sharp planes. Olivia knew from past experience he was impervious to her charms, so she didn't attempt to use any of her usual tactics.

'I didn't know what it was, so yes. I opened it.' Throwing back her shoulders, she crossed her arms over her chest. She refused to feel guilty for looking at someone's private journal decades ago. Especially when that person was a cruel, unhinged, horror of a man. And her brother.

'What Edward is trying to say is that your curiosity is a very good thing.' Ivy took Olivia's cold hands in her warm ones and squeezed gently. Philippa slowly crossed the parlour, giving Edward an unreadable look as she paused next to where Ivy sat. Whatever message passed between them, Edward stepped away from the settee, giving the women space.

The duchess' index finger rubbed endlessly against her thumb. Amethysts dripped from her ears and were wrapped around her neck like a collar, but that delicate collarbone was bare and vulnerable.

Ivy smiled gently at Olivia, somehow sensing how much Olivia needed reassurance.

Because she knows what it's like to be related to a sadistic monster.

'Do you remember what you saw inside?'

Olivia focused on Ivy's question. 'It read like a journal. Each entry described something he'd done. What he would do differently the next time. What he liked. How he felt when it was happening.'

'What about the mementoes? You said there were things pressed into the pages,' Ivy prompted.

Olivia swallowed, feeling the weight of Philippa's gaze even if she refused to glance up and make eye contact.

Yes, Philippa. I'm still angry with you. For being an idiot.

'Some of the things were harmless. A scrap of clothing. A ribbon. But some were more gruesome. A tooth. Hair. Things like that.'

'Trophies.' Reading looked up from his ledger. His whisper of a moustache quivered as he looked at the Commissioner. 'We've seen it before. In rare cases.'

'But those were all cases of the mentally insane,' Edward responded.

'We're talking about the Lord High Chancellor. Second only to the bloody Queen of England. He couldn't possibly hide such madness.' Drake prowled in a tight line, turning to pace back to his wife.

'Or maybe his wealth, power, and position help him create darker shadows where he keeps his insanity cloaked.' Penny lifted her chin. Liam reached over to take her hand in his and squeeze.

'You're right, my love. A beggar on the streets might be labelled a lunatic while a duke is simply called eccentric.'

'Is it possible he would still keep a memory book?' Philippa directed her question at Olivia, but Olivia refused to return her frank stare. Instead, she focused on the fireplace and shrugged.

'I don't know. He has always been a man of habits. I think it's likely.'

Edward reclaimed his snifter of brandy and sipped it, his gaze returning to Olivia, assessing her carefully. 'If he is truly like the other men we investigated, then it's more than likely. Many of them obsessed over their trophies. Some showed more grief from losing their mementoes than they did when facing the hangman's noose.'

Millie stood and joined Ivy and Olivia. 'Dear God. And this man has your daughter?'

'He won't hurt her. Not until he can use it to his advantage.' Olivia knew him well enough to know this was true. It had to be, or she would go mad herself.

'I think you're right, Lady Smithwick.' Reading dipped his quill in a small pot of ink precariously balanced on the corner of the ledger. His calm words created a well of relief in Olivia. She didn't know the man, but to have any reassurance her daughter was safe was an invaluable gift. 'One of the common traits we found amongst the men was a need to plan their, er, escapades, meticulously. He won't make any moves until he is sure he can achieve his ultimate goal. Your daughter is safe, for now. I would bet Commissioner Worthington's life on it.'

'But not your own?' Edward raised his brow at his assistant.

'It's a compliment, sir. My life is hardly worth that of Scotland Yard's leader.' The thin man ignored his employer's glare.

Hannah tapped her muff pistol against her skirts with the same contemplative expression Reading held when tapping the feathered end of his quill against his cheek. 'We need to act soon. I propose a two-pronged attack. We take away his leverage while simultaneously securing the evidence we need to prove his guilt, unequivocally.'

Olivia admired the economy of movement in the small woman and held no doubt about her ability to fight with the same fierceness as any seasoned warrior.

'Of course. Brilliant plan. Why didn't I think of that? Take away his leverage and find irrefutable proof of his guilt, all in time for afternoon tea,' Drake muttered darkly. Millie elbowed him in his belly.

Killian sent his friend a withering glare before softening his features when he looked at his wife. 'What do you have in mind, darling?'

Hannah narrowed her eyes at Drake then turned back to the group. 'We need to draw him out. Once he is away from his house, we can search there for Hyacinth and stage a rescue. Surely that is where he keeps her.'

Olivia nodded. 'It makes the most sense. But he won't just allow us to come waltzing up to his house while he is away. He has access to the Queen's guard.

I'm sure there will be men all over the grounds and in the house. He'll tell the Queen and Hyacinth it's for her protection, but it's to ensure he doesn't lose his prize.'

'What if he brings Hyacinth to us?' Millie's wide smile exposed a dimple.

Drake exhaled through his nose. 'Why do I get the feeling I know where this is going, and I am not going to like it?'

'Because you know where it's going, and you aren't going to like it,' Liam quipped, earning a black glare from Drake.

'How do you propose we get the Lord High Chancellor to do that, Lady Drake?' Reading asked, his brows lifted in innocent inquiry.

'I'd wager I know.' Ivy shared a conspiratory smile with Millie. 'A ball.'

Drake groaned loudly.

'But Cedric doesn't attend balls. He only came to Worthington's gala because he was ensuring Percival didn't botch the plans to abduct the orphans. Thanks to Ivy's courage, he didn't succeed.' Guilt washed through Olivia at the memory of her part in Cedric's horrifying plans. 'Ivy, I can never express my true regret for not finding another way.' Olivia bowed her head, shame making it impossible to meet the eyes of anyone in the room.

Ivy's warm hand rubbed up and down her arm. 'Not another word, Olivia. We've already resolved this. In a similar situation, with no allies and no choices, any one of us would have done the same thing.'

Philippa lifted her chin a fraction. 'And now you have all of us, Olivia.'

I don't have you in any of the ways I want you, Philippa.

Because looking at the duchess in all her glory, Olivia could no longer deny the depths of her feelings. She wanted Philippa for more than just a moment. She wanted her forever.

Impossible.

But it didn't stop the yearning in her heart. Nor a small voice almost lost in the much louder self-doubt.

Why is it impossible? I survived the madhouse. I escaped the clutches of my brother. I convinced the entire beau monde to hold me in their capricious regard despite my reputation as a harlot. Why can't I woo the duchess?

She had no real answer. Because she could. And she bloody well would. She would save her daughter, destroy her brother, and win Philippa's heart. Damn anyone who tried to stop her. Including Philippa.

With that decided, she lifted her head and finally let her gaze meet the one pair of eyes she had been avoiding all night.

'All right. We're going to throw a ball that Cedric can't possibly refuse. Because it will be hosted by the Queen herself. And you are going to convince her to do it.' Olivia smiled triumphantly as Philippa blinked.

'Are you commanding me, Marchioness?' Philippa crossed her arms and tapped a finger against her sleeve like a cat twitching its tail. The entire room fell silent.

'It's about time someone did, Duchess.' It felt glorious to meet Philippa as an equal on the battlefield.

You have no idea how determined I can be, darling. But you're about to find out.

16

Philippa sat in her carriage in one of her best day dresses. It was an expertly tailored affair in royal blue with an overlay of layered organza in shades of shimmering emerald-green and black. Ingenious use of the eye of peacock feathers had been sewn onto the bodice. The colour enhanced her eyes and skin, and the cut drew attention to her figure. It was exactly what one wore when visiting the Queen, especially if one had the audacity to ask the leader of the United Kingdom to throw a soiree for All Hallow's Eve.

Philippa was rarely nervous, but she also wasn't in the habit of asking favours from her sovereign. Whether it was because of Victoria's love of the holiday, her longstanding relationship with the Duchess of Dorsett – Philippa wasn't bold enough to call it friendship – or perhaps because Victoria had been in a grand mood that day, the Queen had been delighted with the idea.

Samhain was only a fortnight away, but Victoria was undaunted. And why should she be? With endless money, manpower, and influence, it would be a lark to throw the biggest ball of the season with only two weeks to prepare. By the time Philippa left, the Queen was already ordering servants hither and thither to begin sending invitations. The High Lord Chancellor Hardgrave and his delightful niece would be amongst the revellers.

Philippa *might* have mentioned the poor young lady wasn't given a proper coming-out, and wouldn't this ball be a lovely time for Miss Hyacinth to make her debut in society? Surely the Lord High Chancellor would be thrilled at

Victoria's specific invitation to his niece, for there couldn't be a higher compliment paid to a young woman on the cusp of her adulthood.

During their entire discussion, Philippa watched for any signs illuminating the Queen's knowledge of Hardgrave's more nefarious activities or any indication where the monarch's loyalty might lie, but Victoria was Queen for a reason. She revealed nothing to Philippa that she didn't intend to show. Of this, Philippa was certain. And so, she left the palace confident Hardgrave would attend the ball with his niece, but less assured on whether Victoria was privy to – or even more troubling, approving of – his actions.

As she sat in the carriage, bumping over cobblestones for the short drive to Belgrave Square, she should have been congratulating herself on a successful mission or plotting the next step in their plan. But instead, she was thinking about Olivia.

I am always thinking about Olivia.

It was a problem she couldn't seem to solve. Even more troubling was who she had not been thinking of. Liza. A truth which filled Philippa with oily guilt. Liza had been the love of her life. The woman whom she had faithfully mourned for the past two decades. But ever since her night on the cliff, something had changed. It felt like Liza was slipping away from her, and instead of feeling hollow, Philippa felt lighter. Which was unacceptable.

On a whim, she stopped the carriage and had the driver change course.

Exiting the contraption before her footman could hop down and set the step, Philippa breezed up the stairs leading to the front entrance of 4 Whitehall Place. She wound through the corridors as Bobbies leapt out of her way. The Commissioner's office had once been the main bedchamber when 4 Whitehall Place was a home. Since it was converted into the Metropolitan Police Force's headquarters, it now housed Commissioner Worthington's very messy office. What would have been a small parlour for the lord of the house was Mr Reading's much neater workspace.

Hopefully, Edward is not out slavering over his new wife like some lovesick fool.

Philippa paused as her heart stuttered. Never in a million years did she think she would be able to forgive Edward Worthington for betraying her and revealing her love affair with his sister. Yet here she stood, her wasted husk of a heart full of joy just thinking about Edward's romance with Ivy Cavendale, a woman who vowed to remain single for all her days. But Ivy had met her match with Edward Worthington, and Philippa couldn't be happier. Both had found healing together and new life within each other's arms.

'But what of me?'

Indeed. Edward has been able to forgive himself and find his partner in life, but I have already found my partner and lost her. How can I possibly move forward with another woman?

Her chest squeezed painfully. Because it was equally impossible to ignore her growing feelings for Olivia.

I can't hold two opposing truths within one body without splitting apart entirely.

Philippa's thoughts tripped back to the day before. Pleasuring Olivia had been divine, but watching her stand up for herself in the parlour when the Damsels and their daring lords had convened was something else entirely.

I respect her. And damn it. I like her. Which is so much worse than being attracted to her. Everyone is attracted to her. The woman is a bloody siren. But how many know the human being living beneath all that beauty? The courageous mother fighting for her child. The terrified sister battling for freedom? The lonely woman aching for a true companion?

A corresponding pang of longing thrummed through Philippa. Shaking her head and pressing her lips together, she pushed through the door and didn't pause at Reading's desk as he dropped his quill and hurried to his feet.

'Your Grace. We weren't expecting... What a lovely dress you're wearing. Are those peacock feathers?'

'I've no time, Reading.' Yet she couldn't stop herself from pausing in a helpful beam of light coming from one of the dusty windows so the smartly attired assistant could better admire the details of her ensemble. Even in the midst of her turmoil, fashion must be given its due. 'And yes. They are.'

'Divine,' Reading breathed.

Philippa quite agreed. Her heart might be disintegrating one beat at a time, but at least she looked dashing.

She didn't have to open Worthington's door because the man did it for her. Standing in the frame, he took one look at Philippa and his eyes softened. A wave of emotion crashed over her, and she feared she might burst into tears in the middle of Scotland Yard. The sheer horror of such an unsightly display kept her emotions at bay.

Damn you for being able to read me like some penny dreadful.

He knew her too well. Better than anyone, for they had been children together, lost Liza together, and while once he dreamed of romance between them, now he loved her with the loyalty of a dear friend. And she desperately needed a friend, though she was loath to admit it. Especially to Edward.

'Please, come in and sit.' He stepped back, making room for her in his cluttered office.

She sniffed, looking for a clear surface. The desk was littered with papers. Several books were stacked haphazardly on the floor next to his seat. The hardback chair reserved for visitors held a leather satchel with its contents spilling onto the floor, a discarded scarf, and what looked to be the remains of half a pickle and pork sandwich wrapped in wax paper.

'I think I shall stand.' Philippa raised a brow and looked pointedly at the chair.

Edward's cheeks flushed red. He rushed to the seat, swiped the satchel and scarf off, and looked around for a place to put them, apparently deciding the overburdened bookshelf was his best option. He crammed both items into a convenient opening on the third shelf between a dusty tome on ancient Roman government and some medical treatise on death and decay.

Delightful.

Philippa picked up the sandwich by the wrapper. 'Saving this for afternoon tea?' She knew her tone was sharper than a sabre, but battling with Edward was so much easier than being vulnerable.

Edward snatched the sandwich and plunked it on top of a ledger on his desk. 'To what do I owe this unexpected pleasure?' His emphasis on 'unexpected' was not lost on Philippa.

Exhaling a breath she hadn't known she was holding, Philippa felt her protective layer of pride deflate right along with her false bravado. 'Am I terrible, Edward?' She forced the words out before she could think about what she was revealing. The Duchess of Dorsett, confidante of the Queen, femme fatale, fiercely independent warrior, was actually full of self-doubt. It was beyond the pale and hardly something she wanted to admit.

Sinking onto the chair, Philippa couldn't look her oldest friend in the eyes for fear of what he might see there.

Edward crouched next to her, gathering her hands in his and squeezing. 'No. You are the very opposite. What's brought this on?'

'I'm forgetting her. How can I forget her?' She didn't have to speak Liza's name. She knew Edward would understand. Which is why she came to him and not one of the other women. Because of their shared grief. He was the only other person alive who knew Liza, loved Liza, and had lost Liza.

The tears came unbidden as Philippa tried to swallow the panic and pain. Edward leaned forward, pulled Philippa into an awkward hug, and to her horror, she clung to him like a child as her body shook with silent sobs. They stayed that way until she was able to slow her breathing and ease her grip on his coat sleeves.

Edward leaned back, searching in his pocket for a handkerchief. He found it, and while it was terribly wrinkled, it was also clean. Philippa dabbed at her face. She must look a total fright. Pressing her lips together, she tried to gather her thoughts as Edward waited patiently.

'I used to think about her all the time. For years and years, I would wake with her name on my lips and sleep with her face haunting my dreams. But it's all changing; it feels like she's disappearing, and I don't know how to keep her here.' She thumped her chest with her fist.

Edward took a measured breath. She knew he was trying to weigh his words so as not to upset her.

'Just say what you need to say, Edward. We are past being careful with one another.'

Shaking his head, Edward's lips twitched in a wry smile. 'One is always careful with a woman as dangerous as you, Philippa. But fine. I will speak plainly.'

'Please.' Philippa nodded.

'It is not for you to keep her trapped in your heart, nor should you stay entombed in your memories of her.'

Anger swept in, a complement to her pain. 'I haven't trapped her there.'

Edward's jaw hardened. 'You have. And you've buried yourself away with her, shutting down any chance for new life. New growth. New love. Because you know the pain of loving someone with every part of your being and then losing them, and you are too scared to face that possibility again.'

He's right. Damn him to the Devil, he's right and he knows it. Smug bastard.

Philippa blinked, swallowed, then tapped a finger against the arm of the chair. 'I am not scared.' But she was. 'And there is no shame in protecting yourself.'

Edward shook his head. 'No. But there is also no chance of happiness when protecting yourself also means living in isolation. You aren't forgetting Liza. It's not possible. You are just letting her go, Philippa.'

Fear washed through her. 'But I don't *want* to let her go.'

A dry chuckle escaped as Edward reclaimed Philippa's hand and squeezed gently. 'No. Because keeping her is a convenient excuse to stay safe within your grief. But you have never been a coward, Philippa. Letting Liza go is scary, yes. But it isn't a bad thing, and it certainly doesn't make you a terrible person. It's necessary. Because she isn't here any more.' His voice broke and hearing his pain helped her to acknowledge her own. 'You are holding onto a memory that has you frozen in the past. And it's time to step into your present. She would want that for you.'

Philippa shook her head, rejecting his words even as they resonated in her heart. 'What if I can't?'

Edward rocked back on his heels. His handsome face broke into a smile. 'Is there anything the Duchess of Dorsett cannot do? Surely not.'

'The duchess isn't real, Edward.'

He brushed a tear from her cheek that she'd missed. His dark eyes burned with fierce emotion. Love. Respect. Empathy. 'No. But Philippa is real, and she has never let fear of the unknown stop her. I didn't think I deserved love after what I did to you and Liza. But I was wrong, and Ivy is the greatest blessing in my life. I know this is a novel experience for you, Philippa, but you are also wrong.'

Philippa pulled back. She hated being wrong. Admitting her own fallibility was her least favourite thing. It was much easier to be right all the time. Except, perhaps, for now. Which was alarming in the extreme. Not only was she blubbering like a ninny; she might also have to admit she wasn't perfect. Madness.

'Excuse me?' She did her best to regain the archness that kept everyone at arm's length. Except Edward. And Olivia. And the Damsels.

Damn. I'm slipping.

Edward stood, walked to his desk, and leaned a hip against it. A paper-weight fell to the floor with a dull thunk. 'You loved Liza. And she loved you. But you are wrong to believe Liza was your *only* chance at love. Your time with her will never be replaced by another, and your love for her will never be tarnished by another. But you can't live in memories, Philippa. It doesn't work that way. Love is not a pie with a certain number of slices. It is a stream with infinite tributaries. The river wants to take you on new adventures, if you are brave enough to let go.'

This has nothing to do with love. I'm attracted to Olivia. I respect her. I like her. I find myself increasingly amenable to spending as much time with her as possible, but that hardly means...

Hellfire.

I do love her.

Her mind recoiled from such a shattering revelation to refocus on criticising Edward. Because that, at least, was manageable. 'That was a terribly mixed metaphor. Pies and rivers. Really.' But his message was no less powerful because of it. Not that she would ever admit such to him. It was bad enough she cried in front of the man. And nearly conceded she was wrong. Dear lord. If he dared share this with anyone, she would be forced to kill him.

'Liza released me from our promises to each other. The last letter she wrote to me, before she went to the asylum. She told me to let her go.' Philippa hadn't planned on sharing that with Edward, but once she spoke the words, she couldn't call them back.

Edward blinked several times. 'Oh?'

'She told me she loved me, and she released me.'

Clearing his throat, Edward's voice was suspiciously husky. 'She wanted the best for both of us. Even if she couldn't have a full life herself, she wanted that for us.' His chin quivered, and Philippa felt marginally better that she wasn't the only one having an emotional breakdown. 'I think the best way to honour her, what she meant to us, is to live life to its fullest, Philippa. Even if it is painful at times. Even if it is frightening.'

Philippa felt something crack around her chest and fall away, like chains being snapped free. She filled her lungs completely for the first time in nearly twenty years. The ache of Liza's absence was not gone. It would never be gone. But there was room in her heart for something new, if she was brave enough to claim it.

'If you tell anyone of this conversation or my emotional lapse, I will eviscerate you and turn your entrails into a necklace for my next gown.'

Edward scrunched his face. 'I very much doubt that would look good. Not even on you, Philippa. And the smell would be ghastly.'

Philippa shrugged. 'Fashion is a fickle thing, Edward. You never know what will be the next craze sweeping through the beau monde.' She stood and looked around his cluttered office for a mirror. Surely amidst all the detritus, there would be one looking glass. There was not.

'You look fine, Philippa.'

She turned to glare at him. 'Fine? Are you trying to insult me?'

Edward chuckled. 'I wouldn't dare. I care too much about my entrails.'

'Fine might be acceptable for the Commissioner of Scotland Yard, but it will hardly do for the Duchess of Dorsett.' Turning, she opened his door. 'Reading, have you a looking glass?'

Reading rushed into the room with one in each hand. 'Of course, Your Grace. And I have a full-length mirror in the other room if needed.'

'Well, at least someone is prepared.' She gave Edward a dry look, her equilibrium somewhat restored, even if she had no idea what to do with her new revelations.

Could she pursue Olivia? Was she brave enough to risk her heart once more? Would Olivia even accept her suit? For a woman who spent most of her life knowing exactly what she wanted, and exactly how she meant to get it, Philippa found herself bumping down love's river of adventure with nary a raft in sight.

17

Olivia stood in the centre of Philippa's grand ballroom wearing a day dress in the lightest shade of rose. Her hair fell around her in a wild tangle of curls, her face was warm from exertion, and sweat trickled down her right leg, tickling the sensitive skin behind her knee.

'If you wished to torture me, I'm sure we could find a rack somewhere that I will happily chain myself to if it means we can stop.' Olivia glared at her nemesis standing opposite her.

Philippa was resplendent in a dark-blue dress, deceptively simple in design. The clean lines and lack of her signature jewels only highlighted the duchess' figure, drawing Olivia's eyes to her full breasts, frustratingly hidden from view behind a row of black onyx buttons running down the front of her bodice. It didn't help that she looked as cool and calm as any lady might when enjoying a cup of tea at an afternoon visit with friends.

'If torture were my aim, trust me, you would know. You cannot fight with your anger. Battles are won here first.' Philippa tapped a finger against her temple.

'Then cease provoking me,' Olivia hissed, stepping back with her right foot into the fighting stance Philippa had taught her.

They had spent the last week practising daily. From the frightful hours of ten in the morning until two in the afternoon, Philippa schooled Olivia in shooting pistols, throwing knives, duelling with swords, and hand-to-hand combat. It quickly became apparent Olivia was dreadful at all of it. But still, Philippa was relentless. She insisted Olivia needed to learn how to defend herself if they were going to take on her brother.

'I will not allow you to be a liability for the rest of us,' were her exact words. Hardly flattering, even if they were true.

But she is right. I will not be the weak link in this chain of warriors.

Clearing her mind of swirling thoughts, she exhaled and focused on pushing volatile emotions out of her chest until she was completely calm.

'You are not as hopeless as you think, Olivia. You just let feelings get the better of you.' Philippa circled around Olivia, forcing her to pivot as she tracked the duchess. But she left Olivia a small opening. Acting on instinct, Olivia sprang forward, tackling her low around the waist. They crashed to the floor in a heap of skirts, tangled limbs, and loose hair, but Olivia was on top, giving her an advantage. She blocked the wild swing Philippa tried to deliver and caught one wrist, then the other, pinning both next to Philippa's head. Sitting low on Philippa's pelvis, she smiled triumphantly. 'I suppose I'm not so hopeless after all. Even with all my uncontrolled emotions.'

Philippa struggled against her hold, but Olivia tightened her knees around Philippa's hips, holding her in place. The duchess' skirts made it impossible for her to use her legs to any advantage.

'Fine. This round goes to you. Now kindly get off.' Philippa spoke through clenched teeth as she bucked her hips, attempting to displace Olivia. But she had been listening to the lessons Philippa delivered and she was ready. Hunkering lower, her blonde curls fell loose, creating a curtain around their faces. They were both breathing hard, and Olivia was acutely aware of Philippa's lithe body undulating beneath her, creating delicious friction against her core.

'No. I don't think I will.' Olivia leaned closer and ran her nose from Philippa's jaw to her ear, inhaling sweet jasmine and spicy frankincense. 'I do have trouble controlling my emotions around you, Duchess, no matter how hard I try.' She whispered the words into Philippa's ear before sucking the lobe into her mouth and biting hard enough to stun the duchess into stillness. 'I find myself wondering what might happen if I stopped trying.' She nuzzled the soft skin just under Philippa's jaw and pressed a kiss where the duchess' pulse beat madly before sucking hard enough to leave a mark.

'I've not seen these fighting tactics before.' Philippa's husky voice urged

Olivia onward. Philippa shifted her hips, no longer trying to escape, but instead making space for Olivia's thigh to nestle between her legs. Olivia bent her knee, pressing into the heat she could feel through Philippa's layers of silk and crinoline. Philippa had taken control of their lovemaking last time. Now it was Olivia's turn. She couldn't admit the depths of her affection for Philippa. Not yet. But she could show the duchess exactly how much she wanted her.

'I've no wish to fight you, Philippa.' Olivia nibbled her way up the elegant column of Philippa's throat, nipping her chin before she paused, her lips a breath away from Philippa's. 'I want to give you the same pleasure you gave me. Will you let me? Will you let go?'

Philippa's body hardened. 'Let go?' Panic filled her blue gaze.

Olivia wasn't sure what her question meant to Philippa, but she knew she was treading on very delicate ground. 'Of your need to be in control. Can you let go and trust me to take care of you?'

Philippa exhaled, the tension in her softening, but Olivia's curiosity was piqued.

What did you think I was asking? What has you so scared, Philippa?

'I don't need anyone to take care of me.' Philippa tried to pull her wrists free from Olivia's grip, but she wasn't giving up so easily. She tightened her fingers, refusing to grant Philippa freedom.

'You don't need me to, but do you want me to?' Olivia raised her brow and waited.

Philippa swallowed, her gaze flicking from Olivia's eyes to her lips and back again.

'Or are you too frightened?' If nothing else would convince the stubborn woman, surely she could provoke Philippa by questioning her courage.

'I'm not scared of you.'

'Prove it.' Olivia bent her head and pressed her mouth against Philippa's, teasing the seam of her lips, waiting for the duchess to open.

Let me in, sweet woman.

Philippa's body softened as her lips parted. Olivia plunged, triumph singing through her blood as she tasted the heady flavour unique to Philippa. Stronger than any whiskey and just as intoxicating.

'Keep your hands where they are,' she demanded between kisses as she released Philippa's wrists and slid her hands down her toned arms, following the curve of her high neckline. 'I dislike the cut of this dress.' Clever fingers expertly worked at the onyx buttons until half of them were undone, and the tops of Philippa's glorious breasts were exposed. Her pale skin glowed in contrast to the dark material.

'Shall I inform Delacroix of your preferences?' Philippa arched a brow, but her uneven breaths and the colour riding high on her cheeks belied the cool words.

Olivia didn't answer. Her attention was focused elsewhere as she traced the lace-lined edge of the fine silk chemise covering Philippa's dark-cherry nipples. She wore an under-bust corset, pushing her breasts up while leaving them deliciously exposed. Instead of pulling down the silk, Olivia stretched it tight. Philippa's budded nipple pressed against the nearly transparent fabric and Olivia bent forward, licking through the material, catching the tip of her breast between her teeth, knowing the silk would dull the bite. Philippa cried out, her hips bucking, but Olivia gave her no quarter, nibbling, sucking, laving the sweet tip until she knew it ached, and then blowing on the wet silk. She sat back to admire her work. The fine material was now completely translucent. Philippa's nipple, dark, swollen and puckered, was somehow more erotic covered in wet silk than nothing at all. Philippa's cheeks were pink, her glorious hair in disarray as she thrashed her head from one side to another, her eyes closed, her wrists still by her head. Knowing they could be discovered at any moment added another thrill. This was forbidden. Naughty. And insanely arousing.

'I wonder if I can make you climax just from this,' Olivia mused, bending to the other breast and administering equal attention until Philippa cried out, her body tensing. Her legs clamped around Olivia's knee. She knew what she would find under the duchess' skirts. Her cleft would be wet and swollen. Needy still, even after one climax. Because a woman's body could reach that shining pinnacle again and again. Each time more intense than the last. And Olivia wanted to see how high she could take the duchess before she finally flew.

'That was... I haven't ever come just from...' Philippa's hands were in Olivia's hair, tugging her away.

Olivia sat back and caught Philippa's wrists once more. 'Oh no. We aren't done yet. I'm just starting.' She put her hands back over her head. 'Don't move, Duchess. Or I'll stop.'

Trailing her hands on either side of Philippa's cheeks, she smiled at the always controlled woman's look of dazed confusion. 'But I already climaxed.'

'Once. Yes. But once is never enough with you. I want to see you come apart again.'

Philippa shook her head. 'What about you?'

'Don't worry about me. I'm perfectly content.' Olivia trailed her fingers to the wet silk, roughly pulling down the material and feasting her eyes on Philippa's naked breasts. She brushed her thumbs over the reddened tips and revelled in Philippa's gasp. 'So sweet. You are so beautiful.'

Philippa bit her lip as a flush covered her pale skin. If Olivia wasn't already falling, this moment would have sealed her fate.

The duchess is shy. And no one gets to see her like this except me.

It was a gift she would always treasure.

Pressing soft kisses against each nipple, she continued her journey south, knowing one day, she would strip Philippa bare and worship every inch of her naked skin. But today, she would be content with this. Gathering Philippa's skirts, she pulled them up her long legs, loving the contrast of black leather boots against pale, muscled calves. When they were bunched around her waist, Olivia let her gaze take in the glory. A dagger was tied high on Philippa's thigh, and Olivia's clitoris pulsed at the contrast of deadly steel pressed against such vulnerable skin. She flicked her thumb over the sharp edge. 'I suppose I shall have to be careful.'

'Very careful indeed.' But Philippa wasn't talking about her dagger, and Olivia's heart cracked even wider.

'People sometimes forget how delicate a strong woman can be. I won't forget. Ever.'

Philippa tipped her chin, granting Olivia permission.

Olivia held Philippa's heavy-lidded gaze for a moment, acknowledging her submission before dropping her view between Philippa's thighs to the dark thatch of hair covering her vulnerable centre. Pink lips peeked from their secret cove, glistening with Philippa's sweet essence. Olivia's nipples tightened as her channel clenched. She pulled up her own skirts, exposing herself to Philippa's gaze as she boldly rubbed the aching bud demanding friction. Philippa's eyes widened, her pupils blown.

'My God, Olivia.' Her husky voice spurred Olivia onward. She worked herself with one hand while the other stroked Philippa's inner thigh until she found her slit, wet and waiting. Slipping a finger into her tight opening, she coated herself with Philippa's nectar and lifted her finger to her lips, savouring the taste as she continued to stroke herself, knowing the sight was only fuelling Philippa's need.

Philippa started to move her hand, but Olivia's sharp look stopped her.

She shook her head and tsked. 'Naughty girl. Put your hands back or I shall stop.' Adding weight to her threat, she started to let her skirts fall back into place, but Philippa immediately returned her hands over her head.

To wield such power over a woman whom no one controlled was exhilarating. Olivia pulled her dress up again and continued her decadent task of self-pleasure. 'Well done.' She traced back along Philippa's silky skin, dipping one finger into the duchess' channel, then another, finally a third. As she swirled her middle finger around her own clitoris, she pressed her thumb against Philippa's, sliding in a slippery circle. Curling the fingers embedded in Philippa's body, she coaxed the duchess higher. When she found a rhythm that made Philippa's breath come in halting moans, Olivia nearly lost control of her own pleasure, but she clenched her teeth and held off as her fingers plunged and plundered, her thumb continuing its unrelenting circles. Philippa held her breath and Olivia knew she was close. She curled her fingers harder, pressing down with her thumb as her own climax rippled through her. Philippa cried out as Olivia let herself shatter, knowing she wasn't alone. They broke together, fragments of their hearts fusing into each other until Olivia couldn't determine where she ended and Philippa began.

* * *

Philippa came back to herself in slow degrees. As she did, certain truths crystallised. She was irrevocably in love with Olivia. She was also completely at a loss as to what she should do about this. With Liza, it had been so easy. They had been friends since childhood, and their deep affection seamlessly transitioned into romance with no risk of rejection. But her love for Olivia was nothing like her love for Liza. Which was a revelation.

Damnation. Edward was right. Love is not a pie. Remarkable.

Because she wasn't taking her love from Liza and giving it to Olivia. This was something entirely new. Something only Olivia could inspire within Philippa. It was uniquely theirs.

Olivia had righted her clothes. She wore the smile of someone who knew their own power, and Philippa found herself warming all over again. Nothing was more desirable than a confident woman.

'You look quite proud of yourself.' She refocused on her own clothing, rebuttoning her gown over her still-wet shift. The memory of what Olivia had done to her breasts was enough to make her fingers stall and her nipples tingle.

'I am. I believe this bout goes to me.' Olivia lifted her hands over her head in an exaggerated stretch. 'I think I'm finally starting to get the hang of physical combat.'

Not able to stop the snort of laughter, Philippa regained her feet and brushed out her irrevocably wrinkled skirt. 'I certainly hope you don't plan on engaging the enemy quite like that.'

Olivia's face grew serious. 'No. Just you.'

Before Philippa could think of a response, a smart knock sounded, followed immediately by Stokes opening the door. The insufferable man didn't wait to be called in, and Philippa arched her brow at him, wishing for a rapier.

'Has your senility reached a level where you've forgotten a servant waits to be admitted into a room? What if we were engaged in something scandalous?' She glanced at Olivia and fought a smile.

Stokes exhaled through his nose. 'Your Grace has yet to shock me, despite the many scandals I've seen, swordplay and fisticuffs notwithstanding. I doubt that will change now.'

Philippa blinked.

Surely he's not giving me permission to engage in scandal. As if I need his approval. A duchess does not seek the permission of her butler.

Stokes straightened his military spine even further. She was certain she heard it crick in the quiet room. 'I thought you might wish to see this rather urgently.' He stepped closer, holding a silver tray in front of him bearing an envelope with the seal displayed. Philippa didn't need to look at the writing to know who sent the missive.

This letter didn't carry the distinctive head of a crow, body of a wolf, and tail of a snake. Instead, it bore the crest of the Lord High Chancellor. Yet they both knew the leader of the Devil's Sons was sending a message.

Philippa plucked the note from the tray as one might pick up a dirty sock. 'Ah. A letter from your brother. How lovely.'

Olivia's flushed cheeks paled, and her eyes grew wide with fear. Just for that, Philippa wished to eviscerate the Lord High Chancellor with a very dull butter knife.

'Shall I have the cook prepare some tea and sandwiches?' Stokes asked helpfully. Which was something the man had never been in all the years Philippa knew him. 'I shall bring them to the front parlour, Lady Winterbourne, as I'm sure the two of you will be more comfortable there.' He had also never cared a whit about her comfort.

She raised an eyebrow at him and wondered if he planned to put more than just whiskey in her tea. Perhaps a dram of hemlock.

'That would be lovely, Stokes. Thank you so much.' Olivia seemed to have collected herself and sent the butler a warm smile.

Stokes turned a shade of pink more likely to be found on the frock of a young miss than the complexion of a staid butler.

Is Stokes blushing? What the Devil is going on here?

'Of course, Lady Smithwick.' Stokes tucked the silver platter under his arm, nodded to Olivia, turned, and swiftly left the ballroom.

'What have you done to my butler?' Philippa knew they should be looking at the note, but certain mysteries required immediate solving.

Olivia shrugged. 'Nothing. He came into the library the other day to bring me tea, and we chatted for a moment, that was all. He isn't nearly as terrible as you make out. Did you know he's an avid fan of penny dreadfuls? We had a delightful discussion on whether *Varney the Vampire* or *The String of Pearls* had a better antagonist. I'm more partial to Sir Francis, but Stokes liked Sweeney Todd. I suppose it's a matter of blood or flesh.' Olivia's eyes strayed to Philippa's neck before she blinked back into focus and looked at the note. 'I suppose we should open that. God. I hate how frightened I am of a bloody piece of paper. Hardly Damsel material, am I?'

Philippa couldn't answer. Not without revealing more than she wished. Because Olivia was far more than just a worthy candidate for becoming one of the Queen's Deadly Damsels. She was the only woman Philippa could imagine spending the remainder of her days with. But blurting out her undying love for Olivia while discussing a threatening letter from her brother, the Lord High Chancellor of England, who coincidentally led the most insidious ring of sex traffickers in London and was also keeping Olivia's daughter hostage, hardly seemed ideal timing. She would wait until the mess with Lord High

Chancellor Hardgrave was sorted. Then she would declare her love for Olivia. Hopefully cosied up in front of a roaring fire with whiskey in their hands. Naked. A much better scenario.

'There is no shame in being frightened. What's more important is what you do in spite of your fear.' Philippa wanted to pull Olivia close and hug her tightly. Instead, she flicked open the note and read it. With each word, her anger increased.

'What did he say?' Olivia's voice was taut with anxiety.

Philippa handed it to her. 'Read it.'

Olivia's eyes darted over the words.

'He's demanding you hand me over. Oh, God. If you don't, he says he will be forced to inform the Queen that the Duchess of Dorsett is harbouring a fugitive to the Crown. Philippa, he'll destroy you.' Olivia's face crumpled. 'He's doing this because you went to Victoria. He must know we are planning something at the ball, and he is trying to force your hand.'

'Mad men are often also geniuses of a kind. We should have expected him to retaliate. I underestimated him.' Philippa tapped her finger against her lip, thinking of their options.

Olivia handed the letter back to Philippa. 'You must do as he asks, Philippa.'

Philippa recoiled at the very idea. A duchess did not cave to the demands of anyone. Certainly not this insidious bastard. 'Acquiescing to a bully only makes him bolder.'

Olivia shook her head, her hair falling around her face in disarray. 'You don't understand, Philippa. He won't stop until he gets what he wants. To defy him puts Hyacinth at risk. He has me exactly where he wants me. Powerless.' Olivia swayed on her feet, and Philippa feared she might faint. 'We must do as he demands. I'm not worth ruining your reputation. I'm certainly not worth the life of my daughter. If we do as he asks, mayhap he will promise to keep Hyacinth safe.'

Philippa gripped her shoulders and squeezed, holding her steady and meeting her stricken gaze. 'Men like your brother never keep their promises, Olivia. You know this. But I keep mine. I promised I would get your daughter and bring her to you, safe and well. I asked you to trust me before, and you said you would. Does that still hold true?' She held her breath, waiting.

Olivia blinked, a tear breaking free and tracking down her cheek. 'Yes. I do. Of course I do, but Philippa, if we fail...'

Philippa pulled her close and pressed a kiss to her mouth. 'We won't. We can't.' She held onto her rage with tenuous control, not wanting to frighten Olivia further. How dare this man threaten her woman? How dare he make someone as fascinating, powerful, and important as Olivia feel insignificant? She would rip his throat open and bathe in his blood.

Pulling away, she forced her lips to curl in a smile she feared was more feral than friendly. 'Come, let us enjoy our tea and discuss how best to move forward.'

She nearly reached for Olivia's hand. She had to clutch her skirts to stop from doing so as she turned and led them out of the ballroom. There would be time for tenderness when the Crow was caught. For now, the duchess needed to keep her armour strong and her blades sharp.

18

Callum joined them for afternoon tea. The young man was twitchy and restless with little to occupy his time in the city. When he found out about the note, his face darkened with rage.

'We won't give in to him, will we? Handing over Lady Smithwick only gives him all the control.'

'But not agreeing to his demands puts Hyacinth at risk.' Olivia's fear ratcheted higher. She had promised to trust Philippa, and she did, but she couldn't see a way forward.

'I will reply to his message and meet with him alone.'

Olivia and Callum spoke at the same time.

'No.'

'Absolutely not.'

Philippa's eyes flashed. 'You cannot join me. Olivia, you must know it's impossible for you to be part of this meeting and Callum, you would only be in the way.'

The young man reddened at such an insult, but he remained silent as Philippa stared at him.

Philippa was right, but Olivia hated the idea of her love meeting with her brother alone. The man was diabolical. She couldn't bear the thought of losing her daughter, but nor could she imagine life without Philippa. No longer was she thinking about escaping the continent when they rescued Hyacinth. How could she possibly leave the one woman whom she could no longer deny held her heart?

'Will you at least promise to meet with him in a public place? He is mad, but not enough to risk hurting you in front of witnesses.'

Philippa nodded her assent. 'I will send a response immediately. Trust me, Olivia. I won't say anything that might put Hyacinth at risk. I swear it.'

Olivia wasn't sure she could maintain her composure. If she could not confront her brother, she knew Philippa was the best alternative. She trusted her with all of her heart, including the piece belonging to Hyacinth. This was hardly the time to declare her undying love for the duchess, but she certainly wished she could.

First, they needed to plan a response to her brother that wouldn't send him into a rage. Once they were assured Hyacinth was safe and Cedric no longer posed a threat to them, or any other person, then she would take Philippa's hand, press a kiss to the palm, and convince the stubborn woman to open her heart and her life to Olivia.

Save my daughter, catch the Crow, win a duchess, and live happily ever after. What could be simpler?

A great many things. Like finding the cure for smallpox. Discovering the mysteries of the cosmos. Understanding why it was currently fashionable to look like one was dying of consumption. Olivia took a long sip of her tea and marvelled at how whiskey really did make a remarkable improvement to the drink.

After drafting and sending a reply to Cedric, it was decided they would invite the entire group of Damsels, their spouses, and Reading to yet another dinner to update them and determine how best to move forward with their plans.

Olivia volunteered to inform Stokes of the dinner party and while the man pressed his lips together in a tight line, he kept any remarks to himself in Olivia's presence.

It would have been a wonderful evening of fine food, fabulous company, witty conversation, and stimulating company if Olivia had been able to focus on anything other than rescuing Hyacinth. But she reminded herself they were one step closer to getting her back.

And then what? How can I possibly entertain ideas of a life with Philippa? What might that even look like? Sapphic love might not be illegal, but it is certainly not allowed in polite society... or any other kind of society.

But there were ways if two women wanted to live together. Countless spinsters shared a home and much more with a female companion. Passionate friendships amongst ladies in the beau monde were more than just encouraged. It was an ideal of femininity. Women's gentle, loving nature demonstrated in the affection they showed their female friends. Men found the whole thing rather endearing, and of course, there was nothing sexual in the love a woman might feel for another woman, so it was completely harmless.

Olivia almost choked on her wine as she reflected on exactly how unsexual her love for Philippa had been in the ballroom. Society was full of idiots. Although these beliefs made it possible for women to hide love affairs in plain sight. It was much more difficult for men, and the consequences more severe. They could face prison or even death. Yet still, a concerned father, husband, or brother could commit any woman into an asylum for immoral acts. Neither Philippa nor Olivia had any men to worry about controlling them, but the beau monde was its own kind of keeper for women with their pedigree. She shook her head. Humans had the capacity for such cruelty toward each other for no reason other than a need to control. Which brought her thoughts right back to her brother.

'What was your response to his letter?' Millie asked Philippa, pausing to lick a spot of chocolate from her fork and capturing her husband's attention without even noticing.

Philippa glanced at Olivia before responding. 'I invited him to join me at Twinings for tea tomorrow afternoon.'

'I doubt they make tea the way you prefer it.' Hannah sent Philippa a sly smile before continuing. 'Choosing a public location was wise. Perhaps Killian and I should join you.'

'We are free tomorrow afternoon.' Penny looked to Liam, who nodded his agreement.

'As are we,' Ivy agreed. 'We've sent the children to Edward's country house until this mess is sorted out, so we have nothing but time.' She smiled at her husband. The handsome Commissioner winked at her from across the table.

'Drake, we have no plans, do we? I would love a cup of tea at Twinings.' The voluptuous redhead revealed her dimples and a gleam of adventure in her gaze.

'Nothing would please me more.' Drake's rough voice softened as he returned his wife's smile, the expression far more fearsome on his scarred face. 'Hardgrave needs to understand he doesn't just threaten Olivia. If he wishes to wage war, we are happy to oblige him.'

Olivia shook her head. While the show of solidarity was more than she could have hoped for, alarm bells rang in her head, drowning out the flow of voices.

'No!' She was too loud, too panicked, but they needed to understand how dangerous her brother could be when he didn't get what he wanted. 'Such a show of force would reveal too much of our hand. If he feels threatened, he will react... poorly. People will be hurt. You must understand, he is relentless in his pursuits.' She pushed aside a particularly bad memory when she once tried to stand up to her brother as a child. Her hand still carried the scar from the candle he held over it until her screams alerted the governess.

Philippa sat at the head of the table. She had placed Olivia to her right. Shifting in her chair, she reached across the space separating them, taking Olivia's hand in her own and squeezing gently. All conversation immediately ceased.

Olivia felt the tension tighten as Philippa stiffened, realising what she'd done. She withdrew her hand, and something cracked in Olivia's chest. Perhaps it was the fragile bubble of hope that had been growing there. Hope that there might be a future for her with the woman she loved. But it was an impossible dream if Philippa couldn't even hold Olivia's hand in front of her closest friends.

Olivia knew Philippa was attracted to her. That was clear in the time they had spent in each other's arms. It was obvious every time Philippa's eyes darkened with need when Olivia walked into the room, or how her breath quickened as Olivia pressed a kiss to her warm skin. But attraction was easy. Devotion was hard. Commitment, respect, dedication. Those emotions took strength and valour to sustain. And while Olivia did not doubt Philippa's power in battle, she wasn't convinced the duchess would ever have the courage to fight for love again.

Pushing down the hurt, she embraced anger instead.

Philippa rubbed her finger against her thumb. The duchess was irritated, no doubt because she had been caught expressing something she didn't want anyone else to see.

Good. I'm glad.

Looking at each member of the table, Philippa's blue eyes flashed in the candlelight, but she said nothing.

'Shall we call in the dessert course?' Hannah asked brightly. The woman who was once Philippa's ward no doubt knew her patroness better than most at the table. What did she think of Philippa's slip? Not that it mattered.

Olivia stood first. 'I suddenly feel ill. Probably the stress of the day. Thank you all for such a lovely evening, but I must retire.' She refused to even look at Philippa as the rest of the party expressed their hope that she would feel better and wished her a good night. Olivia held her head high as she exited the dining room, took the stairs to the family bedrooms, and walked down the hall, opening her door and closing it softly behind her. Only then did she let the tears fall as she slumped against the wall, a doll who had lost her stuffing.

'Stupid, bloody fool!' But she didn't know if she was talking about herself or Philippa. Most likely, both of them.

Her maid came a few minutes later with a pot of willow bark tea. 'Her Grace asked me to bring this to you.'

Olivia wished 'Her Grace' had come with the tea herself so Olivia might throw the concoction back in Philippa's face. But she could hardly subject the innocent maid to such a tirade.

'I don't need any tea. Thank you.'

The young woman's eyes softened. 'Of course, Lady Smithwick. I hope it's not out of turn for me to say, but we're all so glad you're here.'

Her kindness was too much. Tears threatened once more as Olivia's throat ached. 'Thank you.'

The maid bustled around, lighting the fire, pulling back Olivia's bed. She helped her remove her evening gown, take down her hair, brush and braid the thick curls, and slip into a voluminous nightgown that made Olivia feel like a little girl. Thanking the maid, she dismissed her for the evening, scrubbed her teeth with powder of charcoal and baking soda, blew out the candle, and climbed into bed. The faint sounds of voices below reminded her that Philippa was still entertaining her guests. A group of people who were closer to family than just mere friends.

But not my family. They are hers. And when I leave, they will still be here to surround her with love and support. And I will be alone once more.

Feeling sorry for herself never accomplished anything, so Olivia only allowed a few tears to fall before she sniffed and snuggled deeper into her covers.

If they were able to defeat her brother, she wouldn't need to leave the continent, but she certainly had no wish to stay in London. Attending balls and watching Philippa from afar like a lovesick fool held no appeal. When her husband died, he had left her a dowager house in Covington. She could take Hyacinth there and spend her days in bucolic fields of grazing sheep, nursing her broken heart in privacy.

Dear lord, I'm dramatic. Perhaps I shall write some epic verse or Gothic novels to while away my time.

It didn't matter. She would have Hyacinth and her freedom. It was far more than most women ever received, and it would need to be enough. Damn her heart for being so greedy as to want everything.

She drifted to sleep and dreamed of striding along grassy fields. But in her dreams, she wasn't alone. A dark-haired figure walked with her, their hands clasped. Their skirts tangling together in the wind.

* * *

'It would seem this mission has brought you and Olivia together. I'm so glad you were able to get over your dislike of her.' Hannah sat next to Philippa as they transitioned from the dining room into the parlour. She spoke loud enough for the group to hear, and Philippa tightened her hand into a fist and reminded herself of all the reasons it was wrong to punch one's friend in the face, unless they were sparring, of course. Thankfully, young Callum had excused himself, so at least he would not be privy to the conversation.

'I didn't dislike her. I just didn't trust her. And for good reason, might I add.' Philippa endeavoured to keep her voice calm.

'But you trust her now?' Ivy asked, her crystal-blue gaze pinning Philippa to the cushions in a look Philippa was excellent at giving herself. She was less enthusiastic about being the recipient.

'I believe her motives were inspired by love for her daughter and fear she might lose her. She may have acted less than honourably, but her intentions were pure.' Indeed, Philippa more than trusted Olivia. She respected her. Liked her. Loved her. But that was hardly the business of her inquisitive friends.

'When our loved ones are threatened, we are all willing to do things we normally wouldn't.' Drake leaned against the mantel, a whiskey in his large hand. 'There's nothing I wouldn't do to protect Millie.'

'Nor I you, my love.' Millie winked at her husband.

'It brings about an interesting point. I think we all agree that love allows us to do things we otherwise might not be capable of achieving. It makes us stronger. I know on the battlefield, those who fought for love of their land and people were far fiercer than paid mercenaries.' Killian spoke to the group, but his sharp gaze stayed on Philippa.

'Absolutely,' Liam readily agreed as Philippa imagined all the ways she could torture her friends, one after the other. Because they were certainly torturing her. The duchess, whose opinion on romantic love had always been rather dim, was being forced to admit her folly. There wasn't one person in this room she hadn't advised to stay away from the trap of love.

They are enjoying this. Damn them.

'People often think loving someone makes them more vulnerable to attack, but Penny protects me just as much as I protect her. I'd wager I'm far safer with her by my side in any battle than the most skilled fighter. Because I trust her and know she trusts me irrevocably.'

'Who's to say I'm not the most skilled fighter?' Penny raised a brow at her husband before slipping her hand into his. 'There's no one I'd rather stand next to against any foe. Even if I'm only armed with an apple.'

'It wasn't until I met Ivy that I understood how much more I had to live for, to fight for. Knowing how blessed I am to have her in my life, I want to ensure others have that same opportunity. Even those who might not think they deserve it.' Edward raised his brow at Philippa. She would wager he'd practised the look in a mirror for this specific occasion.

Bastard.

'I for one can attest that Lady Ivy has bettered your general mood and demeanour, sir. You are almost tolerable to be with now, and that is a vast improvement.' Reading sipped his sherry and wrinkled his nose, his thin moustache wriggling on his upper lip like a blond caterpillar.

Enough. I will not sit here and be lectured on the virtues of love.

Philippa stood and paced in an agitated track to the fireplace, whirling around to face the group. 'Will you all please stop! I know what you are trying to do.'

Hannah parted her mouth in an expression of mock-innocence. 'What on earth do you mean?'

'You want me to admit that I was wrong about Olivia. Fine! I was wrong. I am not always right, all the time.'

'Just mostly right most of the time,' Edward said.

'Yes, exactly.' Philippa was having trouble keeping her thoughts organised. Her chest felt tight, she couldn't breathe normally, her pulse pounded in her ears, and she had a distinct impression that her voice might be shrill. Her voice was never shrill. Looking at the whiskey glass she had left on the low table next to the settee, she wondered if Stokes really had added hemlock to the spirits.

Ivy approached Philippa slowly, the way one might a spooked horse. 'You do know we all love you, don't you?'

What madness was this? Not only were they needling her to admit her love for Olivia, but now they were declaring their own feelings about Philippa? It was nonsensical. One did not openly discuss their affection for others while drinking port in the front parlour. They certainly didn't declare their love in front of half a dozen of their closest friends when they hadn't even admitted their feelings to the person upon whom their love was bestowed. Philippa couldn't find words, so she shook her head in blatant denial of Ivy's statement.

Millie walked over, putting her warm hand on Philippa's arm and holding tight even as she tried to pull back. 'And we all believe you deserve to find love again.'

She was hallucinating. Probably a side effect of the poison Stokes put in her cup. She was going to kill him. Then sack him. Then bring him back from the dead to kill him again. They should be discussing how they were going to take down the leader of the Devil's Sons. Not Philippa's love life. The very idea was horrifying.

Hannah stood from the settee and joined the trio of women. 'It doesn't matter who you love, as long as they are worthy of you, Philippa.'

Penny stayed next to Liam, but her voice carried easily across the quiet room. 'And Olivia seems exceedingly worthy, Your Grace.'

'Liza would have liked her.' Edward's much softer words hit Philippa like a fist in the belly. Because he was right. She would have loved Olivia's spark. Her stubbornness. Her courage to stand toe to toe against Philippa.

'You don't need to hide your relationship from us, Your Grace,' Reading added. 'I might delight in judging others, but I would never judge you for whoever it is you love.'

'If you want to hold Olivia's hand at dinner, bloody well do it.' Millie squeezed her arm, her wide smile and brimming eyes testament to the woman's affection for Philippa.

But they didn't understand. They thought she pulled back from Olivia at dinner because she was worried about their reactions. That wasn't the case at all.

Dear God. Is that what Olivia thought? Is that why she left?

Dread filled her belly as she realised her mistake. 'I'm not worried about what you think.' Philippa struggled to put her own thoughts into words.

'Ah. Well. That's a relief. We assumed you might actually care about our opinions. How silly of us.' Drake's rough voice was dry as the desert where he once fought.

Philippa never had trouble expressing herself. But tonight was for the books because nothing was happening as it should. The very idea that Olivia might have thought she was embarrassed of her, that she pulled away because she didn't want her friends to know of her esteem, was so patently opposite of how she felt, Philippa was certain she would be sick all over her favourite evening gown.

'I love Olivia.' The words burst forth like water breaking free of a dam. And it felt bloody marvellous to admit her feelings out loud, even if she'd been bullied into doing it by her closest friends.

'Yes. We are all aware.' Stokes had entered the room with his habitual quiet step.

Philippa turned to the door where he stood with a full bottle of amber liquid. More whiskey. Probably full of arsenic. She glared at him before turning back to the others.

'I wasn't trying to hide my feelings for her because of any fears you might not accept us.'

'Really?' Drake raised a broken brow, his scepticism obvious.

'No. I have more faith in you than that. Well, most of you.' Again, Philippa shot Stokes a baleful look as he refilled Killian's glass.

The butler studiously ignored her.

Hannah's smile was full of relief before she quirked her brow in confusion.

'So why did you pull away? Because it looked a lot like you regretted holding Olivia's hand.'

Philippa wished she had her fan. She desperately needed to thwack something. 'I haven't told her how I feel. And I've no idea if she feels the same. I thought I was putting her in an impossible situation. Forcing her to accept such a public display of affection without knowing if she wanted that. So, I pulled back.'

Millie's look of sympathy confirmed Philippa's worst fears.

'Dear God. I made a terrible mistake. Didn't I?'

'Yes.' Ten voices spoke in unison.

Bollocks. What the bloody hell am I going to do now?

Thankfully, she had a plethora of opinions on exactly how to rectify the situation.

The rest of the evening was spent making plans. But not to take down the leader of a nefarious brotherhood. Rather, to woo the heart of a lady.

19

Philippa had no appetite for her breakfast. Her belly was too full of regret to make any room for coddled eggs, crispy bacon, or buttered toast. Instead, she sipped a cup of bitter coffee and appreciated how the flavour fit her mood.

She and Olivia had fallen into a routine of breaking their fast together in the bright breakfast room, but this morning, her only company was a brooding Callum.

'If you continue to saw at your plate like that, you shall be eating porcelain with your eggs. What has you so vexed?' It was far easier to focus on the young lad's problems than think about her own.

'I don't know why I'm still here. You clearly have no further use for me. I should have gone home after I delivered your notes. It's just... I can't leave without knowing she's safe.'

Philippa raised an eyebrow at the man sitting to her left. He had high cheekbones, a strong nose, a firm jaw, and the darkened skin of someone who spent most of their time outdoors. The suit she had insisted on providing him to replace his homespun clothing while he was in London fit his broad shoulders and muscular frame well. The male form held no appeal for Philippa, but she could see how any young lady of the beau monde would find Master Callum an easy target for their flirtations. Yet, he seemed wholly uninterested in any of the pleasures London offered. Killian and Drake had taken an interest in the lad, and when he wasn't traipsing to coffee houses with them talking about God knows what, he was spending his time in the kitchen with her usually taciturn French chef.

'It is not easy when your feelings are engaged with someone who might not reciprocate.' Philippa buttered a piece of toast she had no interest in eating.

The young lad swung his sharp gaze to Philippa, and she realised his eyes betrayed the haunted look of one who had endured hardships belying his twenty-odd years on the planet.

'I have no particular fondness for Miss Smithwick. I just don't like the idea of any innocent person falling prey to the hands of a monster.'

'Ah.' Philippa let the word hang between them for a moment. 'And this comes from your own experience with monsters, Master Callum?'

The young man stood abruptly, nearly knocking over his chair in his haste. 'Please excuse me. I have matters to attend.' He spoke through gritted teeth. Even in the height of his anger, he kept his manners stringently polite. She had to respect his self-control. She had poked a sore spot, and most men would strike, but instead, he forced himself to retreat.

Or perhaps he is trying to escape. But you can't run from troubles. Facing them is the only way through.

Which is exactly what she intended to do as soon as Olivia arrived for her morning meal. In the quiet of the room, she realised how much she'd grown to enjoy sitting with Olivia. Sometimes, they would discuss whatever news made it above the fold of *The Times*; other times, Olivia would recount her latest penny dreadful tale, they would review the schedule for that day, or simply sit in companionable silence. Philippa had always taken her morning meal in her room, but since Olivia's arrival, she found it much more pleasant to eat in the sunny breakfast room on the ground floor. Only this morning, she might as well have stayed abed. Olivia was nowhere to be found.

After loitering over her third cup of coffee until the brew grew cold, Philippa stood and threw her napkin on her plate. This was ridiculous. She wasn't going to faff about all morning like some lovesick swain.

Even if that is exactly what I am.

If Olivia wasn't going to come to Philippa, then she must go to her.

After a lengthy discussion with her friends the night before, one course of action was unanimously decided upon. She needed to apologise to Olivia. Beg her forgiveness. Declare her love. Hope for the best. Not particularly in that order, but all four elements must be present. She could hardly do that if she couldn't first find the woman.

This mission proved more difficult than she imagined. After checking the library, front parlour, back garden and finally tapping at Olivia's door and listening for any noises inside, Philippa was at a loss. The woman seemed to have disappeared. She would have inquired with Master Callum if he had seen her, but he was also mysteriously absent.

Dire times called for drastic measures. Standing in her morning room, she accepted the inevitable and rang for Stokes.

The butler arrived within minutes of being summoned. A rare occurrence for the man, who generally preferred to make her wait as long as possible.

'Have you seen Lady Olivia? I need to speak with her.' He knew bloody well what she wanted to talk about as he had found reasons to dally in the parlour the night before, eavesdropping on her entire conversation with her friends. Odious man.

'She is out, Your Grace.' His expression gave her no clues as to exactly where 'out' might be.

Philippa exhaled through her nose and retrieved the fan from her skirt pocket. She had missed it the night before and found satisfaction in thwacking it against her leg. She would find more satisfaction in flicking it open and using the sharpened edge to threaten her butler with immediate decapitation if he didn't tell her exactly where Olivia was at this moment. Exercising extreme self-control, Philippa chose conversation over carnage.

'Out where, Stokes?' This was hardly the time for her to be flitting about London. The last thing they needed was for her to be spotted out and about. The gossip that would inevitably sprout if she were seen by a member of the beau monde would make it back to her brother, and then what? Of course she would be instantly recognised. Olivia was impossible to miss with all of her glorious, bright locks, her emerald eyes sparkling with mischief, her bee-stung lips begging to be kissed.

Philippa blinked and tried to pull her thoughts back into focus.

'She took Master Callum in the brougham. She said she needed to complete some errands.'

'Is she mad? What if she's seen?' Philippa's voice was becoming shrill. Again.

Stokes curled his lip and sniffed. 'She's far more clever than that. She promised to stay in the carriage with the shades drawn. Master Callum is acting as her footman of sorts and will be the only one leaving the carriage. You really should give her more credit, Your Grace.'

Philippa thwacked the fan harder, taking perverse pleasure in the sting on her leg where the metal weapon disguised as a harmless feminine accessory smacked her through her silk skirts. 'It seems she has managed to win over your very selective regard. Quite a feat.'

Stokes cleared his throat and stretched his neck in lieu of an answer.

'I do give her immense credit. Not that I need to explain myself to you. She is in danger. I only want to ensure she is safe.' Why was she telling Stokes any of this? He was her servant, not her friend.

'One can't protect those they love from every danger, Your Grace. She has Master Callum with her, and she promised she would be careful. She has been trained by one of the most fearsome fighters in all of England, has she not? Have some faith.'

'Who are you, and what have you done with my butler? He's a stodgy, dour, stiff corpse of a man who would never think to compliment me.'

'We are all capable of change, Your Grace.' Clipping his heels together, Stokes executed a sharp turn and walked to the door. 'Even stubborn, arrogant, self-satisfied duchesses.'

'Ah, there you are. I thought you'd been replaced by a much kinder doppelganger.' Philippa shook her head as the man quietly shut the door behind him.

Olivia hadn't returned by the time Philippa needed to leave to meet with Lord High Chancellor Hardgrave. She told herself that, wonder of all wonders, Stokes was right. Olivia was smart. She was becoming, if not skilled, at least a proficient fighter. And Callum would protect her with his life, of that she was certain. It was silly to worry after her. But still, the weight of dread in her belly only increased as she climbed into the phaeton and took the ribbons, turning the horse toward 216 Strand.

* * *

This was probably a terrible idea. But it wasn't Olivia's worst idea. Her worst idea was falling in love with the Duchess of Dorsett, even though the stubborn woman was determined to ignore the fact that she also loved Olivia in return.

But I am far more resolute than you think. I shall not give up, Philippa.

She had woken with renewed hope. After all, most great love stories encountered innumerable challenges. And this was Olivia's great love story. She knew it to the marrow of her bones. She would not give up after one setback during a dinner party.

But first, she needed to attend the meeting between Philippa and her brother to assure herself Cedric didn't do anything completely unhinged. Like kidnap and kill the Duchess of Dorsett.

She knew Callum felt as restless as she did, so she devised a plan to enlist his assistance. He had brilliantly agreed to help her obtain the perfect costume to infiltrate their meeting. She could hardly arrive at Twinings in her usual attire or even dressed in the less conspicuous clothes of a maid. Her brother – and half the beau monde – would recognise her in a flash. But disguised as she was now in the finery of a young gentleman, her breasts bound, her hair trapped underneath a jaunty top hat, her eyes obscured with a pair of wire glasses, she barely recognised herself. In an inspired moment, she'd even drawn on a thin moustache. Reading had given her the idea the night before. It had occurred to her as she watched him meticulously cut his poached turbot that his features danced between the lines of feminine and masculine. She wondered if that was why he insisted on maintaining his whisper of facial hair. But more importantly, she believed she could pull off a similar look, and this meeting between Philippa and her brother was the perfect opportunity to test her theory.

'Remember, it's not just your clothes. You have to walk with your shoulders back, hands at your side. Keep your chin up and look down at everyone. If someone steps into your path, don't pause. They make room for you, not the other way 'round.' Callum spoke low as they walked side by side through the teahouse.

Olivia took a shallow breath. The bandage binding her breasts was almost as tight as her corset. 'There he is. At the corner table by the window.'

Callum paused to scan the crowded teahouse. 'Right. There's a table just to his left.'

'As long as Philippa doesn't see you, we should be grand.'

'Me?' Callum burst into a sharp laugh. 'It's you we need to worry about. This is madness. Why did I agree to this?'

'Because you want to rescue Hyacinth as badly as I do. And you don't value being dismissed as a nuisance when you are far more valuable than that.'

His neck turned a mottled red as he wound around the crowded room. Stopping at a table that was diagonal to where her brother sat, he nodded at the seat facing away from the Lord High Chancellor and took the chair opposite. It was the perfect location, allowing her to listen to their conversation while her back faced their table. Her brother was busy reading a paper as they arrived. Olivia nearly collapsed in a heap when he looked up, his eyes – as green as hers, but hard like a stone – making direct contact with hers. He blinked, dismissing her as easily as he might a gnat. And to the Lord High Chancellor, she was of no more significance than an insect. Just another feckless young lordling like half the other patrons at Twinings.

Olivia sank into her seat and breathed a sigh of relief. It was a brief reprieve as no sooner had she ordered tea for the table than the duchess arrived.

No matter where she went, Philippa caused a stir. Tables grew silent as she passed, then immediately burst into a flurry of whispers. The Duchess of Dorsett was at Twinings. Meeting with none other than the Lord High Chancellor. Queen Victoria herself might have caused less of a fuss. Olivia wondered if she ever grew tired of such constant scrutiny.

No wonder she pulled back her hand last night. The last thing she wants is more attention.

Mayhap it was less about being embarrassed by Olivia and more about wanting to keep private things private. Something to ponder later. When she wasn't eavesdropping on a conversation between her monstrous brother and deadly lover.

* * *

Twinings was bustling with activity. Just as Philippa predicted. No matter what Lord High Chancellor Hardgrave planned, he couldn't very well murder her in plain sight with so many witnesses.

He rose as she arrived at the table, his manners impeccable.

'Lady Winterbourne.'

'Lord Hardgrave.'

'Please, sit. I took the liberty of ordering a pot of tea.'

Philippa looked at the pot and then back at him. 'How lovely.' She could have been commenting on her feelings about dysentery.

'One lump or two?' He poised a sugar cube over the cup.

'None. I prefer my tea as I do my friends.'

'Bitter?' The Lord Chancellor smiled with all the charm of an accomplished politician.

'Strong. And untainted by outside forces.'

'Ah.' He withdrew the sugar.

Pleasantries out of the way, Philippa struck first. 'As delightful as this is, you didn't invite me for a social call. My demands are simple. Release Hyacinth, promise to leave Olivia alone, turn yourself in for your crimes against the Crown, ensure the Devil's Sons are dismantled, and I promise to let you live long enough to face the hangman's noose.' She stretched her mouth into a calculated smile.

Lord Hardgrave smirked with the smug assurance of a man in total control, infuriating Philippa. Which was certainly his plan. 'You have much to learn about the art of bargaining.'

'I wasn't making a bargain. I was simply advising you on the best course of action for your limited future.'

'Ah. Well. Let me make a counteroffer, shall I? Turn my sister over to me now, desist in your investigations against the Devil's Sons, retire to the countryside like a good dowager, and I promise not to systematically destroy everyone and everything you love.'

Philippa examined her nail, feigning boredom. 'You sound just like every other man drunk on his own opinions. Let me remind you, one needs leverage if they expect to win a negotiation. You have nothing.'

'I have Hyacinth.'

Confounded bastard.

Confounded bastard who made an excellent point.

'Surely you wouldn't harm your own niece.' But as soon as Philippa spoke, she realised her mistake. Olivia had warned her, but until this moment, she hadn't been convinced of the depths of his madness. Because he most certainly would hurt his niece. And they both knew it.

'There are so many ways a young lady might lose her life.' He dropped a sugar cube in his tea. 'A tragic illness.' Poured a dollop of cream. 'A fall.' Delicately stirred the mixture with a silver spoon. 'Drowning while taking a pleasure cruise on the Thames.' Tapped the spoon three times before placing it gently on the saucer. 'Of course, those are more pleasant outcomes. She could also be raped. Murdered. Or simply disappear, never to be found again.'

'You would do this to Hyacinth?'

'Oh, by then, she wouldn't be Hyacinth any more. Just a nameless girl in some far-flung corner of the world, being introduced to the myriad twisted desires of wealthy men with endless power and no reservations in exploring their darkest fantasies.'

Bile rose up Philippa's throat. 'What if we promised to stop investigating you?'

'That was only one of my requirements. And why should I believe your promise? The Queen's Deadly Damsels giving up on their mission? That doesn't sound like you at all.'

Because it was the very antithesis of every instinct burning in Philippa. But the words burst free without thought. 'You don't know me. Return Olivia's daughter. Desist in your pursuit of her. I will call off the Damsels. Olivia gets her freedom, but so do you.'

'I thought you weren't bargaining.' Hardgrave sipped his tea. His green eyes, so similar in colour and shape to Olivia's yet wholly different in the madness flashing there, speared Philippa. 'Why would I do that?'

Appeal to his logic. He might be insane, but he loves himself more than anything else. He doesn't want to jeopardize all he's accomplished.

'You have far more to gain by making this accord than by waging war with us. Why wouldn't you agree?'

'Because she is mine.' He growled so softly she barely heard him. 'She has always been mine. Don't you understand? Olivia has defied me from the moment she was born, but I will not abide defiance in anyone. Certainly not my own sister. It's time for her to learn I control her and everything she does.'

Philippa shook her head. 'You don't.'

He drummed his fingers on the tablecloth. 'Oh, but I do. You just haven't realised it yet. Not only do I control her, but I also control you, Lady Winterbourne.'

Philippa curled her lip in a snarl. 'No one controls me but myself.'

'Are you so certain?'

She wasn't. Not at all. Not since she realised her love for Olivia.

She holds my heart in her hands, and I can't control the depth or strength of my regard for her. I can't control my thoughts when I'm around her. I can't control my need to ensure she is safe. I can't even control whether she will love me back. Or stay with me.

But it didn't matter. It was worth the risk. Olivia was worth risking everything. Even Philippa's carefully curated control.

Cedric was still talking. Philippa did her best to refocus. 'I have allowed you and your Damsels to ferret out the Wolf and the Snake because I wanted to eliminate them. Thanks to your efforts, I now have total control over the brotherhood. You stupidly thought you were pursuing me, but I led you down this path every step of the way. I didn't strike against you because you were fulfilling certain odious tasks I needed accomplished. But now it's time for you to stand down, Duchess, or I shall put you down.'

'There is only one person I take orders from, and she wears the crown.'

Hardgrave's lips twitched as a cold, hard fist of doubt wrapped around Philippa's chest and started to squeeze. 'You don't think she is aware of my actions? That the Crown doesn't financially benefit from my enterprise? That political wheels aren't greased by the favours I provide? Silly, Duchess. For such a worldly woman, you are woefully naïve.'

Philippa shook her head. 'I don't believe you.' But the doubt grew and developed sharp teeth biting into her confidence. How well did she know the Queen? How well did anyone know another?

Shrugging, Hardgrave sipped his tea. 'What you believe has very little influence over what is true. Once you have seen me destroy all those you hold dear, perhaps then you will accept my words as fact. Would you willingly sacrifice your friends all for a woman you hardly know? Lord and Lady Killian, Major General Drake and his lovely new bride. Lord Renquist and his maid. Even the Commissioner of Scotland Yard. None of them are safe from my reach, Lady Winterbourne. Surely their lives are worth more than one insignificant woman.'

'You fucking bastard.' The words were weak and useless, but they were all Philippa had in the moment.

Tsking, he shook his head back and forth in slow censure that made her want to reach across the table, punch his throat, collapse his windpipe, and watch him gasp his last breath.

'Such foul words from such a fine lady. Although it makes me wonder. Why do you hold so tightly to my sister?' Lord Hardgrave leaned back in his chair, his eyes darkening with understanding. 'Ah. I see. Men seem to lose their heads when given the chance to fuck her, but I had no idea women could be equally stupid.'

'Be silent.' Heat washed over her as his insidious words burrowed through her armour.

He leaned forward. 'I promise, whatever value she holds between her thighs is hardly worth risking your life and that of your friends. Don't be a fool, Lady Winterbourne.'

Rage swept in, taking with it Philippa's control. 'You've no idea what she's worth. Olivia is more important than you could ever imagine.' She stood and threw her tea in Hardgrave's face, the hot liquid turning his cheek red. Gasps could be heard throughout Twinings as the tearoom went deathly still.

'Oh dear. I slipped,' Philippa snarled. 'Do forgive me.' But she'd made a terrible mistake. She'd shown the Crow her hand. And now he knew her weakness.

The Lord High Chancellor wiped his face, slowly rose to his feet, and dropped the soiled napkin on the table. 'I shall expect you to deliver my package by the Queen's Samhain celebration. There's no telling what kind of mischief might occur if the Devil doesn't get his dues.' He turned to walk away and crashed directly into a young serving boy carrying a silver tray. Cups, plates, a full pot of tea, and several iced cakes tipped from the platter, all of it landing on the Lord High Chancellor's snow-white vest.

The serving boy's face turned pale as he unsuccessfully attempted to clean off the mess with a napkin.

'Get away from me, you idiot.' The Lord High Chancellor shoved the boy to the floor. Without a backwards glance, he strode from Twinings.

'That went well,' Philippa muttered.

20

Olivia sat at the table Stokes had arranged in Philippa's private sitting room. She jiggled her leg anxiously and looked down at her gown. She had dressed carefully for this intimate dinner, but still she wasn't sure the pale-lavender colour was quite right. The scooped neckline dipped scandalously low, leaving her arms, shoulders, and upper breasts bare. A skirt of gauzy satin flowed down her body like water, revealing as much as it covered. Was she being too obvious? Might a more demure ensemble have better suited her purposes?

Extra wood had been laid on the fire as the evening air carried a bite of winter soon to come, but her shiver had nothing to do with temperature and everything to do with nerves.

Of course I'm nervous. I'm attempting to convince the most stubborn woman I know to do the opposite of what she desires. And I'm stooping so low as to use seduction as my tool.

Which was a weapon she'd used often in the past and with great success, but one she didn't want to wield with Philippa now. It felt horribly wrong.

But after listening to her brother threaten both her daughter and the woman she loved, it became clear Olivia only had one path forward. She would not sacrifice Hyacinth, Philippa, or her friends in the hopes of evading her brother. She had tried that course before and failed dismally. It was time to accept her fate. But before she did, she would have one more night with

Philippa. One last evening to take with her and hold close as her future closed around her like a steel trap. So perhaps the seduction served two purposes. Convincing Philippa to see things Olivia's way and giving Olivia memories to cherish for the rest of her days.

She sighed heavily.

'It's all rather depressing.' She spoke to the empty space.

'What is depressing? And why is there a dinner table set up in my sitting room?'

Ah. Well. Not quite as empty as I thought.

'You are entirely too quiet on your feet.'

Yes. Start with fighting words and an arch tone. That will surely have Philippa throwing her skirts up and begging for my mouth between her legs.

Philippa's pupils darkened.

Olivia reconsidered. Fighting and fucking did have so many similarities. Mayhap it wasn't such a terrible strategy.

But she wanted to fuck Philippa about as much as she wanted to seduce her.

So what do I want?

To love her. And be loved. To give herself to Philippa. To receive whatever Philippa was willing to offer in return. To melt bodies, souls, and minds together into one perfect union.

How the bloody hell do I accomplish that?

'You look lovely in lavender.' Philippa walked slowly toward Olivia, her eyes missing nothing. Olivia's skin sparked everywhere Philippa's gaze touched her.

'I wore it for you.' Olivia lifted her chin as Philippa stood next to her. She had left her hair loose, and it fell softly over her shoulder, pooling in her lap. She fiddled with the ends.

'Will you take it off for me as well?'

'Are you hungry? We could eat first.' And Olivia could talk. Convince Philippa to give her up to her brother. Submit to his demands and ensure the safety of all those they loved.

But not the innocent children he will continue to exploit.

Olivia pushed the thought away. She could only handle one devastating compromise at a time.

'I'm only hungry for one thing.' Philippa reached down, caught Olivia's hand, and pulled her to her feet.

Fine. Seduction first. Then I shall convince her my plan is best.

Olivia chose the lavender dress because the cut was flattering, the colour suited her skin, and most importantly, it had buttons down the front, making it easy for her to unclasp the little seed pearls until the bodice gaped. Her corset was ivory, her shift white lace. She revelled in the gasp as Philippa watched her like a hungry cat, ready to lap up every drop of cream.

'I need to speak with you.' Words she hadn't planned on saying yet spilled forth.

Blast.

She was going to wait. But she couldn't make love to Philippa without total honesty. And she desperately wanted to have no deception between them for their last night together.

Philippa tucked her fingers in each sleeve of Olivia's dress and tugged down until the entire thing slipped to floor. She stood in nothing but her corset and lace shift. With the fire behind her, she knew Philippa could see the outline of her body. 'Later.' She traced her finger over the swell of Olivia's breast. Warm, wet heat coated Olivia's core as her belly clenched.

'Now.' If she didn't get the words out immediately, they would be lost forever.

Philippa raised a brow and caught one of Olivia's curls in her hand, twining it around her finger before she tugged gently. 'You are very serious.'

Olivia held onto her focus with an iron grip when her body clamoured to forget conversation and give over to sensation. 'This is a serious subject.'

'In that case…' Tangling her hand in Olivia's hair, she wrapped her strong fingers around the base of Olivia's head and pulled her close, her lips a whisper away, frankincense and jasmine overwhelming Olivia's senses. 'Please, do go on.' She pressed a soft kiss to her mouth, Philippa's tongue whispering over Olivia's full bottom lip.

'You need to agree to my brother's terms.'

Her words were akin to throwing iced water onto hot flames. Philippa pulled back, air escaping her in a hiss. 'I need to what?'

Oh dear. I've done it now.

But there was no turning back. 'You need to agree to his terms, Philippa. Give me over to him at the ball. It is the only way to ensure everyone's safety.'

Yours, the Damsels', my daughter's. He is right. My life is certainly not worth all of theirs.'

'How do you know he said that?' Realisation dawned in her eyes. 'You were there.' But her real message was clear. *You put yourself in danger.*

'I brought Callum with me. And I came in disguise.'

Philippa rolled her eyes. 'Yes, because Callum could protect you from a man like your brother.'

'You were alone,' Olivia threw back. 'Who was protecting you?'

Slipping her hand from Olivia's hair to her neck, Philippa flexed her fingers around Olivia's throat. A thrill ran through Olivia's body. 'I was protecting me.'

Philippa's pupils blew wide as Olivia pressed forward. 'And you would have protected me if it came to that. At your own peril. Which is exactly my point, Philippa. I won't have you put yourself in his path just to try and keep me safe. You are too dear to me. I love you too much. I can endure him. I managed to survive him for my entire childhood. I can do it again.'

Philippa froze. 'You what?'

Olivia tried again. She had to convince Philippa to agree to this. 'I lived with him for my entire childhood, and despite his best efforts, he did not crush me. I can take whatever punishments he's devised as long as I know you and Hyacinth are alive and safe.'

Philippa shook her head, a rogue wave of black and silver broke free from her complicated twist of curls and braids. 'No. Not that part. The other part.'

Olivia frowned in confusion. 'What other part?'

'The part where you said you loved me.' Philippa's voice broke on the last two words.

Damnation. I did say that. Out loud. To a woman who is terrified to love again after losing her soulmate.

Once more in this conversation, she couldn't turn back. The only way through was forward. 'I do love you, Philippa. Completely and irrevocably. But that does not mean you need to return my feelings. I know what we have is temporary, even if my feelings for you are not. And I can accept that. But you must know, in the moments we have together, I will love you for a lifetime.'

Philippa's perfect crimson lips quivered. She pressed them together as her eyes grew glassy with tears. She tried to speak, but Olivia stopped her with a kiss. She didn't want to hear Philippa's apology, or even worse, her rejection.

Instead, she tested the seam of Philippa's mouth and thrilled when she opened to her. Exploring her depths with nips and licks, she grew bolder as Philippa softened in her arms. She might not be able to return Olivia's love, but Philippa wouldn't deny her this moment of comfort and affection. Olivia was certain of that. She took her time removing each of the pins holding Philippa's hair, revelling in the silky sensation as she uncoiled the beautiful strands and let them fall.

Circling around to Philippa's back, Olivia cursed how many buttons were required to keep a woman contained. She worked as quickly as she could, needing to see Philippa undone. As each inch of skin was revealed, she pressed open-mouth kisses, drinking in the fragrance of Philippa, savouring her silky skin, searing each moment in her memory.

Philippa helped peel her dress away. Unlike Olivia's, Philippa's corset was black silk that pressed her breasts high and sculpted her waist. But Olivia wanted to see her true form without the artifice fashion dictated. She unlaced the corset, pushing it down Philippa's body so she stood in nothing but her shift.

'Your turn.' Philippa spun Olivia, unlacing her just as quickly.

Olivia pulled her shift up, whipped it over her head and pretended not to be insecure as she stood naked in front of Philippa. The fire was behind her, warming her back, and Philippa's eyes were just as hot as the flames on Olivia's clavicles, her breasts, her waist, her thighs, her mons. She feared she might melt into a puddle of aching desire just from Philippa's possessive gaze.

'Now you.' Olivia needed to see Philippa just as bare. Just as vulnerable.

As Philippa shed her shift, it was clear she was not quite as naked as Olivia. She had a blade tied to her thigh. A leather holster held a small pistol on her opposite ankle.

'Will you take off your weapons for me? I promise I won't attack.'

'You've already waged your war and won, Olivia.'

Olivia wanted to ask what she meant, but Philippa answered her unspoken question. Bending forward, Philippa unbuckled the strap holding her blade. 'I was determined to remain alone. I thought after loving and losing Liza, that part of me was gone forever. And in some ways, it is. I will never love you the way I loved Liza.'

Olivia swallowed the pain and lifted her chin. 'I'm not asking for that.'

Philippa paused as she worked on her ankle holster, looking up from her task. 'I know. You aren't asking me for anything. But it won't stop me from giving you everything. All that I am now.'

Olivia's knees went weak, and she lurched to the chair, sitting heavily. If she wasn't emotionally overwhelmed, she would find it rather amusing to be sitting on Philippa's button-back chair, the velvet upholstery soft against her naked skin, dinner still sitting untouched on the table to her right. 'Pardon?'

Philippa placed her weapons on her own chair and knelt next to Olivia, taking both of her hands and holding them tightly. She looked up, the firelight highlighting Philippa's high cheekbones, strong nose, delicate mouth, and sharp jawline.

God, she is beautiful.

'Liza will always be a part of me. But who I was when I loved her is not who I am now.'

'Who are you now?'

'A woman who has fallen so deeply in love with you, I'm not sure where I end, and you begin. But I know wherever you are, that is where I will be. And that place will never be at your brother's mercy. So, no. I won't be handing you over to him. And no. We won't be giving in to his demands.'

'What about Hyacinth?' No matter how desperately Olivia loved Philippa, she wouldn't sacrifice her daughter for the duchess' love.

'I keep telling you, we will get her back.' She spoke with such conviction, Olivia couldn't doubt her. Philippa truly believed they would rescue her daughter or die trying. And because the duchess only made promises she could keep, Olivia believed her as well. 'All will be well. Hyacinth is part of your heart, so she is also part of mine. Whether she grows to accept me or not, she will always have a place with us.'

'Us?' Olivia's heart was so full, it stretched her chest tight. She wasn't sure she had room to breathe.

'Yes. Us.' Philippa stood, taking Olivia's hand and pulling her up. 'Will you come to bed with me? Tomorrow, we will plan how to claim our future. But tonight, I just want to be with you.'

Because nothing was certain. They were going to war against an enemy Olivia knew far too well. Tomorrow might only hold death and destruction despite Philippa's promises. But tonight held love. And hope. And dreams of a future. And Olivia needed the strength of that to bolster her for the fight to come.

Olivia brought Philippa's hand to her lips and pressed a kiss on her palm. 'I will come to bed with you. I will walk into the fires of hell with you. Because wherever you are, that is where I will be.' Echoing Philippa's words back to her, Olivia felt the truth of them. 'Lead on, my lady.'

* * *

Philippa was terrified. It was not a feeling with which she was familiar. She was not amenable to it in the slightest. Her corset was jabbing into her ribs. The black and crimson beads sewn into her bodice in a design resembling flames licking up her dress were rubbing against her skin and would no doubt leave marks in the morning. A thousand pins held her hair into a coiffure so complicated, she wasn't sure she would ever dismantle the braids, twists, and curls, and each one dug into her skull. But that wasn't the problem. Knowing Olivia sat in her eggshell ball gown, alone, sequestered in Buckingham Palace's white drawing room while Philippa rubbed elbows with the creamiest of the crop in the throne room until their plan came to fruition was making her want to crawl out of her skin with anxiety.

The grand throne room was lit by five gargantuan chandeliers. The largest and most ostentatious of these hung in the centre of the room with four smaller versions surrounding it. Each was fitted with the controversial gas lighting, taking the country by storm. While many still distrusted its safety, the Queen was convinced it was not just harmless, but far more efficient than candles or oil. Philippa couldn't deny the brightness achieved by this new lighting invention was far superior to previous methods. More crystals than one could ever count reflected the luminescence onto the crowd of revellers.

Well over five hundred guests clamoured against each other, each vying for a coveted spot near the raised dais where Queen Victoria sat in all her splendour, her husband by her side. With so many lords and ladies in attendance, even the lowliest of barons received an invitation and would have bankrupted their household to assure their clothing was fit for the Queen's theme of devils and angels cavorting together.

A roaring fire burned at the far end of the ballroom, giving some heat to the spacious room. The intricately carved panels decorating the walls were gilded, adding to the warm glow from the lights. While the beau monde still raved about Queen Victoria's Georgian Ball, requiring guests to dress in sumptuous attire from that bygone era, for this event, Queen Victoria expressed an inclination for a more haunted theme to honour the closeness of the veil between life and death as the seasons transitioned from autumn to winter. Many guests wore masks in the Celtic tradition, some as devils and others as angels. One young woman was daring enough to fashion wings to her costume, leaving a trail of feathers behind her and causing hazardous conditions on the crowded dance floor.

Philippa wasn't the only lady in attendance wearing dark hues, though none were as bold as her flamed design to honour the tradition of bonfires on this night, or perhaps the hellfire she would face when taking down a true devil. She had already approached the Queen, bowing deeply and expressing her compliments for such a splendid ball. Victoria had nodded regally, then winked at Philippa. In such a public arena, there was little of the familiarity Philippa enjoyed between herself and the monarch during more private meetings, but Philippa hardly expected to be singled out. In point of fact, it worked to their advantage if the beau monde was never quite privy to the depth of their acquaintance. So, after making her expected show of deference, she drifted away from the Queen and the many guests desperately seeking her favour and found a spot on the edge of the crowd where she could more easily watch those in attendance.

She knew Edward and Ivy were keeping an eye on the grand staircase to alert her the moment the Lord High Chancellor arrived. She knew Hannah and Killian were loitering in the music room, guarding the entrance to the white drawing room. She knew Millie and Drake had taken watch in the royal closet in case the Lord High Chancellor attempted to find his sister using a circuitous route. She knew Penny and Liam were somewhere in the crowd, circulating amongst the guests and keeping their eyes and ears alert, as it was clear many of the Devil's Sons were in attendance this evening. And she knew Callum was near the stables, watching the carriages to ensure no one slipped away unnoticed. But still, she wasn't at ease, nor could she be until she and Olivia were back in her home, cuddled together on her bed, celebrating the success of their wild plan.

Dear God, Goddess, Saints, and Sprites, let that be the outcome of this evening.

As a rule, Philippa rarely spoke to deities she didn't believe existed, but it couldn't hurt on an evening when so much hung in the balance to call upon all the forces of good in the hopes it might help their cause.

The air shifted around her, and she felt the press of an arm against her own. Reading, dressed in all black with a mask covering his eyes and high-lighting his thin moustache and rather feminine lips, nodded to her. 'His carriage has just arrived.'

Philippa nodded. 'And so, it begins.'

21

Olivia paced on the marble floor. Her gown of endlessly layered white silk rustled around her legs.

'This is ridiculous. I should be out there. No doubt Cedric has arrived with Hyacinth. I should be with my daughter. Protecting her from him. Standing with Philippa. Not hidden away in this bloody white room in my white dress like some fragile, helpless virgin awaiting sacrifice!' Which was laughable on so many levels.

But that wasn't the plan. And she knew if they had any hope of catching her brother and ending his terrorising reign, she must follow the plan. She could hardly swan about the dance floor in the Queen's throne room when the entire beau monde would recognise her in an instant and sound the alarm.

She took another turn. Slipping her hand into the pocket sewn into her voluminous skirt, she fingered the dagger there and wondered if she had the courage to use it. Could she actually plunge the lethal metal into her brother's chest if it came to that?

If it means Hyacinth and Philippa are safe, and I am finally free... yes. I think I could.

The door on the far side of the white room creaked open, and Olivia froze. She wasn't sure who she expected to see, but it certainly wasn't Hyacinth. And yet, there she was. Standing in the frame of the doorway, with the lights from the corridor creating a nimbus around her head. Her dress was a shell pink, befitting that of a young woman at her first ball. Her blonde locks, nearly as pale as Olivia's, but wavy instead of the wild curls her mother long ago stopped trying to tame, were piled up in a twist that left wisps framing her face. It had only been a few weeks since Olivia last saw her, but she looked different. Her girl had transitioned to a young woman.

Olivia's throat ached as she stepped forward, but before she could reach Hyacinth, another figure appeared behind her. He wore the mask of a grinning gargoyle. His hands were ungloved as he grabbed Hyacinth's bare arm and pushed her further into the room, closing the door behind them. Olivia didn't need to see his face to know who he was. Her brother had arrived at the Queen's All Hallows' Eve Ball.

'Don't move a step closer, Olivia,' Cedric warned. He pulled a gun from his pocket and calmly pushed the muzzle against Hyacinth's ribs. The young woman didn't break eye contact with her mother. Her wide eyes were frightened, but even more terrifying, they were resigned to whatever fate might befall her this evening.

'Do not point that at my daughter.' Olivia's voice was quiet, calm, and full of venom. She wished she had a pistol in her pocket instead of a dagger, though in truth, she would never trust her aim when Cedric held her daughter in front of him like a shield.

Releasing Hyacinth's arm, he pushed his mask off and threw it to the floor. His face was red with anger, his eyes wild. The madness he kept hidden so carefully from the world had broken free this night, and fear washed through Olivia. Because one could not reason with a madman, nor could she predict his actions. 'Do not tell me what to do. You never listen, Olivia. No matter what I do to try and teach you. Your defiance knows no bounds. But that ends tonight.'

'Your cruel acts were hardly lessons, Cedric. Let her go. You made your deal with the duchess. You have me. Now let Hyacinth leave.'

'And abandon my dear sweet niece into the arms of strangers?' As he spoke, he stroked his hand up and down Hyacinth's arm. Her face hardened, and she pressed her lips together, refusing to let any emotions break free, brave girl that she was. Olivia's fear amalgamized into fierce rage. How dare he frighten her child?

'Why are you doing this? What can you possibly gain from hurting her besides an eternity in hell?'

'Your obedience.'

Olivia changed tactics. 'Fine. I will give you my complete submission if you let her go and promise to dismantle your flesh ring. What good does it do you? You don't need the money.'

'Money is nothing when you hold the darkest secrets of the realm's most powerful men. How many dukes, viscounts, barons, and marquises do I control? Imagine what might happen if their involvement in my little operation were to be made public? And of course, I am not tied to any of this. I've been sure to keep my name from any piece of incriminating evidence.'

'Always so clever, Cedric.'

He preened under her false praise. 'There isn't a limit to what information one can learn from a desperate little boy trying to keep his dirty deeds from ever seeing the light of day. I own half the beau monde, Olivia. I control their lives. Just as I control Hyacinth's, and now, yours.'

Olivia shook her head. 'This scheme is madness. You can't possibly expect to get away with this. Too many people know. You will be caught, Cedric. You will be punished.'

His laugh was too high, too shrill. It made Olivia's skin crawl as she remembered the brother of her youth. The same lad who would giggle when a dog got caught beneath the wheel of their carriage, or a maid was beaten for an indiscretion. Something had been twisting within him for far too long, and now it had warped the very fabric of his soul. 'Who is going to punish me? You? Please. You wouldn't dare.'

'Oh, I think she would.' Philippa's voice rang out from behind Olivia. Relief and fear filled her with equal potency. Now, both of the women she loved beyond measure were in the same room, at her brother's mercy.

Cedric tore his gaze away from Olivia to focus on Philippa as she came to stand next to her. His eyes darted back and forth between the women. 'What are you doing here? Your part of the bargain has been fulfilled. Leave us.'

Philippa's lips curled in a smile holding no warmth. 'I don't think so. Let Hyacinth go, and maybe we will spare your life.'

'You forget, Duchess, I am the one holding all of the cards.' Cedric's grip tightened on Hyacinth. 'Take another step and I'll shoot her.'

Olivia's heart fractured. Because he would do it without hesitation. She knew this just as well as he did. A single tear tracked down her daughter's cheek. It shattered Olivia's resolve.

'Oh, I don't know. We might have an ace or two up our sleeves.' Killian emerged from the shadows, Hannah by his side. She held a pistol in her hand pointed steadily at Cedric's head. 'Have you met my wife, Lord High Chancellor? She's a crack shot. I wouldn't test her skills.'

Hannah smiled. 'You say the loveliest things, darling.' She spoke to Killian, but her gaze was focused on Hardgrave.

'I bet I could beat you if we used knives.' Millie came out from behind a heavy set of curtains hanging on the far wall, Drake just behind her, his scar catching the candlelight. She held a throwing knife in her hand and flipped it in the air, catching it by the hilt as she approached their growing circle.

Penny and Liam stood up from behind an emerald velvet settee, both holding pistols. Ivy and Edward rose from their hiding place next to a mahogany desk.

'I've never liked bullies. You remind me of some men I knew in prison. It didn't end well for them either.' Penny thrust out her chin as she stopped on Millie's right side, and Ivy took her left. Liam and Edward stayed behind the women, but there was no doubt in Olivia's mind either of them would tear her brother apart before he took a step closer to their ladies. The Deadly Damsels and their dashing men surrounded Cedric in a crescent with the door to the room at his back.

'Fools. All of you.' His lip twitched into a small smile that froze Olivia's blood. 'Guards!' he called out and, in a seamless move, twisted so Hyacinth was behind him and his pistol was now pointed at Olivia.

With a thundering of feet on the marble floor, the white parlour was flooded with scarlet as the Queen's royal guard swept in from every door. They must have been standing by, waiting for this very moment.

Of course he would stack the deck in his favour.

Cedric never played fair, and he never engaged in a game unless he knew he would win.

Small skirmishes broke out as one guard attempted to grab Millie. Drake punched him in the face before three others wrestled the major general to the floor. Hannah put a choke hold on a young man valiantly trying to restrain Killian before a large guard ripped her off him and pinned her to the floor. Liam took down two crimson-clad men before a third got a lucky shot, bloodying Liam's lip with a sucker punch. Penny launched herself at the man but was intercepted by a fourth who somehow kept his hold on her as she fought like a wild demon to get free.

Ivy's face was pale as she struggled against a guard holding both hands behind her back. Edward stormed toward him, throwing any crimson coat in his path to the side, death in his eyes until she urged him to stand down.

Several more of the guards surrounded Hyacinth, protecting her from the scuffle.

Olivia lurched forward, only to meet the blinding smack of her brother's hand across her cheek. She stumbled back, his weapon unerringly pointed at her chest.

'You bastard!' Philippa moved toward Olivia, not pausing when Cedric swung his gun in her direction. She took Olivia in her arms, her hand running over her wounded cheek before she turned back to face the Crow. 'I am going to enjoy taking you apart one piece at a time.'

'Stay back.' He cocked the weapon, and Olivia knew he would shoot. He wanted to kill Philippa. She was everything he hated. Strong. Independent. Unwilling to bend to his will through threat or blackmail. She was magnificent. And Olivia loved her. One more reason for Cedric to destroy Philippa. He promised so long ago to take everything Olivia loved, and he meant it.

But he won't take her from me. I won't let him.

With a banshee scream, Olivia launched herself at Cedric, aiming low as Philippa had taught her when facing off against a larger, stronger opponent.

Her shoulder crashed into his legs with a painful crack. A gun went off, but Olivia didn't know if it was Cedric's or one of the Damsels'. She didn't care as long as the bullet didn't hit Philippa.

Cedric landed on top of her, and she twisted beneath him, grappling for the dagger in her pocket. She slipped it free, but he grabbed her wrist, slamming her hand against the floor in an attempt to make her drop the weapon. If she let go, he would take the knife and plunge it into her chest. She gripped the hilt tighter, preparing for his next crushing blow. But it never came. He froze on top of her as a gun cocked. Olivia blinked and saw the glint of metal pressing against her brother's temple.

'Get. Off. Of. Her.' Philippa's voice was quavering with barely controlled rage.

Cedric carefully let go of Olivia's wrist, holding both hands up. 'Easy, Lady Winterbourne. Let's not do anything rash.'

'Oh, killing you won't be rash. It will be well thought out. Calculated. Absolutely intentional.'

'Will someone please explain what my guard is doing in the white room, wreaking apparent havoc?' Queen Victoria's voice carried over the din, creating immediate silence.

Olivia wrenched her gaze away from Philippa and Cedric to see the Queen of England standing in the doorway. Her dark-purple gown was voluminous. The cinched waist and large skirt hid any indication of the birth of her fifth child, just seven months earlier. Her hair was parted down the centre and draped in a smooth wave over each ear. A coronet of diamonds and purple sapphires sparkled in the otherwise simple coiffure. Though only five feet tall, she seemed to look down upon the entire melee with the greatness of a giant.

The various scuffles occurring between the guards and Damsels ceased immediately as everyone froze. Olivia was reminded of a theatrical performance she once saw where scenes were stopped mid-action, and the actors stood frozen as if in a painting. If it wasn't all so horrifyingly awful, it would have been quite funny.

'Y-your Majesty.' Cedric struggled up, leaving Olivia on the floor. Philippa kept her gun trained on him with one hand and reached with her other to help Olivia to her feet. 'Your timing is truly fortuitous.'

'Lord High Chancellor Hardgrave. Why is the Duchess of Dorsett pointing a gun at you?'

'I have grave news.'

Olivia felt bile rise as her brother glanced at her, triumph glinting in his eyes.

'Might it have something to do with the small war being waged in my drawing room?'

'This woman, who you have grown to trust over so many years' – Cedric pointed a shaking finger at Philippa – 'has betrayed you most grievously. And she has used her friends to aid her in nefarious crimes against the very crown she was sworn to protect.'

Queen Victoria raised a brow in an expression very like Philippa's. Olivia wasn't sure if she learned it from the duchess or the other way around. 'Really?'

'It is Lady Winterbourne who has masterminded this entire ring of insidious flesh traders and set herself up as the Crow, leader of the Devil's Sons.'

There was a variety of exclamations from Olivia's new friends ranging from disbelief to outright anger. But Cedric spoke over the clamour.

'Worthington's position as the Commissioner of Scotland Yard made him her perfect second-in-command. As the Wolf, he was conveniently privy to the Prime Minister's leads and loyal to his childhood friend above all others, even Your Majesty.'

Edward shook his head in disbelief as Drake demanded Cedric commit a highly inappropriate act upon himself.

Cedric kept making outrageous claims. 'Lord Reynard, a man you took into your confidence once he returned from the war, was their Snake. These three, with help from their loyal lackeys, have been playing you a fool all along.'

All of the Damsels and their men spoke over each other in rebuttal of his accusations.

'Silence!' Queen Victoria commanded. She turned in a slow circle, spearing each of the Deadly Damsels and their husbands with a gaze as sharp as any rapier before returning her attention to Cedric. 'These are serious accusations, Lord High Chancellor. I assume you have evidence to prove this?'

Cedric rocked back on his heels. 'I have an eyewitness to their crimes. One of their would-be victims. Thank God I intercepted my sister before she could kidnap her own daughter and auction her to the highest bidder.' He pulled a piece of parchment from his coat pocket. 'I have Hyacinth's sworn testimony right here. Written by her own hand, outlining their nefarious deeds.'

Rage, grief, and an unholy need for revenge made it nearly impossible for Olivia to form words. 'And what threats did you use to get her to write it, Cedric? Did you promise to hurt those she loves? To destroy any chance she might have at a future? To isolate her from anyone offering sanctuary?' She knew her brother's cruelty and could easily imagine ten different ways he could have forced her daughter's hand, each worse than the last. Striding up to him, she slapped him hard in the face. Grim pleasure filled her at the mark she left on his cheek. 'You need not fear the duchess' wrath. Your death will come at my hand.'

Cedric's eyes gleamed with triumph. He turned to the Queen and gestured to Olivia with the confidence of a man who knew his words wouldn't be questioned. 'Even now, you see how boldly her lover threatens me. It pains me to admit this about my own sister, but she is an invert. Her love affair with the Duchess of Dorsett completes this circle of depravity. I would loathe for it to become public and ruin Hyacinth's chances of ever finding a worthy gentle-man, but Olivia has been privy to all of the duchess' machinations and joined with her in targeting innocents, including her own daughter. Their twisted love affair is only one more example of their immorality.'

Olivia felt the hot tears tracking down her cheeks, but she didn't care. 'I love Philippa with a depth and purity you will never know. The only thing twisted and depraved in this room is you.' She faced the Queen, desperate to convince the monarch of the truth. 'You cannot believe him, Your Highness. Philippa is the most loyal, courageous, honourable person I know. She would never betray your trust. She would never stoop so low as to hurt an innocent.'

Queen Victoria stared at Olivia without blinking. She felt like a bug on a pin and forced herself not to shrink away from such an intense inspection. The Queen's face gave away nothing. She turned slowly to Philippa.

'And what say you, Lady Winterbourne? Serious charges have been laid at your feet. Have you any words to defend yourself?'

Philippa carefully placed the pistol on a side table. She smoothed her hand over her skirt. 'Lord High Chancellor Hardgrave has put forth dire accusations against me, indeed. I wonder if you had to choose between his word and mine, with no other proof than our divergent accounts, which would sway you.'

Tension pulled tight between the Queen and the duchess. Philippa was confronting Victoria more boldly than anyone should dare. Olivia felt certain her lungs would seize, and she would collapse on the spot. It would save the hangman the cost of a rope.

Philippa stretched her mouth into a smile, something wicked sparking in her eyes. 'Thankfully, it won't come to that as I have actual evidence, not the terrified scribblings of a girl in distress.' Turning to look at Millie, the buxom redhead elbowed the guard holding her in his solar plexus. The poor man doubled over, wheezing for breath. Before another guard could take his place, a blade appeared in her hand. She flicked it in the air, catching it by the hilt and waving it at the approaching man like a naughty child trying to steal a piece of candy. 'I would stay where you are, good sir.'

The guard looked to the Queen, who shook her head. He stepped back as Drake struggled against the three men holding him and growled something foul enough to have his captors turning the same colour as their coats.

'Billy, dear. You can come out now,' Millie called sweetly.

There was a scuffling sound as the gold-and-white settee, big enough to comfortably fit three men larger than Drake, shifted, teetered, and screeched on the marble floor before a scruffy boy appeared from under the skirting.

'Cor blimey! It was right dusty under there. For a palace, you thinks the maids would be a little more careful with their mop an' broom.' The dirty lad with a cherub's smile walked right up to the Queen as if she were a street monger in Whitechapel selling sweet meats. ''ere you go, yer greatness.' He held out a leather diary.

Millie cleared her throat. 'It's Your Highness, dear. And one bows when they are addressing the Queen of England.'

Billy doffed an imaginary hat and bent nearly double before popping back up again with a cheeky wink.

Queen Victoria's lip twitched. 'You are a very grubby child,' she said, taking a silk handkerchief from her own pocket and using it to retrieve the diary.

'What the bloody hell is this?' Cedric thundered. His eyes had gone wide and wild at the sight of the journal. He wheeled on Olivia. 'You little bitch!' He lunged for her. Before Philippa could step in front of her, Olivia fisted her hand tight, pulled back her arm the way she had been taught, and punched Cedric as hard as she could. She was aiming for his nose, but her fist landed smack in the middle of his neck.

Cedric stalled in his attack, both hands that were reaching for Olivia clasped instead around his throat as he gasped for breath. His face turned bright red, then dark crimson, then purple. He fell heavily on his arse.

As he writhed on the floor, Queen Victoria flipped open the diary. 'I require my spectacles.' She looked to the guards standing around her parlour. 'You might as well release these people and make yourselves useful.'

The guard holding Hannah quickly let her go and began ferociously searching. His fellow brethren followed suit, upturning every drawer, table, hearth, and desktop until one man held up a pair of glasses with a cry of triumph. He cleared his throat, blushed furiously, and hurried to the Queen, bowing as he handed her the glasses.

'Oi, I see 'ow it's done now. Nice and fancy like.' Billy mimicked the young man's bow.

Millie quickly strode to the boy and pushed him behind her, the sumptuous copper gown nearly hiding him entirely.

'That's lovely, dear, but mayhap we'll practise your courtly manners later.'

Drake joined his wife and cuffed Billy on the head. 'You did well, lad.' He winked at the boy.

The Queen raised a judgemental brow at the trio before returning her focus to the diary in her hands. 'The Lord High Chancellor has sent me many letters during our work together. I noted early in our acquaintance his peculiar habit of adding an extra flourish to his "i"s. It is mirrored perfectly here.' Victoria tapped her finger on the page.

'Because it was written by his hand.' Philippa spoke quietly.

Victoria speared her with a glance. 'That is yet to be determined, Lady Winterbourne. I would remind you, I make the final decisions.'

Philippa bowed her head, but a smile played about her lips.

'If your guard were to search Hardgrave's offices and private rooms, I'm certain they would find other diaries,' Commissioner Worthington added as he strode to Ivy and held her hand. He leaned close, murmuring something in her ear.

'I'm perfectly well, Edward.' Ivy smiled up at her husband. While she looked demure and delicate in her simple gown of ice blue, Olivia knew she held more courage in her little toe than the entire Queen's guard combined.

Killian stepped forward. 'As investigators for the Prime Minister, Drake and I would happily go ourselves to search Lord Hardgrave's home and offices.'

'But we wouldn't want there to be any suspicion about planted evidence,' Hannah added.

A small cough from the corner of the room shifted everyone's focus as Hyacinth wiped tears from her cheeks and strode forward. 'I can tell you where they are. He showed me. He made me read some of them out loud.' Her eyes filled with tears. 'He promised worse would happen to me if I didn't write those terrible things...' Her voice trailed off as a sob choked her.

Finally free to act as she wished, Olivia rushed to her daughter, pulling the young woman into her arms as the girl dissolved into racking sobs.

'He can't hurt you now, darling. I'm so sorry. So, so sorry.'

Philippa still stood next to the Lord High Chancellor, who gargled something incomprehensible as his feet scrabbled on the floor. She lifted her skirt and kicked him hard in the ribs. The wheezing increased in intensity.

Queen Victoria looked from Philippa to the man at her feet. 'Well, this has been a ball to remember. But it is late, and I am tired. I think I shall take this' – she held the diary aloft, shaking it – 'and retire for the evening.' She turned to the head guardsman standing at her right. 'Take him to Newgate until we can sort this out. I'm inclined to believe our Lord High Chancellor will be taking a very long journey to New South Wales in the immediate future. I have heard the treatment of men like Hardgrave can be very rough indeed in prison colonies. Mayhap he will learn some empathy for all those he has mistreated.'

Queen Victoria flipped a few pages in the notebook, her glasses slipping to the tip of her nose. 'It would appear he kept meticulous records of all those who worked with him. How convenient.' She removed her spectacles and looked at the group of Damsels and their men. 'You have work ahead. Best get some rest while you can.'

Queen Victoria swept to Philippa, whispering something to the duchess that had her cheeks warming in a blush. She dipped her head in a flustered bow. 'Thank you, ma'am.'

As the Queen passed Olivia and Hyacinth, she paused, placing a small hand on Hyacinth's shoulder. 'You have shown courage and strength tonight, child. I am always amazed at the resilient nature of humanity. You will heal from this, I promise.'

Hyacinth ducked her head, tears falling freely though her sobs had mellowed to shaky breaths. Olivia squeezed her arm tight around Hyacinth's waist, grateful to finally have her daughter back, devastated she hadn't been able to protect her from her brother's reach.

Queen Victoria looked once more into Olivia's eyes, but this time, there was a warmth and understanding there that shocked Olivia. 'No mother should see her child suffer, though we all must endure it. Even the Queen. For that, I offer my greatest sympathy. But while a mother's love can be the most terrible of things, it also has the power to heal the deepest wounds. I have found when facing adversity, it is my close confidantes who offer me the support and sanctuary I need to replenish and revive. Never be afraid to draw close to your friends.' She looked meaningfully at Philippa, then back to Olivia. 'Goodnight, Lady Olivia. I hope to see you again. Mayhap it will be the next time I visit with the duchess.'

Queen Victoria left with the royal guard fanning around her like a crimson shield.

'In all my giddy daydreams, I never thought I'd ever meet the Queen. Me. A lowly maid who was raised in a prison.' Penny shook her head, her face dazed.

'There is nothing lowly about you, darling Penny. And you keep forgetting. You are a marchioness now.' Liam pulled her close, pressing a kiss to her forehead.

'I don't know what all the fuss is about.' Billy ducked out from behind Millie's skirt. 'She ain't 'alf so 'oit'-toity as the duchess.' He nodded to Philippa.

Philippa crossed the room and took Olivia's hand in hers. 'I think it's time for us to go home.'

Olivia looked at their joined hands. She glanced at Hyacinth, but she was too lost in her own emotions to notice what her mother was doing. But she hadn't missed when Olivia declared her love for Philippa in front of everyone. It was a conversation they would need to have. Later. When Hyacinth had been given the time, love, and support she needed to recover. Right now, Olivia was going to let Philippa lead them out of the palace, into her carriage, and home to Belgrave Square.

* * *

When they arrived home, young Callum announced quietly that he would be going Cornwall, seeing as Miss Hyacinth had been safely returned to her mother. Olivia tried to convince him to stay a bit longer and enjoy some of London's amusements now Hyacinth was no longer in danger, but he was determined to get back to his mam.

Philippa handed him a heavy bag of coins and gave him free use of her carriage the next morning to take him to the train station. He turned crimson and tried to hand the purse back, to which Philippa merely raised her brow.

'One does not refuse the gratitude of a duchess. Certainly not this duchess.'

He murmured his thanks, walked over to Hyacinth, and hesitated as though he might say something to the girl, who couldn't manage to meet his gaze. In the end, he only nodded at her, gruffly telling her how glad he was she was safe, then strode out of the room. That had been several hours ago.

Now Philippa sat in bed, waiting for Olivia to return from tucking Hyacinth into her new room. Despite the fear and horror of the past few hours, a warmth filled Philippa's chest. She frowned, unfamiliar with this new emotion. Unlike the fear she felt earlier in the evening, this was quite pleasant.

Is this contentment? Is that what I'm feeling? Dear God, is this what Hannah, Millie, Ivy, and Penny have been blustering on about for so long?

No wonder they defied Philippa's orders to avoid love. This was absolutely bloody brilliant.

Olivia padded into the room. She wore a pale-rose quilted robe over a white nightgown. Philippa couldn't wait to strip her bare and lie together, skin against skin, hand over her lover's heart, breathing in rhythm with her other half. She patted the blanket next to her.

'I've had a revelation,' Philippa said as she pulled the covers back for Olivia to tuck next to her in the obscenely large bed.

'Wait, before you tell me, I have to know something.'

'All right. I suppose my earth-shattering epiphany can wait.'

Olivia grinned, then quirked her brow. 'How did you get his diary?'

Philippa pulled her close, running her nose along Olivia's cheek, nuzzling her neck until she squirmed. 'When you were spying on me the other day at Twinings, did you happen to notice the young lad who bumped into your brother as he left?'

'The one who spilt his tray all over Cedric's waistcoat?' Olivia gasped, and delightful things happened to her breasts, just visible through her nightgown. 'Billy!'

Philippa nipped Olivia's earlobe. 'Billy,' she confirmed.

Turning her head to give Philippa better access to her neck, Olivia sighed. 'I can't believe it's finally over.'

The quaver in her voice pulled Philippa out of her desire and instilled a stronger need to comfort. She ran a soothing hand down Olivia's arm.

'He can't hurt you any more.'

'I never thought I would actually be free.'

'Always. You will always be free. You can do whatever you wish. I only hope you wish to be with me.'

Olivia reached out, tucking a strand of hair behind Philippa's ear. Her soft touch made something quiver in Philippa's chest. 'I never want to be anywhere but right here. In your arms. You are the future I didn't dare dream of finding.'

Tears threatened. Philippa valiantly swallowed them down. 'I never thought I would be free either. To love again. But I know Liza would have been so happy for me. For us.' It was too late. The tears were falling. Olivia leaned close, kissing each drop.

'I'm so sorry you lost her. But I'm so grateful we have each other now.'

Philippa cleared her throat, turning the conversation to other emotionally fraught issues. 'How does Hyacinth fare?' After Callum's exit, the young woman had asked her mother to help her ready for bed. She seemed oblivious to her surroundings as Olivia had led her up the stairs to Hannah's old room. Now it would be Hyacinth's.

Olivia's smile was shaky. 'Hyacinth needs time to heal. She was able to tell me that Cedric never touched her, so we have that to be thankful for. It was as I suspected. He was a doting uncle until just before the ball when he needed her confession. He frightened her with his diaries and threats, and broke her trust, but he didn't break her foundation. She is a strong woman. With time and love, she will heal.'

'Do you think she will ever come to accept me? To accept us?' Yet another unfamiliar emotion swept through Philippa. She realised she was not a fan of insecurity in the slightest, nor the anxiety it brought along with it as an uninvited guest.

'Well, she did ask me if we were going to be living here now.'

Philippa held her breath, terrified to ask how Olivia answered.

'I told her that is what I wanted.'

'And?' she wheezed, still unable to release the air trapped in her lungs.

'She told me your house is finer than any other she's seen, including her uncle's. She also wanted to know if you would teach her to fight. I think watching you go after Cedric the way you did woke something within her. She is hurt right now, but she's also angry.'

Air rushed out in a puff. 'I understand that kind of anger. So do you. Of course, I'll teach her to fight. I'll teach her everything I know. She'll be the deadliest Damsel of us all.' And she would. Philippa would make sure of it. Never again would Hyacinth live in fear of her power being taken away.

'Then that's a start.' Olivia brushed her fingertips over Philippa's mouth. 'I love you, Duchess.'

'I love you too, Marchioness.'

Olivia flipped, giving Philippa her back. Philippa wrapped her arms around Olivia, squeezing tight, her fingers dipping into the loose neckline of her nightgown, stroking the soft underside of her breast.

'You were going to tell me your revelation,' Olivia murmured, wiggling her bottom to nestle against Philippa's pelvis.

'Oh. Yes. Well. I just realised that sometimes, it's quite wonderful being wrong.'

Olivia burst into a startled laugh. She turned her head, and Philippa marvelled at the perfection of her profile. 'I promise I won't tell anyone that the indomitable Duchess of Dorsett has a few flaws. Never fear, my lady. Your secret is safe with me.'

'My entire world is safe with you.' Philippa pressed her lips against Olivia's in a kiss that was more than just two mouths meeting. It was two hearts intertwining. Opposite elements fusing into something completely new. Two souls knitting together for the rest of this life and into the next. Forever.

* * *

MORE FROM DARCY McGUIRE

The first book in another spicy historical romance series from Darcy McGuire is available to order now here:

https://mybook.to/ConsultantsCrown1

AUTHOR NOTE

If you or someone you know is having thoughts of suicide, please reach out for help.

Canada/US: Suicide or Crisis line call or text 988
UK: Call NHS at 111
AU: Lifeline Australia call 13 11 14
NZ: National help line call or text 1737

ACKNOWLEDGEMENTS

I would like to thank my family for always supporting me, no matter how bogged down I get in finding the right combination of words. I also couldn't do this without my Boldwood team, especially my talented editor, Megan Haslam, my fabulous copyeditor, Emily Reader, and my brilliant senior marketing executive, Niamh Wallace. While this novel touches on some of the challenges inherent in being a member of our invaluable LGBTQ+ community in the 1800s, it weighs heavily on me that individuals are still being persecuted today because of who they love. Love is always a gift. It is never wrong. It is never dangerous or harmful. Each person's right to love within the bounds of equal power and informed consent should always be celebrated and protected. I want to acknowledge the brilliant individuals in our vibrant LGBTQ+ community, their countless contributions to better our world in every facet of society, and their intrinsic right as human beings to be seen, heard, respected, and valued.

ABOUT THE AUTHOR

Darcy McGuire is a high school counsellor who grew up in the wilds of New Zealand but happily settled in the Pacific Northwest. In between dodging territorial geese, gathering duck eggs, taking the dog for long walks, Darcy loves writing about fierce female protagonists who may dodge daggers and bullets but never seem to escape Cupid's Arrow.

Download your exclusive bonus content from Darcy McGuire here.

Follow Darcy on social media here:

facebook.com/AuthorDarcyMcGuire

instagram.com/authordarcymcguire

ALSO BY DARCY MCGUIRE

You're cordially invited to

The home of swoon-worthy
historical romance from the
Regency to the Victorian era!

Warning: may contain spice 🌶

Sign up to the newsletter
https://bit.ly/thescandalsheet

Boldwood

Boldwood Books is an award-winning fiction publishing company seeking out the best stories from around the world.

Find out more at www.boldwoodbooks.com

Join our reader community for brilliant books, competitions and offers!

Follow us
@BoldwoodBooks
@TheBoldBookClub

Sign up to our weekly deals newsletter

https://bit.ly/BoldwoodBNewsletter